STEM TO THE WIND

STEM TO THE WIND

Frederick A. Heyes

VANTAGE PRESS
New York

This story is based on twenty-six years of service in the Royal Navy and closely follows an early period of World War II in the Mediterranean.

While the actions of some characters are true to life, this recounting is not intended to cast unwarrantable reflection on any officer or man but to represent certain historical events as they occurred.

FIRST EDITION

All rights reserved, including the right of reproduction in whole or in part in any form.

Copyright © 1991 by Frederick A. Heyes

Published by Vantage Press, Inc.
516 West 34th Street, New York, New York 10001

Manufactured in the United States of America
ISBN: 0-533-09454-2

Library of Congress Catalog Card No.: 90-90473

0 9 8 7 6 5 4 3 2 1

To Bessie, whose background support kept me sane during the war years

STEM TO THE WIND

CHAPTER 1

On a carpet of Mediterranean blue in the formation of geese in flight fifteen sleek destroyers moved eastwards. Enhancing the grandeur of the scene, and seemingly portraying purpose through a visual symbol, five larger ships followed the V, making it an advancing broad arrow. The nerve centre of this potent force lay in the first large ship; its wings lay in the second.

In this second vessel, recently completed, Britain's shipbuilding craftsmen had by varying devices incorporated the lessons of the war to date, and on her joining the fleet there had risen from her flat top an umbrella of planes. They ended the heyday of a high-flying enemy. Bombs now fell few and wide, and whatever disfavour this bulky craft had engendered in the bloodshot Italian gaze, she was riding fair in the eyes of the British fleet.

Prior to her arrival on the scene, the British fleet and convoys had been subjected to high-level bombing attacks from dawn to dusk, and the sea route from Gibraltar to Malta and Alexandria had been known as Bomb Alley; meanwhile in the offing there had been the ever-present menace of the powerful Italian fleet.

After the failure of Italy's prolonged bombing attacks it had been expected that their fleet would venture out. The British navy was scattered about the world, and here in the Mediterranean it was vastly outnumbered. A determined attack by the Italian fleet could overwhelm the British and leave the fortress and naval base of Malta in enemy hands.

What was holding them back? They needed to get rid of that nuisance of an aircraft carrier.

Perhaps they feared Britain's locating device, later to be known as radar, which was holding their airmen at bay, and had so recently helped to blunt the nose of Goering's Luftwaffe in the epic battle over Britain.

Had Mussolini's airmen been granted a clearer, undisturbed view of the carrier in the clear sunlight of this 1940 autumn morning, even they might have cast an approving gaze. For then, despite her new camouflage paint, in the clear lines below her weather deck they would have seen beauty and an assurance of speed. They would also have noted with surprise that one of the portholes in the row on the port side was open.

The porthole let daylight into the engineers' office. At that moment a young engineer in a brown overall suit entered with an obvious look of inquiry on his face.

Sublieutenant Kelling had left Keyham Engineering College three months before and, to his great joy, was sent to join the new carrier. At the age of twenty-one he was a fair-haired, energetic young man who had made a name for himself on the college rugby team. Slightly above average height and slim of build, he exuded a healthy freshness, even in the heated machinery spaces below. This morning his problem was not the design or operation of machinery. Nevertheless he sought his usual source of information. Throwing down his gloves and removing his cap from his perspiring brow he approached the only other occupant of the office, one dressed like himself but with a form tending slightly to stoutness.

Commissioned Engineer Mayson's rather pale face was a register of years in heated machinery spaces, but he still had a good head of sandy hair, brushed neatly back, and his steel grey eyes in his pleasant open face seemed to smile as he looked up from a ship's drawing lying on the desk.

"Well, well! What's cooking now?"

Kelling's eyes lit up in a smile as he met the steady gaze of the older man. It seemed his old friend could read his mind. He leaned back on the high desk and looked down at his boots.

"I'm not quite sure this time, Mr. Mayson—it's something I've pondered since we came to sea. Tell me, do you think the men in our department are as happy as they should be in a fine ship like this? Mind you, I know they're doing their job well enough, but there's a lack of verve about it. Morale down there isn't good. When you watch the upper-deck ratings at work you see the difference—they seem to enjoy what they are doing."

Kelling would have had more to say but he became aware that the commissioned engineer was gazing steadily at him and smiling gently.

Mr. Mayson had served twenty-five years in the Royal Navy, first as an engine room artificer, and then as warrant engineer, which rank he had attained as the result of a competitive examination in which he was one of eight selected out of nearly three hundred candidates. After ten years in warrant rank he was automatically promoted to commissioned engineer. Three years had passed since then. He had served with a succession of sublieutenants and watched them move up a promotion ladder quite different from his own. Some he had served with again after they had become lieutenants and lieutenant commanders. Now, at the age of forty-three, he was still junior in rank to a sublieutenant.

He appreciated the friendship of Kelling, and it pleased him to have the young man's confidence.

"Well, Sub," he said, "you're reading the signs correctly. Morale in our department could be better. The point is, what is the reason for that, and what can we do about it?"

Mr. Mayson would have continued but he heard a heavy yet lively tread nearby and the ship's commander (E), dressed smartly in his blue uniform with three shining gold rings on the sleeves, swept breezily into the office. At the age of forty-five he was the head of the engineering department, and generally referred to as "the chief." He was a rotund man of above-average height, with a good head of dark brown hair, greying at the temples, and his round face had a fresh, almost boyish appearance, marred only by a slight sag in the fullness of his cheeks. As he strode the length of the office, his cheeks moved in harmony with each bouncing tread. He was in a mood to stir things up, and as he reached his desk he turned: "Kelling!"

Kelling stiffened to attention. "Yes, sir."

Mr. Mayson picked up his gloves and torch and disappeared.

"Have you got the fittings for my door curtain yet?" The chief had designed a system of pulleys, string, and weights for automatically closing his cabin door curtain.

"Yes, sir, and an engine room artificer will do the job this forenoon."

"And damn near time, too."

Kelling started to slink out of the office, but the chief suddenly realized that he was alone. Kelling didn't manage to clear the threshold.

"Kelling!"

"Yes, sir."

"Where's the senior? Where are the messengers?" The chief glanced around the office and his rage increased. "Where the hell's the writer and everybody?"

Kelling was about to reply when the commander (E) cut him short.

"Tell the senior I want him."

Kelling disappeared, glad to get away.

Meanwhile the chief was busy going through the papers from his IN basket and cursing certain unknown individuals who had been using his pens and other desk gear in his absence.

The senior engineer soon appeared wearing a white overall suit. He held the rank of lieutenant commander and was a tough-looking man who always seemed to be up to the eyes in work. Of medium height with broad shoulders, he had dark brown hair and, unless he shaved twice a day, a dark stubble about his handsome, rugged face. His job was to take charge of the engine room department in a practical way, the commander (E) being more or less a consulting engineer, dealing with correspondence and the office side but nevertheless the head of the department.

As the senior entered the office the chief looked up.

"What speed are we doing, Senior?"

"Two-thirty revs, sir; we've just increased."

"Yes, so I noticed."

"Look here, Senior, this office is a damned disgrace. Where's that writer and those damned messengers? Look at this desk again. Every blighter who comes into the office uses my gear. It's not damned well good enough. Look at that pen!" The chief stood holding the pen under the senior's nose.

The senior knew the chief's moods. "Very good, sir, I'll see about it."

"Well, get all the engineer officers together and tell them about it."

"Very good, sir."

At that the matter subsided and the chief carried on working through his IN basket. His desk was a strange sight to behold. The worry of his life seemed to be that other people kept using his writing materials, sometimes failing to return a pen or an eraser. Consequently he had brought his inventive genius to bear. A notice on his desk warned others not to borrow his gear. His pens were tagged "Commander (E)," and his pencils and erasers were tied to his desk by pieces of string anchored by desk pins. These devices did not safeguard the materials, but they served to remind prospective borrowers that they had better not be caught. The trouble was that the chief did not spend much time in the office, but other people did.

The senior still remained in the office, sitting at his desk and looking through the engine room register. The chief got up to leave and in walked Heathcote, the engineers' writer.

Heathcote had served more than twenty years in the navy. He knew his job down below as the chief stoker in charge of boiler rooms, but his last five years had been spent in the specialist job of writer. He was not looking as well as he had in the past. His work on taking over a new ship had been very heavy, and he was looking forward to the time when things settled down and his job became more or less routine.

He stood smartly to attention as the commander (E) passed. The chief suddenly remembered that he had missed Heathcote earlier on and called back as he left: "Senior, find out where this man has been and tell him to be here when I arrive mornings."

Heathcote smiled faintly and walked rather wearily to his desk beside the senior. The senior had progressed to a new occupation: He was tearing up a great pile of typewritten material. He glanced at the writer.

"You know, Heathcote, the old boy likes to see somebody in the office when he arrives mornings; for heaven's sake, man, buck up!"

"I've been here since seven o'clock, sir. I only slipped away because the captain's office wanted me about our stationary demands."

"Yes, I see," said the senior in a slightly milder tone, "but wait till the old man comes before you go in future." Then he added: "I've decided to scrap these orders of mine."

"What? Again, sir?"

"Yes. I find there are a lot of other things that should be included."

"But couldn't they have been added?"

"I'm afraid not, as they have to be dropped in under the various headings here and there. I'll alter my originals, seeing they are in pencil, and you can type them again." The senior shoved an armload of papers into the wastepaper basket. "You'd better get on with them right away, then. We need to get them out."

Heathcote emitted a feeble, "Very good, sir," and looked sadly at the pile the senior had jammed into the bin. Those quickly discarded papers represented hours of overtime work.

The senior picked up his gloves and torch and left.

Heathcote looked up and out of the porthole. According to the ship's standing orders this porthole should have been closed, but the commander (E) had left instructions for it to be open when he arrived in the morning. Now Heathcote gazed out upon an almost-flat, calm sea, but in his mind he was seeing other things. He saw behind him weeks of incessant toil; of striving towards a state of orderly efficiency in his work, without which he could never be happy. And still work surrounded him—in drawers, in files, on shelves, in ledgers and in registers—much of it required "at once" or "as soon as possible." His mind strayed over the past, and his heart sank at the apparent futility of it all. But he fought off the depression and allowed himself to take in the view. The blue waters of the Mediterranean sparkled in the sunlight and rebuked him for his gloom. What was *he* fretting about? These waters would smile long after he had gone his way. But Heathcote was not to stand meditating for very long.

Blurp! blurp! blurp! Blurp! blurp! blurp! Blurp! blurp! blurp!

There it was again, the high-pitched, staccato sound of the electric horn calling all stations to action. The ship's locating device had detected aircraft some miles away approaching the fleet.

Heathcote quickly shut the porthole, dropped the deadlight over it, and screwed the whole up tight. He grabbed his respirator and lifebelt and ran. Overhead and about was the bustle of men running, preparing gear, giving orders, each man conforming to routine in the organized ship's party to which he belonged: gun's crew, flight deck, fire and repair, pumping and flooding, medical, and food supply.

Men between decks stood quietly about, waiting. Over the ship's sound system came the calm voice of the paymaster, speaking from the bridge.

"Well, our fighters have gone up to intercept. There is no report from them as yet. It is a lovely day with a few white clouds about high up." He paused. "And that's about all for the time. I will let you know when we get a report."

John Soames, leading stoker of the Number Three Fire Party, voiced the sentiments of some of his messmates. "Curse those Italian bastards! Coming over at this time of day. I wonder if they know I've got the afternoon watch in the boiler room."

Soames was an old-timer and had his Long Service and Good Conduct Medal, granted him, so he said, for undiscovered crimes.

Young Stoker Hicks could not resist taking a poke at "Old Stripy" (as he called Soames). "It's about time some of you old blighters kept a watch. You've been ashore most of the war."

"Whaddya mean, you little twerp? I was going to sea before you—"

Bang! Bang! Bang! *Bang!*
Bang! Bang! Bang!
The paymaster's voice broke through the noises of war.

"Well, our AA guns have opened up. There are about six enemy planes high up among the clouds. I can't see much of them from here. Our fighters are up there but there is no report from them yet."

The steady bang of the antiaircraft guns continued, keeping the bombers up. Occasionally a different sound was heard, a heavier but less metallic boom. The men between decks knew the difference. There was a general air of agreement: "Bombs."

The paymaster's voice came through again. He opened in his usual way and halted occasionally. "Well,"—a pause—"those bombs all fell wide of the mark. The nearest ones dropped off our port beam"—another pause—"between us and the destroyer screen." A longer pause followed, then came the excited report: "Our fighters have sounded the tallyho! They've gone in to attack!"

The sound of the AA guns ceased.

Able Seaman Tuckett, working in the hangar, was, in naval parlance, "kicking himself," wishing he had a job on the flight deck. "Wonder if Bowman is up," he said. "He'll soon scatter 'em."

Tuckett was referring to Sublieutenant Bowman, who, in a short active career of two months, had made a reputation for flying into anything, always shooting something down, and coming out unscathed.

Inside damage-control headquarters a small staff of men assisted the damage-control officer. Reports had come in from the various parties throughout the ship: "Watertight doors and hatches in Number One Section closed." "Number Two Repair Party closed up correct." Times of all reports were jotted down and passed on by telephone to the second damage-control position for duplication. This latter job was carried out by the engineers' writer, Chief Stoker Heathcote, beside whom sat the master-at-arms receiving the incoming telephone reports.

Throughout the ship between decks there was a general air of quiet waiting. Then came the click of the shutter that covered the microphone on the bridge, a sound that, heralding the broadcaster's voice, could be heard in quiet periods.

"A report has just come in: Our fighters have shot down one enemy bomber."

Men between decks voiced their satisfaction about this in their various ways. A hefty leading cook belonging to one of the first-aid parties was not to be outdone. "That's the bloody stuff to geve 'em!"

The broadcaster's voice broke in on him. "That bomber is coming down!"—a tense pause—"He's diving into the sea!"—pause—"And—there he is; it seems he is sinking right away. Anyhow, whoever is in it cannot be alive, judging from the way he hit the water."

Behind the paymaster's voice could be heard, faintly, the cheers of the flight deck party.

After a brief silence the microphone clicked again: "There's another plane coming down! It's a good distance away— Don't know yet if it is an enemy plane or not— And there's a parachute coming down too! The plane has crashed into the sea. The parachute is slowly falling. It's quite a sight"—pause—"good thing to get a picture of. I see a few cameras busy on the flight deck."

Silence followed, soon to be broken by the sound of explosions. The noise, distant but heavy, came repeatedly: Boom! Boom! Boom! Boom!

Lieutenant Tangry, the engineer of the after fire and repair party, was puzzled momentarily: "What the hell's that?"

"Depth charges, sir," replied a chief stoker of his party, an old destroyer man.

"Oh yes, so it is. Submarines about, eh?"

The paymaster made his voice heard over the distant explosions.

"Our fighters are all safe and are coming in to refuel. That second plane to fall was an enemy bomber. A third bomber was damaged. The noises you can hear are depth charges. The destroyers seem to be tearing up the ocean for miles around"—a long pause. "Sorry for that man with the parachute!"

No, there was little sense in any ship stopping to pick up an enemy survivor, for she would then offer a better target to enemy submarines.

The sound of the depth charges ceased and the paymaster spoke again.

"We are now altering course into the wind. There are three fighters revving up on the flight deck ready to take off before the others fly on."

Commander Sands, on the bridge, reported to the captain. "I'm going below now, sir. I'll be moving aft this time."

The captain nodded and smiled. "Right you are, Commander."

The commander made his way down through the various decks to the main deck. As the senior executive officer on board he was second in command. It was his practice to move about the ship when the men went into action. He kept the captain informed of his whereabouts as closely as possible. He was a smart-looking man, tall and dark, with an athletic build. He was responsible for the internal organization of the ship. It was a job he seemed to enjoy, and he carried it out very efficiently. His ready smile more than offset the slight severity that crept into his manner occasionally. All members of the ship's company were ready to jump to any order he gave. They knew how fortunate they were. With a captain like Captain Graham and a commander such as this, who could do less than his best?

Commander Sands was ably assisted in his job by his first lieutenant, Lieutenant Commander Courtenay, a pleasant, easygoing officer generally known as "Number One."

The commander made his way to damage-control headquarters. Damage control was chiefly an engine room department concern, but the commander had done much in the initial organizing of it. Since then he had not had much to say in the matter, nor did he concern himself with the organization of the engine room department as distinct from damage control. This latter was a matter for the commander (E) alone, and to him Commander Sands looked for cooperation in keeping all departments working in harmony.

On entering damage-control headquarters the commander was surprised to find so many people there, most of all the commander (E), whose action station was the second damage-control position, the machinery control room.

The other officers and men stood to attention as Commander Sands entered. He quickly waved them to sit down, and set about relieving himself of his respirator, life belt, and steel helmet before perching himself alongside the warrant shipwright on an extension of the electrical rating's desk.

The warrant shipwright, Mr. Ganer, generally known as "Chippie," usually kept close to the commander in action. The other officers present, apart from the commander (E), were Mr. Brinnell, the bos'n, and Lieutenant Morton, the damage-control officer. The latter was busy making an index system intended for use in recording damage in action. It was a unique system that had originated in the commander (E)'s inventive mind, and the young officer had been urged to press on with it.

The chief was happily ensconced in an easy chair with his

chubby legs crossed and his back to the bulkhead beside Lieutenant Morton's desk. A wardroom library book rested on his upthrust knee. It was cooler here and more comfortable than in that machinery control room two decks down. He folded his book and looked up.

"What's the latest, Commander?"

"Well, we seem to be on our course again now. There were no signs of hostile aircraft when I left the bridge. I fancy it is all over bar the shouting. We will secure from action stations soon if we have no further signs of attack. I want to pipe the hands to dinner at eleven-thirty if possible."

"And when do we expect to get in?"

"It all depends. As you know, if the weather remains suitable we have to take a crack at Rhodes tonight. If everything goes off all right we should be back somewhere southeast of Crete at dawn. Then we have to cover a convoy from Greece."

"Does that mean we may get into harbour tomorrow night, sir?" asked the bos'n.

"Yes, all being well, we should. And now I must get back to the bridge."

As the commander moved out the chief turned to Mr. Ganer. "Look here, Chippie, when are you going to fix the headrest for this chair?"

"Sorry, sir, but my staff are busy just now on important work around the ship."

"What do you mean, important work? There's nothing more important than my chair at the present time."

"What about the work you have asked to be done for damage control, sir?"

"Such as what?"

"Well, there are those keyboards, and the repair party tool boxes."

"Oh to hell! There's no hurry about them for a day or two."

"But the jobs are well under way, sir, and you said you wanted them done as soon as possible. My staff are busy on those cabin modifications, too, and there is a long list of items in the defect book I can't get started on."

"Well, how's that man getting on with my camel saddle?"

"He's polishing it now, sir; it should be finished today."

Mr. Ganer's reply seemed to give the chief some satisfaction. The camel saddle was a curio he had acquired ashore in Alexandria, and he prized it very much. There was one particular corner of a certain room at home in which he intended to stow this reminder of his world travels. He smiled a little and heaved himself to his feet. Then he turned slowly to gaze thoughtfully at the highly coloured canvas and the two wooden uprights that formed the back of his collapsible easy chair.

Mr. Ganer saw his chance and slipped out. The bos'n was about to follow suit when the chief suddenly became alert.

"Mr. Brinnell!" he exclaimed. "Come here!"

The bos'n, who had reached the doorway, walked leisurely back.

"Look," said the chief, patting the two uprights. "Chippie is going to fit two extensions to these to make the back a foot higher. I was going to have a strip of canvas fitted across the extensions to form a headrest, but we can do better than that. Get your sail maker to make a canvas bag. Then go up and see the navigator and ask him to let me have one of his meteorological balloons. We'll push the balloon into the canvas bag, lace up the open end of the bag, and inflate the balloon—just to make a nice soft cushion. You'll have to get four loops made and sewn on to the bag to slip over the extensions."

The chief straightened his back and smiled proudly, for

this was a real gem from his inventive mind. The bos'n smiled, too, but remained silent.

"All right, Mr. Brinnell," said the chief, "now you and Chippie get together about this, and tell him to get busy on those extensions."

"Yes, sir."

The bos'n left and the chief went back to his library book.

Down in the machinery control room the senior was busy with the main machinery. He was not concerned with damage control, but a staff of three ratings, stationed there to assist the commander (E) in this job, stood idly by. The senior looked more than ever up to his eyes in work—turning this telegraph, altering that indicator—and all the time trickles of sweat ran their winding path through the bristles about his face, to drip from his chin or pass down his neck to soak into his undervest. It was quite warm in the compartment, for it was situated over the engine rooms, but the senior could not keep still. He had an abundance of energy that must be worked off.

Through the broadcasting system came the sound of the bos'n's pipe, followed by the voice of the bos'n's mate.

"Hands secure from action stations."

With action stations over, Mr. Mayson, who had the afternoon watch below, went to get an early lunch. As he entered the mess he heard the pipe, "Hands to dinner," and wondered how it originated that officers called it lunch and the men called it dinner. He joined two of his messmates at the table, and as he sat down he felt a pat on his shoulder and heard a voice from behind.

"Afternoon watch, eh, Mr. Mayson. Wear the old one out first, I say."

Sublieutenant Kelling had been invited in by Mr. Langley, warrant engineer, to join him over a glass of beer.

Mr. Mayson turned and smiled. "I'll take a lot of wearing out yet, Sub, and what about you—and the chief's door curtain?"

"Couldn't do it because of action stations, but I've got a man working on it now while the chief's in the wardroom."

Mr. Langley chimed in. "Good for you, Sub. You'll get along in the navy."

The two officers' messes, wardroom and warrant officers', were situated adjacent to each other on the upper deck beneath the hangar. A friendly harmony existed between them due, primarily, to the personalities of the two presidents: Commander Sands of the wardroom, and Mr. Mills of the warrant officers' mess.

Commissioned Warrant Officer Mills was nearing the age of fifty, fairly tall and well built, with a weather-beaten face and a good head of dark hair streaked with grey. He was generally known and addressed as "Torps," being the ship's torpedo gunner, and he exuded a bluff heartiness that was truly appreciated by his messmates.

In the lounge area at the ship's side, clear of the dining table, several warrant officers, including Torps, were enjoying a prelunch drink from the bar and discussing the war situation. A feeling of optimism prevailed in the mess, engendered by the ship's performance since joining the fleet, but there was no hiding the fact that the war outlook was far from bright. With the exception of Greece, busy stalling the Italians in Albania, the British Empire stood alone, holding two powerful dictators at bay. The Luftwaffe, beaten off in daylight attacks, were pounding Britain at night. In the Battle of the Atlantic, German submarines were threatening Britain's lifeline to the New World. Meanwhile the British army, vastly outnumbered in the Western Desert, had fallen back to Bardia, near the Egyptian border. Italian forces threatened the Nile Valley, and with a determined push might overrun the naval base of Alexandria and the Suez Canal.

Here in the Mediterranean, one escorted aircraft carrier was about to attempt its first operation against the enemy ashore. It would be a risky business, and several queries were raised about it in the mess. Then Sub-lieutenant Kelling got inquisitive. He called across the lounge to the president.

"How about it, Torps—will we be using the 'latest' tonight?" He was referring to a new type of mine, recently received on board.

Torps took a sip at his noggin of gin. "Not tonight, Sub. I'm told the planes will only be bombed up. As far as I can see this is only an initial tryout for our Swordfish planes. There are much better targets for our mines and torpedoes. We hope to chop down on the supplies to the Italian army pretty soon, and take the pressure off our chaps in the desert."

Later in the afternoon Mr. Mayson, walking aft to examine the steering gear, noticed that the wardroom doors were closed. The pilots and observers were receiving their instructions for the attack on Rhodes.

CHAPTER 2

Darkness. It was the period between sunset and moonrise and the ship was on her course, steaming in the direction of Rhodes. Somewhere in the surrounding blackness were two modern cruisers and a small screen of destroyers. This naval force steamed at twenty-eight knots, each unit keeping its position relative to the others, while the whole force unerringly made its way through dangerous waters to a predetermined point.

Inside the hangar of the carrier fleet, air-arm mechanics were making the final adjustments to eighteen Swordfish bombing planes and filling the fuel tanks. On the flight deck dead silence reigned and the guns' crews stood motionless at their guns. Shortly after moonrise the flight deck party were piped to muster on the flight deck. Very soon the aircraft lifts were brought into operation, and the planes came up from the hangar one at a time. On reaching the flight deck the wings of the planes, which had been folded back to facilitate stowage in the hangar and passage by lift, were unfolded and secured. Chocks were removed from the wheels and the machines were ranged up at the after end of the flight deck.

The engines of the planes were started, thoroughly warmed through, and then stopped. At midnight they were started again, and shortly afterwards the pilots and observers appeared in their full equipment. The engines were given a thorough racing while the ship turned into the wind. Soon the steady breeze could be felt blowing directly head-on, and the pilots and observers took up their positions in the planes. At a signal from the flight deck officer the first plane taxied forward a little, then the engine raced up to a roar and the machine picked up speed and ran forward down the centreline of the flight deck. It had barely passed the bridge structure before it was in the air, carrying its load of bombs—and two brave men. The other planes followed at steady intervals. The whole operation was carried out without a hitch. And the moon rose high.

The ship altered course, turning out of the wind, and soon she was steaming steadily again at twenty-eight knots.

There was an air of quietude between decks. Men at action stations conversed in lower tones than usual. The ship's company knew that they had approached an enemy naval base, and there was the chance of running into a hostile naval force. Should that happen now it might be disastrous, at least to the planes in the air, for to land on-ship they needed the carrier to be steaming steadily with her stem to the wind.

The ship was now moving away from Rhodes and there were two hours of waiting ahead—waiting for the return of the planes. Before they flew off there had been a general feeling of tense excitement about the ship, a feeling such as that experienced by a small boy who had reached the pantry without anyone knowing: The array of good things lay before him; could he get busy, do justice to himself, and then get clear away? Now it was different. There was no excitement about this waiting period. One wondered how those young men in the air were doing. How many of them would come back?

In the wardroom pantry the stewards were busy, and up in the galley the cooks were preparing large quantities of ham and eggs, a favourite dish for the young airmen.

Inside damage-control headquarters the chief dozed in

his chair while Lieutenant Morton worked away persistently at the index scheme. Chief Stoker Heathcote and the master-at-arms were busy cutting up sheets of white notepaper into pieces about four inches square. The stoker messengers were painting across one corner tip of each piece—some pieces red, some blue, others green, and a few black—in accordance with the chief's idea for recording damage. He had seen the damage-control officer, during the first action practice occasions, taking down reports on a signal pad and had promptly told him to stop it. The chief had suddenly become inspired. He explained his idea to the damage-control officer. It was quite simple: Reports coming in about fire would be recorded on red-coloured paper; those about flooding on black; those about structural damage on blue; and electrical reports on green. Each report would be duplicated and one copy sent to the second damage-control position. The warrant shipwright was told to produce a board, fitted with four paper clips, for each control position. Each board would rest on a desk; the paper clips would be painted—one red, one blue, one black, and the other green. Reports of one colour would be grouped and held by the same colour clip.

Heathcote and the master-at-arms with their helpers were pressing on with the work; the commander (E) wished to try his idea out in practice.

Commander Sands broke the monotony for the ship's company when he arranged with the paymaster and the cooks for a large copper of cocoa to be boiled in the galley. When the cocoa was ready for consumption the ship's broadcasting system came into use again; a subdued voice called, "Cocoa is ready for distribution in the galley."

Jugs and cups were quickly produced, messengers hastened to the galley, and soon all men were sipping away at the thick, piping-hot cocoa.

Time went slowly by until two-thirty A.M. when the bos'n's

pipe was heard, followed by the voice of the bos'n's mate calling softly, "Flight deck party, muster on the flight deck."

The flight deck party prepared for the landing on of the planes. Lifts, and the machinery for operating the arresting gear, were manned. The arresting gear consisted of steel wire ropes stretched across the flight deck. When a plane landed on-ship a hook in the tail caught one of these wires, which, with a springlike action, brought the plane gently to rest.

On the bridge, high above the flight deck on the starboard side, the captain stood with the flight commander, the officer in charge of the fleet air arm on board. Both knew that they should hear the returning planes soon: Their approach had been detected on the locating device.

They had not long to wait before they caught the faint drone of distant machines, and soon the planes were in view, circling low over the ship in the bright moonlight. Small lights were switched on as guidance for the pilots, and the great vessel turned into the wind.

Very little time was taken in this flying-on process. The pilots and flight deck personnel had been well trained. A simple signalling system seen from the stern of the vessel informed the planes when all was clear for them to fly on.

As the first plane came down, the flight deck party stood on platforms at each side of the flight deck, a few feet below deck level. The plane made a perfect touchdown at the after end of the deck, ran forward a little, and caught one of the arrester wires, which brought it to rest. The flight deck party ran in and unhooked the tail hook from the wire, and then signalled to the pilot, who taxied the plane forward. Forward of the bridge the pilot and observer jumped quickly down and went to the flying operations room, situated in the bridge structure, to report to the flight commander, who had moved down from the bridge and was waiting. Other men of the flight deck party pushed the plane on to the forward lift, folded back the wings and chocked the wheels. It was then lowered to the hangar, where the hangar party removed it and sent the lift back up to receive the second plane then touching down.

Up on the bridge the captain and Commander Sands looked down, silently keeping count as the planes flew on. The process was being carried out without a hitch, the flight deck party working like clockwork. Here, too, was evidence of superb work by the pilots and observers.

Another plane touched down and the captain mentally noted, *Thirteen.* There were still planes in the air; the losses, if any, had been few.

Very soon the sky was clear of planes and no other aircraft could be detected by the ship's locating device. Seventeen had returned safely. Captain Graham knew that the chances of the remaining plane ever coming back were very slim.

In the air operations room the crews of two aircraft said they had seen one plane flying low, silhouetted against the flames of burning buildings below, apparently damaged and trying to make a landing.

The ship was now turning out of the wind. Soon the small naval force of which she was a part was steaming away on a course and at a speed that would both be known to the men in the missing plane.

In the wardroom there was little evidence that one plane had not returned. This was something to be talked about later. Each man hoped that the missing plane had made a safe landing. Consequently the young airmen set about showing each other, and everyone, how lighthearted they were. There was a babel of noise over the mess table as they talked about their experiences of the night. Many of their nonflying shipmates sat around, deeply interested and asking a question occasionally.

The raid had been a great success, although there was little shipping in the harbour. Docks and warehouses had been strewn with bombs. The army barracks had been left blazing and was probably completely gutted.

Young Blakeney had been given a target that had caused envy amongst his friends. This fair, quiet, studious-looking young officer had been told to go for the house of the Italian naval commander-in-chief. Judging by his self-confident smile it seemed he had been successful in his mission. Someone called over the table to him, "How did you get on, Blakey, old boy? Did you find the target all right?"

"Oh yes, we found the target. The trouble is, some of you chaps dropped your eggs a good bit before we did and probably scared the c-in-c away."

"You're about right there," said one of the observers. "I expect he took those first bombs as a starting signal and set out on a marathon race across the island."

There was a roar of laughter over this. It did not take much imagination on their part for these young men to get a mental picture of the Italian admiral legging it across country in his bare feet, and clad only in a nightshirt.

From beneath came the steady drone of the propeller shafts.

Through the microphone came the sound of the bos'n's pipe, followed by the call, "Hands secure from action stations."

Two hours to go before dawn, when the ship's company would be called to action stations again. A good thing to let the men off watch get a couple of hours' sleep. Dawn would bring increased danger of enemy attack.

CHAPTER 3

Nine A.M. The aircraft carrier with its escorting cruisers and destroyers had rejoined the remainder of the fleet. In the distance, to the northwest, the rugged mountains of the island of Crete stood out clearly. Two hours before, over on the horizon to the southwest, the early morning light had revealed the smoke and the many black dots that indicated the position of the convoy from Greece. Since then the fleet had been cruising about off the southwest coast of Crete, while the convoy with its escorting destroyers made good headway towards Port Said. The fleet, on its way to Alexandria, would afford covering protection.

At a signal from the flagship the fleet altered course to the southeast and steamed away from the vicinity of Crete at a speed of twenty knots. It was a calm, sunny day. The men found it rather surprising that there had been no signs of enemy reconnaissance planes following the attack on Rhodes. It had been expected that the enemy would locate some units of the fleet soon after dawn and at least carry out high-level bombing attacks. For this reason fighter aircraft had been sent up soon after dawn. At present there were six in the air, forming an umbrella for the fleet, and six more were ready to fly off at short notice. But the ships proceeded on their southeasterly course unhindered, and the ship's companies enjoyed the midday meal without interruption.

By twelve-forty-five peace reigned about the mess decks

of the carrier. All men not actually required for duty were lying down resting, catching up on lost sleep. Hammocks were not slung in the afternoon. As soon as the midday meal was over and the dishes had been cleared away, men found the most convenient places about the decks, tables, and stools on which to sleep. Each man removed his boots and used spare clothing from his kit to form a pillow. Officers off duty removed their boots and lay, otherwise fully clothed, on the bunks in their cabins. Thus the ship's company was ready to go to action stations at short notice.

At 1:12 P.M. the expected call came. The high-pitched note of the electric horn sounded, and tired men hastily donned their boots. The language about the mess decks was in the best (or worst) tradition of the navy as the men expressed their ill wishes toward the Italian air force, but they reached their action stations quickly.

Inside damage-control headquarters the chief sat unperturbed in his armchair, waiting for quietude before opening his library book.

Over the sound system came the voice of the paymaster.

"Well"—the usual pause—"there isn't much to report— Unidentified aircraft have been detected approaching the ship about forty miles away." Pause. "They closed in once to"—pause—"about twenty-five miles, and that's the nearest they have been so far— As you know, we have six fighters in the air. There are six more revving up on the flight deck ready to take off if required." Pause. "I cannot see the convoy from the bridge; it is well ahead of the fleet now. And"—pause— "that's about all. I'll let you know if I get another report."

A click followed as the shutter closed over the microphone.

Soon the paymaster's voice was heard again.

"Well—There have been no further signs of hostile aircraft. The planes that were first detected have gone out of our range. They may have been reconnaissance planes"—pause—"which took a peep at the fleet and flew away as quickly as possible. And"—pause—"that's all for now."

The chief grinned all over his rotund face. "I don't blame the blighters for flying off, either," he remarked to the office in general.

No, one could not blame the Italians. They knew now that if they sighted the flat top of an aircraft carrier it was fatal to linger in the vicinity.

By 2:00 P.M. the men off duty had gone back to their afternoon sleep, pleasantly surprised.

Throughout a peaceful afternoon the fleet steamed steadily to the southeast. The convoy with its escort was several miles ahead. Occasionally the fleet would turn into the wind—what little there was—and speed up so that planes could fly off from the carrier's deck, making way for others to land for refuelling.

The afternoon watch is not popular in the navy. Men who keep night watches form the habit of sleeping in the afternoon. That afternoon there were two engineer officers on watch: Lieutenant Leyton was controlling the machinery and Mr. Mayson was roaming the machinery spaces keeping a watchful eye on moving parts. Except for watch-keepers below, the engine room department seemed completely at rest, but when Mr. Mayson called at the engineers' office he found Heathcote and two messengers hard at it. Heathcote had removed his uniform jacket and seemed to have all the available desk space covered with stacks of papers. He stopped his typing and looked round as the engineer entered.

"Hello, sir. Got the afternoon?"

"Yes, Heathcote. What's the matter with you? Can't you sleep?"

"Not me, sir. I have to finish the defect list before we get in. I've got the senior's standing orders finished, though."

"Well, good for you." With that Mr. Mayson went his way. From what he had seen of the defect list he knew that the chief stoker might be at it till midnight, and he had had little sleep the night before.

CHAPTER 4

Dusk. The fleet steamed into the wind while the last of the planes flew on in the rapidly fading light.

The ship's company had been at action stations for the last half hour. It was always the practice to prepare for action at dawn and dusk, for these were ideal times for attack on surface vessels by undersea craft or by aircraft. The carrier could give no night-fighter protection.

As the last plane was taken below, the gun's crews stood alert at their posts, peering into the gathering gloom.

The men at action stations between decks regarded the proceedings as a matter of course. Every day at dusk they went to their stations, remained about half an hour, and then fell out. Lighting conditions were the same to them as they were at any other time of the day; portholes with their covering deadlights were always closed.

Mr. Mayson had checked his pumping and flooding parties at their stations and was now sitting on the edge of a desk in damage-control headquarters. It was a place he avoided as much as possible. On this occasion he was refreshing his memory of the ship's watertight subdivision and pipe systems, but there was little need for him to refer to the plans; he knew his ship from stem to stern, from keel to bridge. On first joining her he had put in many hours studying the plans, sections, and profiles. Then had followed many more hours of work throughout the ship, checking that the drawings were correct in every detail.

The commander (E) sat comfortably, engrossed in a fresh library book, and dead silence reigned in the office.

Then suddenly the voice of the paymaster came through. He spoke hurriedly. Everyone stiffened to attention.

"Unidentified aircraft are closing in rapidly!"

Mr. Mayson drew in his breath. This was obviously a follow-up of the Italian reconnaissance flights of the afternoon.

"By gosh, that's good timing!"

The damage-control officer looked up. "We must have roused the Italians this time, Mr. Mayson; it seems they are trying something new."

"Yes, and it could be torpedoes."

A brief silence followed, then could be heard the sound of the shutter being opened at the microphone on the bridge; but whatever the paymaster had to say, it was never heard. His voice was drowned by a terrific hammering roar, a noise such as would be made by a thousand pneumatic road picks working in unison. The ship's multiple pom-pom guns had opened up with everything they had. Loose paint and dust, shaken free from the deck heads, showered over the men between decks. Men looked at each other with a mute tenseness.

The guns ceased firing.

Mr. Mayson braced himself. He felt he might have an important job to do soon. Low-flying aircraft coming in close and no bombs dropped could mean only one thing: torpedoes.

The guns opened once more with a prolonged roar. Then they stopped.

Lieutenant Morton set about clearing his desk of gear so that the film of light debris could be wiped off.

The shock of the silence, which was almost eerie after the sustained noise of gunfire, was wearing off when the paymaster's voice came through the microphone.

"A report has just been received that HMS *Wexborough* has been hit by a torpedo. The fleet has been attacked by a number of torpedo-carrying aircraft. It is not known how many, but three were sighted from"—pause—"this ship. The fleet put up a terrific barrage of fire. It was quite a"—pause—"fireworks display, with the"—pause—"tracer shells showing up the lines of fire of all the guns. Our gunners shot down one plane. It was hit by"—pause—"a good burst of fire and fell into the water in burning pieces. A second plane was hit and will probably never reach home as it was almost crashing into the water when last seen." Pause. "And that's about all"—pause—"I can tell you at present—except—that it is getting quite dark now"—pause—"and there are no further signs of hostile aircraft."

HMS *Wexborough* was a modern, high-speed cruiser and the news caused quite a stir among the ship's company. Men between decks gathered together and queried each other. "How did they come to miss us, the biggest target and the best prize of all?" "Wonder if she's still afloat." "Who's her skipper?" "How long's she been out here?"

One thing was obvious to all: The Italian air force had shown it could do better than high-level bombing. They were daring men who flew those torpedo-carrying planes.

Very soon the paymaster's voice was heard again.

"Well—another report has come in—and HMS *Wexborough* is still afloat. She was torpedoed on the starboard side and is listing"—pause—"badly to starboard. Preparations are being made"—pause—"to take her in tow."

Two hours later the damaged vessel was being towed slowly, by another cruiser, in the direction of Alexandria; and by midnight it seemed fairly certain that the crippled cruiser would be saved. She had ceased taking in water and the weather remained fine.

In the engineers' office Chief Stoker Heathcote tapped

away at his typewriter. He had sent the messengers to their hammocks; there was nothing more they could do to help. Occasionally he removed his horn-rimmed glasses and passed a hand over his eyes, squeezing his temples between fingers and thumb. His thin, rather longish face was pale except for two unnatural red spots high up on his cheekbones. Over his head the bowed form of his hammock hung, but it was 2:30 A.M. before Heathcote reached up, removed the lashing rope, and climbed in.

CHAPTER 5

The night passed and dawn action stations came and went without incident. Men crowded on deck to get a glimpse of the damaged cruiser. She showed up clearly in the early morning light, about two miles off the port beam and being towed by a sister ship. She was well down in the water and listing to starboard, but appeared to be making good progress. Three destroyers maintained a protective antisubmarine patrol, moving swiftly about in the surrounding waters.

The rest of the fleet, including the aircraft carrier, steamed slowly towards Alexandria: a battleship leading, followed by aircraft carrier, battleship, and the remaining cruiser. These four ships were protected against submarine attack by a screen of destroyers steaming in V formation.

Mr. Mayson, keeping the morning watch below, was surprised when at seven o'clock the revolution telegraph ran up to maximum speed. He left the engine room and made his way to the control room, and as he walked down the steel ladder Lieutenant Stanning, who was controlling the machinery, looked up and grinned.

"I thought you'd be down soon."

"Yes," said Mr. Mayson, "what's it all about—flying off planes again?"

"No, we're not flying off; I fancy we're heading for harbour. Don't know just where we are but I think we're near enough for shore fighters to cover the fleet now. Bridge will let us know soon if we're going in."

"That's good. We may get ashore today after all, but I'd better go aft and see how those stern glands are at this speed."

"Right-o, Mr. Mayson."

In the engineers' office a stoker messenger was busy scrubbing the deck. Chief Stoker Heathcote had taken an early breakfast and now came along to see how the job was going. He wanted to get started on his registers as soon as the office was cleaned.

This morning he was lucky, for he had Angus MacLeod ("Speedy") on the job. Speedy came from Greenock, but, as he told his divisional officer, Mr. Mayson, his memories of Greenock were of an orphanage and several foster homes, and many people who had helped him along. He had joined the Royal Navy for the duration of the hostilities only, and would soon be promoted from second-class to first-class stoker. He stood about sixty-five inches in his shoes, but was a sturdy, deep-chested young man, just twenty years of age. His hair was very dark and he had a pair of dark bushy eyebrows over keen, dark brown eyes. An outstanding thing about him was the speed with which he got through any task he was given, this without appearing to hurry. The senior engineer had given him his nickname and had claimed the lad as his own personal messenger in action.

Speedy wiped dry the last patch of office desk, threw his soap, scrubbing brush, and cloth into the bucket, and straightened his back.

"All finished, Chief."

Heathcote entered the office.

"Well done, Speedy. Better go and get your breakfast. Be back here at eight o'clock."

"Thank you, Chief," and Speedy disappeared with the bucket.

At nine o'clock the low-lying, sandy shores of Egypt could clearly be seen. Mr. Mayson had relieved Mr. Langley and had finished breakfast. He stood talking to the other two warrant engineers, Mr. Kirklane and Mr. Prout, in the engineers' office. On checking up together they found that it was Mr. Prout's turn for duty on board that day. That did not worry Mr. Prout, who rarely went ashore. He was a heavily built man, on the short side, and nearing forty years of age. Because of his bulk he had been nicknamed "Tiny." He was a reliable engineer, but he had adopted an outlook on life that a few years earlier he himself would have criticized. It was an attitude that seemed to say to anyone who cared to listen: "Why should I worry? I'm in a blind alley. What does it matter if I'm keen or not? I'll still have to go ten years, and then they'll make this thin ring on my sleeve a bit thicker. Why break my neck helping senior officers to promotion?"

The older warrant officers, of nearly all branches, sooner or later found this suffocating state of mind creeping over them, and whether or not this state of affairs was understood by the powers that be, with the growing threat of war two concessions were made. The first one altered the regulations so that the best warrant officers could be promoted to commissioned rank after eight years, while the worst ones must go twelve years. The remainder would be promoted at some period between eight and twelve years, depending on how capable, in comparison with each other, they were considered by Admiralty. The second concession was much better. It provided for promotion direct to lieutenant of certain outstanding warrant officers below the age of thirty-seven. While this opened the way to a small percentage of the younger men, it only tended to demoralize the older ones, more so those who were still keen; it told them they were too old at thirty-seven.

Mr. Mayson had been well over the age to qualify for

promotion to lieutenant, but an old shipmate of his, Lieutenant Stanning, in his own words, "just got in under the wire," and by reason of eight years' service as warrant engineer, he was now the most senior engineer lieutenant on board, ranking next below the senior engineer. At the age of thirty-seven he was a slim, wiry individual, and with his background knowledge—acquired in service as boy artificer through to first-class artificer, and then to warrant rank—he was a pillar of strength in the engine room department.

Mr. Prout was leaving the office when Mr. Langley walked in.

"Hello there, Tom Langley," said Mr. Mayson. "Have we reduced speed?"

"Oh yes, Harry, we're down to one-eighty revs." He grinned at his three messmates and remarked, "Bit of a change for all of us to be here at this time of the morning. All I need is a new pencil and I'm off."

Harry Mayson looked at the clock, and then to Mr. Kirklane.

"Come on, Jim, let's go."

"I'll soon be with you, Harry. Got two items for engine room register."

Jim Kirklane was the youngest of the warrant engineers, having been promoted to that rank four months previously at the comparatively early age of twenty-eight. In peacetime this would have been an outstanding achievement in view of the competitive efforts of more experienced men. The advent of war brought a greater demand for warrant officers, and more of the younger candidates for this rank were meeting with success. However, Mr. Kirklane's name had appeared near the top of the list when the examination results were published, so he had something to be proud of, and the chance of promotion to lieutenant (E) lay before him. There was nothing in his makeup to hinder his prospects, for he had all the attributes of a fine officer, and tact and judgement worthy of one more mature in age. His appearance, too, would be a help. He was above average height, with a clear, fresh complexion and a good head of hair brushed neatly back from his rather high forehead. Wherever he went he possessed a quiet confidence that was sensed by anyone in his company.

He handed his items for the register to Heathcote, patted the writer's back, and left in a hurry.

Heathcote smiled. He knew the senior would be along soon, and, perhaps, the commander (E).

The senior never seemed concerned that he rarely saw the other engineers in the office. On one occasion the chief had decreed that all engineers off watch should be in the office when he arrived at nine o'clock in the morning. For a time this order was complied with, but more often than not the chief never arrived at nine, nor was he there by half past. Meanwhile all engineers off watch were waiting in the office, idle. The result was, after a few days, that the waiting officers started to slink away at about nine-fifteen to attend to their various jobs. Finally the chief's order was disregarded entirely and the office was avoided about this time. In fact the office seemed to be avoided at any time that the chief might be there. They could always contact the senior down below on the job.

The ship was approaching the entrance to the swept channel, and the change in the drone of her propeller shafts as she reduced speed was noticed by the senior engineer as he entered the office.

Heathcote turned in his chair.

"Good morning, sir."

"Morning. Have you finished the defect list?"

"Yes, sir."

"Let me see it."

Heathcote handed over one complete copy, which the

senior took without comment, sitting down as he did so. He pulled back the sleeves of his overall suit almost to the elbow and started to read, but before he had scanned the first page he heard the commander (E) arriving. No mistaking that tread.

Heathcote stood to attention and saluted.

The senior turned and stood up. "Morning, sir," he said, saluting.

"Morning, Senior," said the chief breezily. "Where's the defect list."

The chief bounced down into his chair and the senior handed him the list.

The chief started to glance rapidly through the pages and the senior wandered to and fro in the office. This was something Heathcote did not like. He knew the senior's moods. Senior was a different man when in the presence of the chief. On those occasions he would seek to impress the head of his department with his own excellence. The fact that he often succeeded in impressing the chief may have encouraged the practice. On this occasion Heathcote was the victim. The senior cast his eyes over the desks, cupboards, and shelves. There were a few drawings lying open on the drawing desk, and a few small machine parts in one corner of the deck.

"Heathcote," he said, "it's about time this office was cleaned out properly."

The chief must have heard but he took no notice. Heathcote walked up close to the senior and spoke quietly; he did not want the chief to hear.

"We scrubbed out the deck this morning, sir, and cleaned the desks. You know how it is—the gunfire last evening made everything dusty. I intend to have everything out of the shelves this forenoon."

"Well, it should have been done earlier."

"But—" said Heathcote, and he got no further, for the chief cut in.

"It's no use making excuses, Heathcote," he said, without looking up. "The senior's always after you for something. Now get the damned place cleaned out!"

Heathcote closed up the fair engine room register on which he had been working and walked out to tell the messengers to get busy at once instead of waiting till the chief left. His pale, haggard face gave no indication of what his thoughts might be.

The senior picked up his gloves and torch in preparation for leaving.

"I'd better get down below now, sir; we should be manoeuvring engines soon."

The chief read on and flipped over another page before replying. "Right you are, Senior. If I'm not here I'll be in my cabin."

"Very good, sir."

The ship had passed through the boom defence and was approaching her berth. Men not required for duty had fallen in two deep on the weather decks and flight deck. There were many ships in the harbour—a few British cruisers and destroyers, an ammunition ship—anchored well clear of all others—a hospital ship, freighters, mail boats, oilers, colliers, tugs, one or two minesweepers, and some ships of the French navy. These latter consisted of an old battleship, looking spic-and-span in a new coat of grey paint, four useful-looking cruisers, and a destroyer or two; all still flying the tricolour of France but taking no active part in the war—just waiting.

The engines stopped as the ship approached her buoys near the coaling jetty. Men looked shorewards with a thrill of anticipation at the tall, neat-looking buildings standing out above the dockyard and the shipping secured alongside. In the near vicinity a few feluccas—sailing boats about twenty feet long—drifted about, each being handled admirably in the light breeze by its respective brown-skinned gentleman dressed in something resembling a nightshirt.

    Across the harbour an oiler was preparing to leave her berth and to come alongside, after the carrier was secured, to deliver oil fuel.

CHAPTER 6

As soon as the ship was secured fore and aft the bos'n's pipe was heard. This time the bos'n's mate did not hurry with his piping, for the call was intended for all ears. There were several trills and a few long, drawn-out notes before the call came.

"Clear lower deck!" Pause. "Hands to muster on the flight deck!"

From all parts of the ship all men not required for important watch-keeping duties moved off promptly by way of the many ladders up to the flight deck.

On the bridge Commander Sands stood watching the men as they congregated below him. A microphone and loudspeaker had been rigged on the edge of the bridge. As the last few men arrived on deck, the master-at-arms reported to Commander Sands on the bridge, "Lower deck cleared, sir." At that, Commander Sands reported to Captain Graham, who was waiting in his sea cabin. Very soon the captain appeared and Commander Sands took over the microphone.

"Ship's Company— Ship's Company—atten*tion!*"

Over a thousand officers and men came smartly to attention.

The captain nodded and Commander Sands turned back to the microphone.

"Ship's Company, stand at ease! Stand easy!"

The captain took over the microphone and started to speak in his usual calm, confident way.

"Well, men, I have brought you up here because there are a few things I have to say to you at this time.

"We are now a little over three months in commission, and I must say it has been a very successful three months. The work has been hard, particularly during the first month, when everyone had to become acquainted with a new ship and with all the modern and improved fittings and machines we have on board. I have been very pleased with the way you tackled this job. There were times when I felt that you were being overworked—and it couldn't be helped—but I was quite cheered by the show of zeal and energy you maintained throughout. You have now reached a high peak of efficiency and the ship has broken all records for the flying on and taking off of aircraft.

"Fortunately, during this early shaking-down period we have escaped damage from enemy action. In fact—and as you know—the boot has been on the other foot, and we have served out a considerable amount of punishment to the enemy. This, I trust, we shall continue to do, but apart from this a good deal of valuable work has been carried out the importance of which may not be so apparent to all of you. Valuable convoys have been escorted, so far without the loss of a single ship."

The captain paused, but not for loss of words; he knew what he was going to say next. He appeared to be calmly surveying his ship's company before going on. A close observer might have noticed the gleam in his eyes as he took stock of his officers and men. These men, he knew, must know the seriousness of the war situation. He himself had no illusions about it, for this was the Dark Hour in the history of the Empire. He recognized, in the men before him, those superb qualities that had carried their forefathers through the grim periods of the past. It warmed his heart and lightened his burden.

Captain Graham turned back to the microphone and went on:

"You will all be aware of the general war situation at present. Apart from Greece, who is giving Italy more than she bargained for, the British Empire now stands to fight alone, and we have a tough job before us. You will remember the words of our great Prime Minister when he said: 'I have nothing to offer but blood, toil, tears and sweat.' Well, I don't altogether agree, for we have no reason for tears aboard this fine ship. I want you men to cast behind you any thoughts of an early return home. Keep your mind on the job ahead, the job of hitting this vile enemy whenever the opportunity arises. We are in a good position to hit him, too, for we are almost at full strength with both bombers and fighters. Whenever we put to sea we have an excellent destroyer screen and battleship protection. So we have every prospect of giving the enemy further proof of our presence in these waters.

"I would now like to add a word of caution. So far I have had no complaints about the conduct of the ship's company ashore. From what I already know of you I do not anticipate receiving any; in fact, I feel rather proud of my ship's company. I have no doubt that when you get ashore—some of you—today, you will want to relax and have a good time. This I hope you will do; it is good for you, and I intend to give all the leave I can while we are in harbour. However, while you are enjoying yourselves be careful in what you are saying. You have seen a fair amount of action now, and much that you could talk about would be useful to the enemy. It is very likely that enemy agents are operating ashore here, so when you are tempted to take that 'one over the eight,' just stop and think; that extra beer may loosen your tongue. If you hear one of your shipmates talking too much, just poke him in the ribs and tell him to keep his mouth shut.

"Well, men, that's about all, except that I must tell you again how pleased I am with your efforts so far. Just keep it up, and God be with you."

So ended the captain's speech, and the heart of every man who listened was with him, come what may.

As the captain left the bridge Commander Sands took over the microphone and called the ship's company to attention. The captain went aft to his quarters and Commander Sands ordered ship's company at ease; he had a few instructions to give on routine matters. He, too, spoke calmly, and in a clear voice.

"Before I dismiss you there are a few small points I will remind you of. As you know we are still within bombing range of the enemy. Consequently the duty watch must be ready at all times to close at action stations. All AA armament must be manned at once in the event of an air-raid warning. Men on shore should get off the streets and find what cover they can. Care must be taken to keep the ship properly darkened. If any man sees a light showing outside the ship he is to report it to the officer of the watch at once.

"We expect provision and store lighters alongside at twelve-thirty today, so the hands will be piped to dinner at eleven-thirty and will fall in on the flight deck at twelve-twenty. There is a lot of work to be done this afternoon, so put your backs into it, men. The sooner the goods are brought up from those barges, the sooner I can pipe leave.

"That's all. Now carry on to your parts of ship."

The ship's company dispersed. The officers and men were very quiet as they walked away. They carried with them the comforting conviction that they were part of a well-led and well-organized team.

Before the flight deck was cleared the bos'n's mate piped

the hands to dinner. Very soon the mess decks forward were crowded with men. It seemed they were all talking at once. Mess kettles, dishes, and cutlery being rattled to their respective positions added to the bedlam.

Able Seaman Tuckett, who had been one of the last to leave the flight deck, brought good tidings to his messmates. As he passed through the watertight doorway leading to the mess deck he sighted his bosom pal, Dusty Miller.

"Cor blimey, Dusty," he yelled, "did you see the motorboat come alongside?"

"No! Why?"

"Why? She was gunn'ls under, almost—umpteen bags o' mail aboard her!"

"Mail!" The magic word swept the mess deck like wildfire.

"Mail? Who said so?"

"How many bags?"

"Are they serving it out yet?"

Then a less happy note from the mess-deck grouser: "Bloody near time we had some mail! Where the hell's it all been till now?"

But he was not to be allowed any latitude today. "Why ask? Who do you think would write to a miserable bloke like you?"

Men teased each other lightheartedly. One of the older men, a leading seaman, stood at the end of his mess table serving out the men's dinner. He paused with spoon upraised.

"By cripes," he said, "if I don't get a letter from my Old Dutch this time I'll stop her bloody allotment!"

His messmates laughed heartily at this. They had heard his talk before about his wife and his three children and knew how much they meant to him.

At the mail office two marines and a regulating petty officer, assisted by a few young ordinary seamen, were busy sorting out the mail into pigeonholes marked with the numbers of the messes. Very soon men from all parts of the ship formed a queue waiting for the first issue of letters, which would start as soon as the pigeonholes were filled.

In the wardroom anteroom things were loosening up. Some officers from other ships had arrived on board and were being entertained by the ship's officers. The commander (E) was very much in evidence as he greeted the ship's guests with cheery bonhomie. Stewards walked around among the standing officers carrying trays of wines, spirits, and beer.

By teatime the last of the stores and provisions had been stowed below, and the lighters were being towed away. On the other side of the ship the oiler's lines were being cast off. Happy men were crowding into the washrooms. They knew that leave would be piped soon and, to use their own terms, they wanted to be on "top line" to go ashore.

While the men were at tea the call came. There was a long blowing of the bos'n's pipe, which caused a stillness about the mess decks. Then came the voice of the bos'n's mate calling louder than usual, almost exultantly. Perhaps he was watch ashore himself.

"Do you hear there? Leave to the starboard watch from sixteen-forty hours till oh-seven-double-oh tomorrow; chiefs and petty officers oh-seven-three-oh!"

On the seamen's mess deck a hefty able seaman was the first to recover, and he had a good pair of lungs.

"Blimey," he shouted. "All-night leave!"

Then the significance of the pipe was fully grasped by the remainder and they gave vent simultaneously to one mighty cheer:

"Hurra-a-a-a-a-a-a-ay!"

It joined forces with other cheers from other mess decks and tore up through the hatchways and over the harbour.

And the custodians of nearby feluccas turned inquiring heads towards the aircraft carrier; they probably guessed that they would soon have fares to take ashore.

Men of the duty watch—the port watch—were resigned to staying on board, but the news of all-night leave cheered them up. They knew that there was a good chance of them having the same privilege the following night or, failing that, on the next time in harbour.

There was little time for the starboard watch to get ready. Men finished off their tea, and soon there was a clamour of steel locker doors and drawers as they took out their best suits. Shoregoing friends called across to each other, making their plans for the night. Able Seaman Tuckett and his friend Dusty Miller were among those heading for shore. An able seaman of the port watch called over to where they stood brushing each other down.

"Where are you going, Dusty?"

Able Seaman Miller squared off his chum's collar.

"Oh, up the canteen I expect, for a game of billiards and tombola."

"Don't tell me you're going drinking that filthy canteen beer again."

"And why not? There's no bad beer, you know. We'll drink to your health tonight, so just keep the ship afloat till we get back."

The ship's bugler sounded the call for liberty men to fall in, and immediately there was a slamming of locker doors, followed by the sound of hurrying feet passing up the steel ladder. Then the port watch had the mess deck to themselves.

Men of the starboard watch were soon crowding down the gangways and into the ship's motorboats. There were so many men going ashore that the boats would have to make second trips. As the ship's boats left with their loads of happy men, feluccas were manoeuvered alongside the gangway with remarkable skill. Men who did not want to wait for the ship's boats piled into the feluccas and paid five piastres each for the trip to shore.

On the warrant officers' cabin flat Mr. Langley and Mr. Brinnell, the bos'n, were discussing a forthcoming run ashore. These two were much alike in build and appearance; both were of medium height, the bos'n a little taller but not quite so broad across the shoulders. He was a couple of years younger than Mr. Langley and had more colour in his face, a difference probably due to the difference in occupations. The bos'n's weather-beaten face made his pale blue eyes all the more noticeable.

Tom Langley, at the age of thirty-seven, had five years' seniority as warrant engineer. His fair hair was thinning at the crown, but there was something youthful about him, reflected in his alert grey eyes; something that suggested a constitution on which life and time could make but slow progress.

They were to be joined shortly by Harry Mayson, Jim Kirklane, and Torps. The men were heading for shore with the pleasant prospect of an evening's entertainment in the company of nursing sisters from an army hospital. On previous calls at Alexandria the warrant officers' mess had, through Mr. Langley, established a friendly relationship with the hospital nursing staff.

Tom Langley had a flair for getting to know people. Whenever he returned to a port of call there were always friends on shore who welcomed him heartily. Here in Alexandria the war had scattered people, but some of Tom's friends remained and he had made new ones, including the nurses at the hospital.

It was while seeking an old school friend of his wife that he had first made contact with the hospital nursing staff. He had landed alone on the night the ship first called at Alexandria, intending to look her up. She was a teacher of

English at the Italian College and he had visited her there once before whilst serving on a different ship. As he walked down the old familiar road he wondered if the college were still operating now that the Italians were at war. He was surprised when, on reaching the gate at the entrance to the grounds, he was checked by a sentry who inspected his identity card and asked his business. He learned that the college had been turned into an army hospital. He was permitted to pass and entered the hall. The hall porter, a tall Egyptian dressed in a light khaki coat and trousers, red fez and sandals, ushered him into a small library. After a few minutes the door opened to admit a trim little woman, about forty years of age, wearing a light grey dress and a snowy white head covering. Seeing the naval uniform, she smiled.

"I am the assistant matron," she said. "Is there anything I can do for you?"

Tom Langley introduced himself and explained the reason for his visit.

"Well," said the assistant matron, "Miss Alice Burns. I think we might learn where she has gone. I remember her by sight, but one of the sisters, Sister Brown, was very friendly with her during the changeover here. Excuse me."

She went into the hall and Tom heard her speaking on the telephone. Soon she was back.

"If you will wait here a moment Miss Brown will be along."

When Sister Brown appeared Tom wondered if he had been sandbagged. She stood about sixty-four inches high in her shoes. Her grey uniform, fitting snugly at the waist and sufficiently full at the bosom, did nothing to spoil the outline of her superb figure; but Tom hadn't yet taken that in. He was too busy gazing at a pair of thoughtful, blue grey eyes and a stray curl of burnished gold that peeped from beneath the loose-fitting, snow white headdress. And she was smiling at him. He noticed that one of her ever-so-white teeth, a front one in the upper row, appeared to slightly overlap the tooth beside it. That small flaw seemed to add to her charm. She had that serene, womanly expression that can appeal only to the best in man and can make him quietly happy. She stood just inside the door, one hand resting in the palm of the other, holding a folded sheet of notepaper. Then she spoke, and her voice matched her appearance: It was a young, friendly, pleasant voice.

"Good evening."

"Good evening," said Tom, feeling he had been a little rude. "My name is Langley—Tom Langley."

"And I am Susan Brown. I hear you are a friend of Alice Burns—but didn't you know she has changed her name? She's in Cairo now, married to a major in Intelligence there: Major Russell Anderson."

"Well, that *is* news! My wife and I have lost touch with her since the war started, and we wondered how she was faring."

Miss Brown carefully tore off the address from the top of the letter she held. "There," she said, "that's her address in case you want to write or visit her, but I think she may be down here soon for a weekend."

"Good. And thanks for the address—and everything."

"Oh, you're welcome. I'll be writing to Alice soon. I'll tell her I've met you."

Tom picked up his hat. "Right-o. Thanks." He looked around the library. Miss Brown watched him calmly.

"I suppose this is the only part of the college that hasn't been changed very much—and I'm glad it hasn't. You know," he went on, "when I was last here practically all the books were in Italian—that's one thing that has changed, I notice—but there was one volume in English: Winston Churchill's *History of the Great War*. I remember starting to read it and got so intrigued that I bought a copy as soon as I could."

Miss Brown smiled. "Would it interest you to know that the book is still here?"

Tom watched the young nurse move along the shelves to find the heavy book, and the sight of the original volume in those small, capable hands gave him a thrill of pleasure.

"Thanks," he said, taking the book. "That's the one." He looked over a few pages and started to read, then realized that that was inappropriate. "I mustn't take up too much of your time." He returned the book to its shelf. "It's been nice seeing the old place again."

Miss Brown looked at her wristwatch. "I must be going, I am on night duty, but call again sometime. You can use the swimming pool and the tennis courts in the evening."

"I'd like that very much," said Tom.

"Well, come up tomorrow. Come to tea and bring a few of your friends. We can swim or play tennis or just sit around."

"That's very kind of you, Miss Brown. There are two of my friends aboard who would be delighted to come, and they both like tennis."

"All right, then. Come about four, or a little sooner if you can."

"Right-o—but there's always the chance of a sudden call to sea— I'll phone you from the ship about three o'clock."

"That will be all right," said the nurse. "Good night now."

Tom stepped ahead and opened the door. "Good night, Miss Brown, and thank you."

And so it had happened that Mr. Mayson, Mr. Kirklane, and Mr. Langley spent their first happy evening at the hospital—the start of a friendship between the members of the warrant officers' mess and the nursing sisters. Thereafter, each time the ship entered harbour, contact would be made with the hospital nursing staff, and nursing sisters would be entertained on board in the warrant officers' mess, or parties arranged on shore.

On this occasion Torps, as president of the mess, had been in touch with Mary Thompson, a senior nurse, and tentative arrangements were made for a party on shore. Torps would phone again on arrival ashore to complete the arrangements.

Tom Langley and the bos'n were waiting on the cabin flat for their messmates when a bell rang indicating that the shoregoing boat had left the lower boom to come alongside.

Tom Langley raised his voice. "How're you doing, chaps?"

From a cabin nearby came the voice of Torps. "Be with you in a minute, Tom."

Mr. Mayson walked out of his cabin, ready.

An electric razor ceased to buzz in Jim Kirklane's cabin and he called, "Coming, chaps!"

They sat on the wooden canopy of the motorboat as it sped shoreward. Harry Mayson spoke to Tom Langley, who sat beside him. "Torps and I will be talking to the girls on the phone to arrange a meeting after dinner. They have arranged to have dinner at the hospital now, and the matron gets annoyed if they change their minds."

"Well, Harry, try to fix a date with Agnes and Josie for Tim and me, or, if they are not free, with any of the other girls who would like to come dancing. Tim here wants to wander around awhile."

Harry Mayson nodded and smiled. The pair were inseparable on shore. "Tom and Tim the tramps under way again, eh?" Then he turned to Jim Kirklane.

"And what are your plans, Jim?"

"Well, I'll be contacting Susie as soon as I can, so I'll come along to the phone with you."

Jim Kirklane and Susan Brown had something in common. On first meeting, a hint of recognition between them led to the discovery that they had attended the same school in Manchester, she three years after him. Since then they had been very happy in each other's company.

"Right-o, Jim," said Harry. "We can phone from the Grand Trianon."

"And what about dinner?" asked Torps. "Shall we all meet later at the usual spot in the Grand Trianon, say, about seven-thirty?"

Tom Langley nodded and looked at Tim. "Suits me," said Tim.

"And me," said Jim Kirklane; "but where do we go after?"

"I think the girls would prefer the Carlton," said Torps. "We'll see what they say."

There was a sudden whirring roar of the boat's engines as she nudged alongside the pontoon. All officers jumped out and made their way through Number Six Gate, passing the Egyptian policeman on guard there. Once outside, the officers piled into a line of waiting taxis—all except the bos'n and Tom Langley.

The instance that had led to Tim Brinnell's friendship with Tom Langley had occasioned him some surprise. Late on a hot afternoon Tim had been taking a walk, wearing civilian clothes, through the maze of narrow streets that constituted the native quarter, and he had been far from comfortable for reasons other than the heat. He hadn't been sure just where he was, and it was obvious to him that the natives were aware of that. Early in his walk his curiosity in the unusual surroundings had led him from one narrow thoroughfare to another. He saw native coppersmiths patiently working copper into all kinds of pots and urns and, in some cases, exquisite ornaments. There were rows of workshops, each consisting of one little ground-floor room with no front to it; they were like adjoining caves in the base of long, and sometimes high, cliffs; the cliffs, of course, were the rows of ancient houses. In most cases the floor of the workshop was of beaten earth.

It was of great interest to Tim to see native workmen in bare feet, dressed in red fezzes and long gowns, working at trades he had thought belonged only to Western civilization. An Arab and his boy helper worked over fire and anvil, while his neighbour skilfully plied a fourteen-inch flat file over a steel bracket held in an engineer's vice. Arab workmen sat behind sewing and weaving machines. Others squatted on low stools and made boots, shoes, and slippers. Along the narrow streets native vendors carried their wares upon their heads or over their shoulders, advertising them in monotonous, sing-song voices. These were the poorer-class salesmen, but they carried a variety of things: native-made slippers and leather belts; baskets of oranges and other fruits; cakes and pastries, some made in the form of ringlets of varying sizes.

As Tim progressed, he slowly acquired a following of evil-looking natives who pestered him incessantly. Some offered to take him to all kinds of entertainments which, according to their descriptions, would be very novel in their lewdness. Others, mostly boys, tried to sell him "feelthy peectures." He shook off these offers, but as his following grew he became uneasy. He increased his pace and tried to find his way out of the native quarter, but each street he tuned in to seemed no more familiar than the one he had left. Eventually he turned a corner and found himself in a slightly wider thoroughfare lined on one side by handcarts. Here were the more well-to-do salesmen. He entered this street without hesitation, trying to appear as though he knew his way. Ahead on the opposite pavement a few small tables had been placed, around which sat natives drinking coffee. A loud, wailing, nasal Arab voice floated out from the coffee shop; the owner had tuned in his radio on some religious programme. As Tim drew level with the coffee shop he slowed down to look across, then he stopped in his tracks. He stood and stared.

Across the way, over the heads of the customers seated

outside, he could see clearly the interior of the coffee shop. There was a wide doorway with three stone steps leading up to it. On each side of the doorway a wide, curtainless window allowed full view. The place was packed with natives; some sipped coffee, some just talked, and others smoked away at their hookah pipes. At a table in line with the open doorway sat a figure dressed in European clothes. There was no mistaking that blue sports coat, the grey flannel trousers—and the attitude. That was Tom Langley, all right. He sat almost facing the doorway, with an elbow resting on the table beside him, and one ankle resting on his other leg above the knee. Two other people sat at the same table. One was an elderly native dressed in a clean white robe, a red fez, and sandals; he smoked a hookah. He had a fine, almost white beard. The other native was younger and of Egyptian origin. He wore European clothes—except for a red fez—consisting of a well-worn black coat and an equally well-worn pair of dark grey tweed trousers. An old khaki shirt completed his attire, for he wore no shoes. He had a fine, intelligent-looking face, dark brown eyes, and straight, jet-black hair. He was a healthy-looking young man of about twenty-two years of age with skin like a sunburned European's.

The bos'n hesitated, getting over his surprise. Then Tom Langley saw him and jumped to his feet. He walked to the door and waved Tim over. The bos'n walked over with considerable relief: He noticed that his band of followers was dispersing. When he reached the pavement near the coffee shop Tom called to him:

"Come on in, Bo'. What the hell are you doing around here?"

The bos'n laughed, a little nervously.

"Well," he said, climbing the stairs and raising his voice to compete with the sound of the radio, "I might ask you the same question."

between the rows of covered stalls, picking their way among crowds of natives and Europeans. Here one could buy almost any kind of dry goods, of almost any quality. The merchants were of various nationalities, among others, Egyptian, Indian, Greek, Jewish, Syrian, and French. Although the thoroughfares were very narrow—not more than eight feet wide—there was something pleasant in wandering through them. Brightly coloured carpets of excellent quality and textiles of all descriptions hung over the stalls and, in some cases, partially over the thoroughfares, so that people might feel the quality of the merchandise in passing. And in the air was that faint, clean, friendly odour of newness; this, together with the absence of noise usually associated with markets, gave one a feeling of peace and loosened the purse strings.

Behind the counters, in some of the stalls, craftsmen—tailors, dressmakers, weavers, woodworkers and leather-goods makers—worked away with the tools of their trades. Tim Brinnell had an entertaining ten minutes haggling with a native of India over the price of two tennis shirts, made locally from Egyptian cotton. Tom Langley stood by enjoying the proceedings and was pleased to see the bos'n make a fairly good deal.

They left the marketplace and made their way across the *place* (square) named Mohammed Ali—a large open thoroughfare surrounded by fine modern buildings—to enter rue des Soeurs. The street was more commonly known to sailors as Sister Street, and the farther one traveled down this wide, straight way, the more one's surroundings deteriorated: There were high-class shops near place Mohammed Ali, while the other end of the street bordered on the poorest of the native quarter.

A little way down the street they entered Spud Murphy's shop. It was a long, high, narrow store running well back from the pavement. There were long, glass-topped counters on each side, and overhead hung a variety of leather goods. Spud was busy parcelling up a pair of shoes for a customer when he caught sight of the two officers.

"Hello, Tom," he said. "I have message for you. Your friend Harry, he ring— You wait, I tell you."

He hurried to give his customer change and then came from behind the counter carrying a slip of paper. He was a lively little man of about forty years of age. His round, clean-shaven face was always ready to break into the smile that revealed a double row of gold-filled teeth. He walked up and shook hands with Tom and was introduced to Tim. Then he put his hand on Tom Langley's elbow and ushered him to the counter, where he put down his slip of paper.

"Look," he said, pointing to the paper, "Harry says, 'I am in Grand Trianon. I go shopping now but if Tom come in you tell him I come back here seven o'clock.' And then he say, 'Tell him ring thiz numbair.' "

At that Spud Murphy jabbed his emphasizing finger at a number on the paper chit and cast an anxious, inquiring look at Tom.

Tom smiled and put an arm around the Egyptian's shoulders.

"Well done, Spud, that's fine. I know that number—it's the Grand Trianon bar. Hmn. Wonder what it's all about."

He turned to Tim and then back to the little Egyptian.

"Did he say anything else?"

Spud Murphy meditated for a while, shaking his head slowly. Suddenly he looked up.

"Oh yes, he say your friend come from Cairo."

"Good old Spud!" said Tom. "Well done!" And Spud made a fine display of his gold fillings.

Tom looked at his watch. "Quarter to seven, Tim. If we shove off now we can walk up and meet Harry by soon after seven."

When they reached the door Tom looked back.

"How about that suitcase, Spud. Hundred and fifty?"

The little Egyptian gave him a happy smile. "Ah, you make joke," he said, and he went to help his assistant tend to his customers.

"Well," said Tom as they moved up the street, "this is a stroke of luck. I've been out here over two months now and this is the first time Alice has been able to get down while we've been in harbour. I didn't realize it was Friday until now. She'll be down for the weekend."

They reached the Grand Trianon soon after seven o'clock and pushed open the swing doors of the bar to find Harry Mayson and Torps handing their purchases over to the care of the Greek manager. The bos'n handed over his parcel as well.

"You got my message then, Tom," said Harry Mayson.

"Yes, Harry, and thanks. That was real good news."

"Well, come over and sit down and I'll tell you the rest of it."

The four hung up their caps and coats and sat at a small table away from the counter. Drinks were ordered and Harry Mayson handed round his cigarette case.

"Well, Tom," he said, "I rang up Eileen Hall at the hospital and arranged the date with her. Mary Thompson is coming along as Torps's partner. Eileen knew that Alice Anderson was in from Cairo, so she brought Susie to the phone. Susie was jumping glad to know we were in. She said she and Alice had arranged to go out to dinner at Glymenopoulos, where Alice is staying, and she asked to speak to Jim. The end result is that Jim has gone to join them for dinner and will escort them back to meet us here about nine o'clock. Susie said she is sure that Alice would be glad to come."

"Good show, Harry!" said Tom. "How about Josie and Agnes? Can they come?"

"Yes, they'll both be here."

"That's good," said Torps. "An extra girl can only improve the party. There'll probably be a few chaps joining us before the show's over."

The four glasses on the table were nearly empty when Torps looked at his watch.

"Well, chaps," he said, "what about some dinner?"

"Yes," said Tom Langley. "Tim and I thought of going to Harry Maroli's place. Feel like coming along?"

"Suits me," said Torps. "How about you, Harry?"

"Oh yes, that's fine. Let's go."

Harry Maroli was a Greek, and he kept a restaurant on the front, facing the sea. He was happy to see the four officers. Since the treacherous attack on his country by the Italians he had had a great hatred for the countrymen of Mussolini and a great liking for the British. The fact that an Italian kept the restaurant next door did nothing to lessen his hatred. But the Italian next door did not hate anybody, except, perhaps, the posturing fool who was leading his country to disaster.

As soon as the four were seated Harry Maroli's stout form waddled to the table to see that they received proper service. He was dressed in black, and the coat he wore, a short one of black silk, distinguished him from his waiters, who wore longer ones of white drill. His authority over his staff was strengthened by that coat, and probably by his row of chins, which were not easily countable, for the downward flow of them was cruelly interrupted by a close-fitting butterfly collar of spotless white.

Torps looked up from the menu. "What's special tonight, Harry?"

"Roast chicken," said the Greek. "Very good."

"Did you hear what I heard?" asked Tim.

"That's good enough for me," said Torps.

"And me," said Harry Mayson.

"Right," said Tom Langley. "Roast chicken for four."

Harry Maroli then took the remainder of their orders. Seeing that they conformed to his own suggestions gave him great pleasure, for that was proof of the officers' confidence in him. He passed the orders in Greek to a hovering waiter, who then hurried away as though his life depended on his speed in serving them.

Tom Langley looked at the Greek proprietor with a humorous gleam in his eye.

"Got any Chianti, Harry?"

Harry Maroli looked for a moment as though he might explode. He swallowed hard before he realized he was being teased.

"Chianti!" he said. "No Chianti in my place! Next door, that bloody Italian—he have Chianti. I gif you Greek red wine—better than Chianti!"

"That's just what we've come in for, Harry. Will you send the waiter along with a large bottle, please?"

The Greek smiled and went away.

The bos'n grinned. "You shouldn't do that, Tom. Old Harry is so proud of his red wine. I believe it means as much to him as his roast chicken."

"Yes, I know. His wine is first class, and these Egyptian chickens aren't much bigger than pigeons, but old Harry turns them out fit for a king."

The waiter hurried in with the wine and filled four large glasses with the mellow, deep red liquid.

Harry Mayson lifted his glass high and looked through it with an appraising eye.

"Well, chaps, here's success to temperance."

The others followed suit, sipping slowly, making the smooth wine linger on its way. It imparted a gentle glow and a feeling of well-being.

The waiter brought the soup and departed. There was a crackling sound as strong hands broke the crisp outer shell of the small, light brown rolls of bread.

The bos'n paused before biting into a well-buttered half roll.

"I wonder how Jim and Susie are doing."

Harry Mayson looked up. "Oh, they'll be as happy as a pair of kids. They might not have been, though—I thought Jim was lucky to get ashore tonight."

"Why, how's that?" asked Torps.

"Well, there are two boilers being cleaned and Jim is in charge of the boiler rooms."

"But you have a duty officer aboard to look after that, haven't you?"

"Oh yes, there are two aboard: Lieutenant Tangry and Mr. Prout. For that matter the boiler cleaning is normally left to the man who knows most about it—the boilermaker—and he's aboard. The trouble is the commander (E) never goes down there, consequently he believes that the more people he keeps on board the better everything will be—for him, anyway. It only needs one engineer to inspect the job when it's finished."

"That's right," said Tom Langley, "and I remember Jim couldn't get ashore last time we cleaned boilers. Could be the chief got too many gins at lunchtime and forgot to hold Jim back."

Torps nodded. "Could be. Anyhow, let's leave the ship in the water. We're ashore now." He called over to the waiter. "Bring on the chicken, Johnny, we're starving!"

Yes—leave the ship in the water. There she lies in the care of the port watch, and in the boiler room men of the engine room department are busy. A portable fan blows a cool breeze into the steam drum of each boiler. Inside these hot steel drums the stokers work. Rivulets of sweat run down their pale, grimy faces. Thin singlets cling to their bodies, and sweat from their arms runs down over their hands and hinders their grip on the steel handles of the tube-cleaning brushes, but they heard their captain speak today and they work with a will. Tomorrow may bring, for them, a trip ashore.

CHAPTER 7

Before midnight the Carlton was full to capacity. Patrons had crowded in in anticipation of the floor show, due to start at the stroke of twelve. The small dance floor in the centre of the hall was packed with happy couples. Civilian clothing was the exception, and the variety of uniforms added to the gaiety of the scene. Here were represented the fighting forces of the British Isles, South Africa, Australia, New Zealand, Rhodesia, and Poland, as well as the nursing services of their armies and navies.

On the side of the hall opposite the bar, three tables had been pushed together to accommodate a large party. Mr. Mills and his partner, Mary Thompson, sat talking and watching the dance floor. At the other end of the table was the only member of the party not dressed in uniform. She sat with her elbow on the table and her chin resting lightly on her hand, listening to her old friend Tom Langley. An unusual person, that one: not pretty unless you looked at her clear blue eyes and fine, light brown hair. She had a rather snub nose and slightly prominent upper teeth. She said she would like to reduce her weight by about ten pounds but Tom didn't agree with her in that. There was nothing about her to suggest more than average intelligence, and yet, at the age of thirty, she could speak nearly every European language fluently and was rapidly mastering Arabic.

"Well," she said, "it's nice seeing you again, Tom," and

she reached over the table to touch his hand. "I've often wondered how you were faring in the war. I wrote to you and Ethel over a month ago, though I couldn't be sure your family would still be in Plymouth in view of the threat of air raids. Anyhow, if she received my letter she will know that Russell and I are married."

Tom smiled. "And that will surprise her, but she'll be just as happy to know it as I was. Is Russell based in Cairo?"

"Yes, but just now he's visiting some headquarters in the desert, behind the front lines there. But how about your family, Tom? You say you haven't heard from them recently."

"No, and it's got me worried. I can only hope it's because they're moving—anywhere out of Plymouth."

Tom sat silent for a moment, gazing moodily at the table, then he looked up and met those steadfast, clear blue eyes and smiled. "Anyhow, let's forget it for now. That's nice music we're hearing."

"So it is, Tom. Let's dance."

The band was playing a slow fox-trot, and they found the floor had cleared a little. Harry Mayson and Eileen Hall were leaving the floor as they arrived. Eileen was a dumpy little person, very little over five feet tall, with round, rosy cheeks and a merry smile.

"You won't catch much of this dance," she said. "This is the third encore."

Alice and Tom danced away, moving easily on the crowded floor.

Tim Brinnell caught their eyes and his face lit up in a happy smile. He was obviously enjoying himself, and his partner, Josie Weir, simply radiated happiness. Josie was a tall, dark, slim young woman who had brought with her, from her native city of Edinburgh, a rather serious expression. But tonight the seriousness was absent and she was a source of joy and wonder to her friends.

Following them on the crowded floor Jim Kirklane guided Susie, and she followed his every move with an easy grace. She had removed her tunic and looked cool and comfortable, her white silk blouse with collar and tie enhancing her beauty. The deep gold of her hair shone. Her blonde head reached just a little higher than Jim Kirklane's shoulder.

And in the centre of the floor another couple performed. Sublieutenant Kelling had entered the Carlton to see the floor show and had been invited to join the party. But the centre of a small, crowded dance floor is a difficult place in which to perform. There is more room in which to move, but that area becomes a small, contested no-man's-land. Kelling and his partner, Agnes Andrewes, were two of the contestants, and several bumps from competing partners, coming in rapid succession, disorganized them and set them laughing outright. Then the music stopped and a few tinkling notes indicated that the dance had ended.

As the floor cleared Torps busied himself seeing that everyone was comfortably seated. He shifted chairs about so that the whole party should have a good view of the floor show.

"Here we are then, children," he said. "All merry and bright now?"

The reference to children brought a few happy chuckles from the party. Then Susie leaned over to look along the table. "How could we be otherwise with Torps to look after us?"

"Hear, hear!" said Harry Mayson.

"Now then, boys and girls," said the smiling Torps, "you'll spoil me with kindness."

The spotlight came on, the lights around the hall dimmed, the band struck up the tune "Whispering," and a couple appeared on the floor.

They were experts—they danced gracefully in perfect

harmony. Except for the soft music all was still. The war was forgotten. Yet, a few score miles away in the Western Desert, British Empire forces held a vastly superior enemy at bay.

CHAPTER 8

The men's canteen was a sight to behold. Several hundred men in naval uniform packed the large room. There was a bar at one end behind which three bartenders worked with great haste, serving bottles of beer to the customers. The floor of the hall was littered with small, oblong pieces of paper of all colours. At the other end of the hall, opposite the bar, three petty officers sat behind a long table. Three queues of men filed slowly to the long table, purchasing blue tickets at five piastres each. In a clear space in the centre of the hall was a small, high table at which sat a leading seaman. He held a bag, full of small wooden discs, which he raised above his head and shook vigorously. The air overhead was thick with smoke, but windows had been opened to allow it to clear. About the hall small wooden tables had been placed. These and the windowsills were littered with beer bottles, many of which were what the sailors called "dead marines": empty ones.

Around one table at the side of the hall a small group of men stood and watched Able Seaman Tuckett. He divided a small bundle of Egyptian pound notes equally into two and passed one stack over to his friend Dusty Miller. Then together the pair started to count a small pile of silver coins. The few men standing around were their messmates, except for one who came from the stokers' mess deck: Speedy, the senior engineer's messenger. Friendship between the two able seamen and Speedy appeared to be growing rapidly.

Able Seaman Tuckett was known to most of his shipmates as "Smiler." The name was well deserved, for he smiled all day long no matter what happened. And he smiled now no more and no less than at any other time. He looked over the heads of his friends toward the three queues at the end of the hall.

"Here, Dusty," he said, "we'd better get moving. I'd better buy the tickets again while my luck's in. And what about the beer? Where's Speedy?"

"Here I am, Smiler," said Speedy, edging his way forward.

Smiler passed over some silver coins. "Go and get some beer, Speedy—and you, chaps—go on, give him a hand to carry it back."

Half a dozen men went off to the bar and Smiler went to buy the tickets for the next game.

"Cor blimey," said Dusty Miller, "his luck's in tonight. Good thing for me we always agree to split fifty-fifty at tombola."

"Yes," replied one of his messmates, "you're a jam-strangling pair of blighters tonight. That's three times he's won now, isn't it?"

"Yes—two lines and one house. I wouldn't be surprised to see him win the big house now."

Soon the sale of tombola tickets had ceased and the petty officers at the table were totalling up the cash received. The leading seaman in the centre of the hall gave his bag of discs a final shake. The discs were numbered from one to ninety, and he meant to see that they were properly mixed. When satisfied about this he untied the end of the bag.

"All ready now?" he yelled. "Eyes down for the first number!"

About the hall the men waited, pencils in hand, ready to cross off any numbers on their tickets as they were called. Each ticket had fifteen numbers in three rows of five.

"First number—three and nine! Thirty-nine."

"Blood!" said Speedy, seeing the number on his ticket.

The leading seaman continued calling out numbers, pausing a little between each one. Some of the numbers had been given rather humorous nicknames, and he seemed well versed in these.

"Two little ducks! Twenty-two!"

"By itself, Kelly's eye! Number one!"

When the twelfth number was called Smiler had crossed off four numbers on his top line. One of his shipmates saw him hurriedly using his pencil.

"Blimey," he said quickly. "Smiler's sweating again."

The calling of numbers ceased and Dusty Miller looked at his chum's ticket. He saw the only uncrossed number on the top line: number ten.

"Oh," he said, "that's what you're waiting for—marine's breakfast, eh?"

"That's him, Dusty—egg and a rasher."

The voice of the leading seaman was heard again.

"Do you hear there? Amount of the house: four pounds, seventy piastres the line, twenty-three pounds, fifty piastres the full house! Eyes down for the next number!"

The bag was given a good shaking and another number taken out.

"Legs eleven! My girl has a pair and they're lovely!"

From across the hall two voices yelled in unison: "*Here you are!*"

The leading seaman raised his voice above the noise that followed.

"Line called on number eleven!"

The two winning tickets were handed up to him and were checked correct against the numbers taken from the bag. Soon the calling of the numbers started again.

"Top of the house! Nine-oh! Ninety!"

Smiler had missed winning the line but his luck still held. As the numbers came out his pencil was busy. Very soon he was waiting for two numbers only, while most of his friends needed six or seven. Number ten had still not been called; the other number he required was seventy-four. His friends watched their own tickets and kept their ears cocked for these numbers.

"All the threes! Thirty-three!"
"Seven and five! Seventy-five!"
"Ah-h-h," said the little group softly.
"Four and seven! Forty-seven!"
"Seven and four! Seventy-four!"

The group gathered around to watch Smiler cross off the number. "He's sweating again on that bloody marine's breakfast," said one.

"Suffering cats!" said another. "Twenty-three blinking quid!"

"By itself—number nine!"

Smiler and his friends were scarcely breathing.

"Royal salute! That's two and one! Twenty-one!"

Small beads of perspiration stood on Smiler's brow, and the pencil trembled in his fingers. Among the great number of men in the room there were probably several who were waiting for only one number, and many more who required only two.

"Half a crown! Two and six! Twenty-six!"

About the hall those who had the number on their tickets cross it off, but still no call came; dead silence.

"All the eights! Eighty-eight!"

Dusty Miller crossed the number off his ticket. Breaking a breathless silence, he whispered excitedly in Smiler's ear, "I'm waiting now—number fifteen!"

The leading seaman pulled another disc out of the bag, glanced at it, and placed it on the table before him. Then his voice rent the silence, and to Smiler's mind it came like a roaring flood.

"Marine's breakfast! Egg and a rasher! Number ten!"

A tiny pause followed while the whole world went round. Then Smiler and his friends yelled together:

"*Here—you—a-a-a-a-a-a-are!*"

A loud buzz of conversation broke out over the room. Men looked over from all directions to see Smiler emerge from his band of friends. He walked up to the centre table carrying his ticket. The leading seaman at the table hardly made his voice heard.

"House called on number ten!"

Envious men heard the ticket being checked. Some had been there all evening and had never had the thrill of nearly winning, let alone the pleasure of shouting, "Here you are." "Same bloke again," said one. "He's the jammiest son of a gun I ever heard of." Others threw their tickets on the floor, some in disgust, some with a smile. Others, again, were not much concerned; they were pouring out the beer. It was nearing midnight, when the bar would close.

Smiler soon came back with his winnings and promptly set about splitting fifty-fifty with Dusty. He handed some silver to his messmates, asking them to bring another round of beer before the bar closed. The division of the money completed, and Dusty Miller pushed his half into his trousers pocket and beamed around.

"Crikey," he said. "I've never had so much money in me life before." He grinned at his chum. "No use hanging around here now, Smiler. You've just about cleaned this place out."

"Yes," said Smiler, "might as well shove off soon, but let's have one more drink with the chaps before we go."

"All right. Here they come now. Cor blimey—they've bought enough beer to last all night!"

"Oh, there'll be lots of chaps to help 'em with that. But where are *we* going, Dusty?"

"Well, what about some steak and eggs and chips or something, and after that we could go to a cabaret—they don't chuck out till about two o'clock."

"Yes, all right, but we'd better book rooms for the night first."

"Blimey, yes," said Dusty. "Let's find a posh hotel, the best one in the blinkin' place."

"And what about Speedy? Shall we ask him to come?"

"Oh, yes—Speedy! Where is he?"

"Here I come," said Speedy, arriving in the wake of the beer carriers. "Who wants me?"

"I do," said Dusty. "Smiler and me are going to push off in a minute. Coming with us?"

"Yes, I'd like to. Where are you going?"

"Some big eats first— But come on, let's have a quick beer with the chaps. We're wasting time."

CHAPTER 9

That night the Italian air force played a dirty trick on Dusty Miller and his two friends, but it might well have been worse. When the air-raid siren sounded the trio were sitting in splendour in a good-class restaurant, each smoking a cigar. They were in no fit shape to rise in a hurry, for in true sailor fashion they had polished off large platefuls of steak and eggs and chips, together with trimmings in the way of greenstuffs and tomatoes. Helpings of apple pie had followed before the cigars were set aglow. With the first wail of the siren the Egyptian proprietor rushed by them to pull a light steel screen down over the doorway, and a waiter turned out most of the lights. The proprietor seemed slightly annoyed because the sailors showed no signs of excitement, but that didn't upset them, either. *They* were slightly annoyed because their chances of seeing a floor show in a cabaret had receded. Another small matter was not quite right for Dusty: He could find nothing under the table on which to place his feet—except the floor. Otherwise everything was fine for all three.

Dusty puffed a huge billow of smoke up into the air. "Might as well stay here now," he said. "They'll try to drop their bombs on the ships. Bet the port watch'll have a bloody howl on tonight—going to action stations at one o'clock in the morning."

"Yes," said Speedy, "especially the chaps who only came off watch at midnight."

The siren ceased its wailing and silence fell. This quiet waiting period prevailed everywhere in the port area. The last turn of the floor show at the Carlton had been brought to an abrupt end when the siren sounded, and now many of the lights were out. Most of the patrons remained seated at their tables. After about fifteen minutes Harry Mayson stood up. "If you'll excuse me, folks, I'll slip out for a minute to see what's happening."

"Well, come back soon, Harry, and let us know," said Torps. "We don't want to sit around here too long."

Harry Mayson had reached the door when the antiaircraft guns started firing. Soon he reentered the hall and beckoned to the others to come and join him. As they reached the main exit from the building the sound of antiaircraft fire grew more intense. There was more light in the street than that given out by the waning moon: A score or more of searchlights had been switched on; the beams from these converged on a point in the sky high up over the harbour. At this point an enemy plane twisted and turned in an effort to vanish into the surrounding darkness. Meanwhile the guns continued their steady barking. A second plane flashed into view. One of its wings passed through a searchlight beam.

"Well this is as good as a floor show, anyway," said Jim Kirklane.

The searchlights jostled about the sky holding the plane in view for several minutes before it slipped away into the darkness. Two, perhaps three, planes could be heard in the sky. The beams of light began to probe independently for these, but the sound of the planes seemed to be fading. Suddenly there was a great flash of flame and a heavy explosion close to the shore end of the breakwater. A stick of bombs had struck the rocks in the water close by. Very soon another heavy but muffled explosion occurred somewhere in the harbour. They learned afterwards that it had been another stick of bombs that dropped in the water well clear of all ships. The searchlights still played about the sky but the antiaircraft fire had ceased. The raid seemed to be over when suddenly another explosion occurred, this time in the town and well clear of the harbour.

"Oh, hell! That's something new," said the bos'n. "They've never dropped a bomb on the town before."

"No," said Tom Langley, "and I don't like it—for more reasons than one." He left the group and walked across the road to the sea wall. Soon he was back again. "There's a fairly large fire in the town," he said, "and judging from the position of the glow in the sky I think it is in the native quarter. By gosh, most of those houses are teeming with people!"

"Oh, what a shame!" said Susie. "There's nothing we can do, I suppose?"

"Not in a case like this," replied Mary Thompson. "The ARP organization will be dealing with it."

"Well," said Torps, "it isn't much use going back into the Carlton now, so what are we going to do? I think this raid is over."

"We have to call at the Grand Trianon to collect our parcels," said Harry Mayson. "Anybody feel like walking? We could walk round and then when the all clear goes take taxis from the stand there."

No other proposals being put forward, the whole party moved off. As they reached the Grand Trianon the siren sounded the all clear. Soon the traffic was moving about the streets again.

"Time we were going home, then," said Mary Thompson, looking round and seeing everyone apparently ready to leave. Her remark brought forth a smile or two for it was one that might have been made by Torps himself. Indeed these two made ideal partners, she being tall and well built and—at the age of forty—several years older than any of the other nurses.

As the party walked over to the taxi stand Alice Anderson sought out Tom Langley and walked beside him. "Tom," she said, "I am staying out at Glymenopoulos so you had better not come all that way. I'll be at the hospital tomorrow for tea with Susie. Can you come?"

"Oh yes, I think we'll still be in harbour."

They reached the taxi stand and gathered as a group.

"What about tomorrow?" asked Mary Thompson. "Any of you boys coming up to tea?"

A general discussion followed, and Agnes Andrewes made her way to Tom Langley's side. "Tom," she said, "if you come up tomorrow bring John with you."

"John," said Tom, "who's John?"

"That's me, you goof," said Sublieutenant Kelling.

"Oh ho! we have a dark horse in our midst. Right-o Agnes, I'll bring him along—if he's not duty aboard."

"Oh no, I'm free, and I'd like to join you. Thank you, Agnes."

"Good for you, Sub," said Tom. "What are you going to do now? Feel like walking back to the jetty? It's grand out tonight, and by the time we get down there these chaps will be coming back in the taxis. Then we can all pile into a felucca and go aboard together."

"Right-o, let's walk."

"Don't wait at the jetty for me, Tom," said Jim Kirklane. "Susie and I are walking back to the hospital."

There followed an opening and slamming of taxi doors.

"Good night, Alice," said Tom.

Good nights came in chorus as the taxis moved away, then more good nights between the four left standing. Tom Langley and Kelling stepped briskly away. Susie and Jim moved off hand in hand along the seafront, and that wily old henchman of Cupid, Mr. Moon, played his light on a Mediterranean shore, and his charm on two hearts in tune.

CHAPTER 10

The work of cleaning boilers had been pressed on through the night and the starboard watch was busy finishing off the job.

In the forenoon leave was piped for the port watch from 1:00 P.M. until midnight. Mr. Mayson, who was one of the duty engineers on board, knew from this that the ship was likely to leave early in the morning.

After seeing the boilers closed up and tested in the late afternoon he went up to the flight deck to take a walk in the fresh air. The sun was shining, but as he faced the light breeze blowing from forward he realized that the evenings were getting colder. He was just getting into his stride when the bos'n's pipe sounded, followed by the call, "Hands to bathe the port side!"

There were a few dozen men pacing the deck, but most of them hurried below to put on their bathing costumes. Mr. Mayson remained, just to watch. *A bit late in the year now for bathing*, he thought, but he knew that the water would be much warmer than the breeze.

Soon men were gathering by the guardrails on the port side of the decks nearer the waterline, ready to dive at the sound of the bugle call. One young ordinary seaman hurried on to the flight deck and stood poised at the side, waiting. The few remaining men on the flight deck, including Mr. Mayson, gathered near to watch him make the high dive. They had not long to wait. The bugle sounded: "Ta ta tah! Ta ta tah!"

Almost instantly a few dozen men hit the water and started to churn it to fury as they raced away from the ship's side. The young ordinary seaman on the flight deck had no time to lose. With the advantage of height he dived clear over the men below. For an instant after he hit the water there was a neat round hole where his feet had followed the rest of his body under, then a small column of water, disturbed by the dive, plopped down and filled the hole, leaving only a slight swirl as evidence. It wasn't so much a dive as an insinuation. And the young sailor wasn't under very long. He broke surface to find many of his shipmates close by in their race away. Someone threw two water-polo balls from the ship, and the swimmers made a thrashing rush and struggled for possession of these. Very soon the two balls were being thrown about and the men were thoroughly enjoying themselves.

Mr. Mayson had been feeling strangely depressed all afternoon. He wondered if he was developing a cold, or could it possibly be the war? Deep inside he carried an unshakeable optimism regarding the outcome of the war. He knew who would win it. How it would be won was a different matter, for the odds were so great and nothing seemed clear ahead. He did not like to admit that the war situation could cause any lowering of his spirits. He was therefore surprised to note the tonic effect the sight of the men disporting in the water induced in him. His own reactions confirmed that he had been subconsciously perturbed about the course of the war. There was something in watching hearty British manhood at play that put his mind at ease. In their whole outlook, in their robust, hardy nature, these were the ideal men to fight in opposition to aggression and treachery. Just looking at them he received an assurance of that. What a tough job the enemy had undertaken! *Yes, by gosh!* thought Mr. Mayson, *This is Britain's material, the stuff with which the war will be won.* He found himself smiling, laughing at the antics of the men in the water, and realized what a fool he had been all afternoon.

After about twenty minutes the bugle sounded the retreat and the swimmers made for the ship's side. Mr. Mayson had some divisional records to write up so he went aft to his cabin and set to work. He was still at his desk at seven-thirty when his door curtain was pushed aside and a head appeared.

"Come on, Mr. Mayson, that's enough of that. What about a gin?"

"Oh, come in, Lieutenant Tangry. Sit down while I stow this stuff away."

Lieutenant Tangry had to bend his head to clear the doorway. He stood over six feet in his socks, and deplored the fact that Her Majesty's ships were so constructed that he was compelled to adopt the shape of a question mark in order to make his way about between decks. He was a fine specimen of manhood, broad of shoulder and without an ounce of superfluous fat. His face was on the lean side, but his complexion must have been the envy of many friends of the opposite sex. In Mr. Mayson's opinion he was, at the age of twenty-five, a damned smart engineer officer.

He sat down on Mr. Mayson's bed-settee and watched the older man stow his papers. There was a mutual admiration between these two. Though drawn from different classes of English social life, each knew, and appreciated, the calibre of the other.

"All set then, Mr. Mayson?"

"All set, sir. Let's go."

As they entered the wardroom anteroom, several officers nodded and smiled a good evening to Mr. Mayson. Lieutenant Tangry called to the steward, who quickly produced two gins. The ship's radio-gramophone was turning out selections from *Lilac Time*.

"Hmm," said Mr. Mayson taking a sip, "very nice."

"What's very nice, Mr. Mayson, the gin or the music?"

"Well I was referring to everything in general, and certainly the music."

"Oh, so you like that sort of thing, do you? It's quite nice, but I must get you to come along and hear some real stuff."

"Well, I'll try anything once, but I don't think we'll be able to go ashore for some time, do you?"

"No, perhaps not, but I wasn't thinking of going ashore. I have the stuff in my cabin. Come down after supper and I'll play a record for you."

"All right, thanks. That's very good of you. I'll come down after I've finished the night rounds. Will that do?"

"Of yes, of course."

Several of the officers moved into the wardroom for supper. Mr. Mayson looked at the clock.

"By gosh," he said, "I didn't realize it was so late." He put down his empty glass.

"Yes, you old warhorse, and you'd still have been down there with your nose in those papers if I hadn't come and rescued you; but do stay and have another one now."

"Oh no, thanks. I'm afraid I must go. See you soon after nine."

A few bags of mail had arrived on board in the evening, and Mr. Mayson found two letters in the rack for himself and one for Tom Langley. The latter he placed in Tom's cabin where that wanderer would find it on his return from shore.

After supper he went back to his desk to read his own mail before doing the rounds. The news from home wasn't good. There had been only a few light air raids on Plymouth, but raid alarms had been frequent, due to enemy reconnaissance flights. These had caused Mr. Mayson's wife and family to spend much of their time in the tiny air raid shelter in the back yard and Mrs. Mayson was concerned about the effect this might have on the children's health. However, so far they were all keeping well, though often tired in the morning. The oldest girl, now seventeen, had left school and started work with a business firm as a shorthand typist. Her sister, three years younger, had one day fallen asleep at her desk in school, so now, when she or the boy seemed overtired in the morning, their mother kept them home.

Mr. Mayson's second letter was from his oldest girl, and it caused him no end of amusement. In her enthusiasm about her job she forgot to mention anything about air raids. She liked her boss and was doing fine. Of course, everyone had to start at the bottom, she supposed, if they were going to learn a job properly. She thought there was plenty of room for women in business in these modern times, and didn't her dad think so too? Mr. Mayson read through four pages of delightful chatty prose and spent a good few minutes in meditation, gazing at the folded letter and occasionally smiling and shaking his head as though to say, "Well, I never!"

After carrying out the rounds of the engine room department he went to Lieutenant Tangry's cabin, and found that worthy well extended on his bed-settee, reading a library book. The rattle of the brass rings holding his door curtain brought the lieutenant quickly to a sitting position.

He pushed a chair over to his guest. "Here we are then, Mr. Mayson."

The older man sat down and took in his surroundings. The cabin was arranged very much like his own. It was rectangular in shape and long enough for a bed-settee and a clothes cupboard on one side. On the opposite side was a chest of drawers and a washbowl, and in between these two ship's fittings the lieutenant had installed a cabinet of his own, on top of which he'd set a portable gramophone. A writing desk was arranged along the short side opposite the door, and it was this part of the cabin that held Mr. Mayson's attention the longest. About a foot above the level of the desk was a neat little shelf on which stood a framed photograph of a remarkably pretty girl. She seemed to smile out of the silver frame in a most natural, friendly way, and it was with reluctance that Mr. Mayson transferred his attention to Lieutenant Tangry, who, while still sitting on the edge of the bed-settee, had reached over and opened the cabinet opposite, from which he was selecting a record.

Mr. Mayson was surprised on seeing the interior of the cabinet. There were so many records that it had been necessary to index them. This had been done very thoroughly: The cabinet was divided into sections marked alphabetically, and each record holder had a small white tag with a number clearly visible.

The lieutenant replaced the index book and took out a record.

"I hope you will like this one, Mr. Mayson. Of course I am playing my favourite one first." He stood up and started the motor.

"Which one is it?"

"It's the Allegro movement from the Concerto in F Minor by Bach."

"Well, it seems I shall have to show my ignorance; I'm afraid I don't know what's coming."

"Never mind, Mr. Mayson, there's plenty of stuff here that you'll like. Hear this one and then take a look through the index."

The two men sat still during the playing of the record. It was obvious that the younger man was enjoying the music immensely: He was lost to everything else. He sat a little sideways on the bed-settee with his elbows resting on his knees. He appeared to be listening intently with one ear. In this position he presented a side view to Mr. Mayson, who noted the firm yet unaggressive jaw, and the high forehead with the dark brown, wavy hair brushed straight back from it. And in the line of sight immediately above the head of the stooping figure was the smiling girl in the silver frame. Her pleasant, friendly smile seemed to be saying, "Yes, he's mine."

When the music stopped the older man realized that he had allowed his mind to wander. Many times had his eyes passed from the profile of Lieutenant Tangry to the photograph of the smiling girl and back again.

The lieutenant sat for a little while in happy reverie before reaching over to lift the needle clear of the record.

"Well," he said, sitting back, "did you like it?"

The commissioned engineer had been waiting for the question, but he hesitated before answering.

"Well—there's no doubt it's good music, and probably the more I heard of it the more I'd appreciate it."

Lieutenant Tangry screwed up one eye and shook his head as though to say, "That's the real stuff, old boy." He handed over the index: "There you are. Now it's your turn."

Mr. Mayson found much that he liked in the index, but he quickly made his choice, and soon the two officers were listening to Peter Dawson singing "The Cornish Floral Dance." It was something both men enjoyed, and at one point Mr. Mayson felt compelled to add his own voice: "Fiddle, 'cello, big bass drum, bassoon, flute and euphonium," patting the deck with one foot and beating time with his right hand. When the music ceased the older man rose and lifted the needle clear. Then he removed the record and replaced it in the cabinet. As he straightened his back his eyes again met those of the girl in the silver frame.

"Do you know," he said, "that's a remarkably fine photo." He turned to Lieutenant Tangry. "Friend of yours, or sister?"

And thereby Mr. Mayson put an end to all record playing for that evening.

The lieutenant's rather serious expression vanished as

he smiled tenderly and looked at the photograph. "She's everything to me, Mr. Mayson. She's my wife."

The older man sat quietly.

"Oh," he said, "I'd never thought of you as being married." He looked at the photograph again, and back to the lieutenant. "Well," he added, "if I'm any judge of character you're a darned lucky fellow."

"You *are* a judge of character, and I think I'm the luckiest fellow in the world." The younger man paused, still looking at the photograph of his wife. After a brief silence he spoke softly, like a man talking to himself. "Her nature is as sweet as her picture. As lovely as she appears there, so she is in all her ways, and she's always the same."

"How long have you been married?"

"Nearly two years now—two years that have been too short. It is four months since we said good-bye to each other, and every day seems like wasted life to me."

"I think I understand."

"Of course you do, Mr. Mayson; I know you have a wife and family; but tell me, does it ever get any better? I mean, does one find any compensation in this life for being separated from the one person you want to be with? Will I feel any easier, will there be less heartache, when there is a child or children at home? Will it lighten her burden? For I can read between the lines and I know she feels the same as I do, though her letters are always cheerful."

The older man sat quietly, his head bowed slightly and his jaws clamped together. He shook his head very slowly.

"No," he said, looking up, "it doesn't get better. You do get reconciled to your lot, in a way. That is, you learn all kinds of dodges to fool yourself, and they do ease your heartache a little. While you are away you work hard and play hard. You seek plenty of company and go to see everything worth seeing in the places you visit. You write long, cheerful letters telling her all about these things. And a good partner like yours—and mine—is doing the same thing at home. Then there is an old dodge I have found useful when I have to leave home. It always works. During the last two or three days before leaving home you watch for the early signs. You feel damned low yourself but you say nothing. Then it comes, in a quiet moment: The unhappy future looms before her mind's eye and suddenly she clings to you. She starts to tell you how awful it is going to be with you away. She's fighting not to break down, and that's when you have to show her how strong you are. So you grab her by the shoulders just before the tears come, and shake her gently, and smile and say, 'Hey, come on! We have all day today and the best part of tomorrow before we start thinking about good-bye. And we're going to enjoy it together, aren't we? So come on, my lassie, to blazes with the day after tomorrow! We'll be unhappy then, not now.' And because she's a fighter she comes up trumps. She smiles and says, 'All right, what shall we do tonight? The dance at the Whatsitsname, or go to a show?' That's round one well and truly won, and from then on if you keep busy during the daytime, before you can properly realize it you are saying good-bye at the dockyard gate, or the jetty, or perhaps the railway station. There may be a tear or two but she's still remembering that other fight she won, and soon you are on your way; both of you better fortified to meet those miserable days that follow your parting."

Lieutenant Tangry had been listening intently and watching Mr. Mayson's face all the time. His eyes shone as he reached over and clasped a large, strong hand on the knee of the older man.

"Mr. Mayson," he said, "you're priceless!"

It was clear that the lieutenant was feeling happier, but he followed up with the subject.

"And it doesn't get better after the children come along?"

Mr. Mayson shook his head. "It doesn't for you or your wife. You see, although she has the company of the children she has increased responsibility, and no matter how strong a woman thinks she is, she still needs support in rearing a family. And she needs this more when something ails the children. If only *you* were there, how different it would be! Her child is in pain—has a toothache and is crying in the night. She wakes up to the full realization that she is minus the one person she needs. Her heart aches for the child and it aches for you. Then there comes the time when she realizes that the children need your influence. She showers so much love on them that sooner or later they try to take charge of her. She has both jobs to do—yours and her own—and it comes hard. I have seen the strain of this clearly in my wife's face when I have arrived home after long spells away. It always gives me pleasure to see it disappear after a few days."

There was a pause for a moment, then the younger man looked up.

"Yes, I think I see—and all this interests me very much. You see I am trying to decide whether I shall continue in the navy and make it my career, or leave after the war and take my chance in outside life with millions of other men who will be doing the same thing. I think I shall leave—I like my home too much. And—it's a bit harder now because"— he glanced at the photograph of his wife—"Mrs. Tangry will become a mother before very long."

"Ah!" said Mr. Mayson. "Now I see."

The lieutenant looked up quickly.

Mr. Mayson smiled. "Excuse me if I seemed rather brusque, but I understand how you feel, and I hope you get home soon. It would make all the difference to Mrs. Tangry—and to you. In any case may you be more fortunate than I was."

"Why? Nothing serious, I hope."

"Well—no, and yes. Both of my girls were two years old

before I saw them. And it was quite a time before either of them could accept me as somebody who mattered very much."

"What a shame!" said the lieutenant quietly.

"It was different with the boy," Mr. Mayson went on. "I arrived home after a spring cruise in the Home Fleet, just in time for the big event. Then I had a shore job for two years, so he and I sort of grew up together. It was grand. And my luck still held, for I went to another Home Fleet ship for a year, so I saw quite a lot of him at just the right time."

Neither man spoke for a while; each was busy with his own thoughts. Then Mr. Mayson went on. "Have you ever thought of what you would like your first child to be, boy or girl?"

The lieutenant smiled. "Well, both my wife and I seem to have taken it for granted that it will be a boy."

"Well, if you are to have as much pleasure with a boy as I have had with mine you will not be disappointed. Mind you, I think just as much of either of the girls, but in a different way. They seem to cling to their mother more. It may be a result of my coming into their lives later. On the other hand it may be because of my own vanity, something that makes me seek the boy's company more; a fact the girls can't help but notice. You see, in the eyes of my son I am the finest chap in the world. His dad is Robin Hood, Oliver Cromwell, and Sir Francis Drake all rolled into one. Another thing, his dad wears a sword, like an admiral. And didn't his dad go to the King's Review? 'Bet he'll soon be an admiral,' he tells himself, and so on. Of course my son will be growing out of a lot of that now, for he's nine years old, but he'll still be my grand little friend. I'm glad he doesn't know I bought my cocked hat and sword secondhand."

Their eyes met, and both men smiled. Mr. Mayson continued.

"Yes, you can have many happy days watching your son grow up. I remember coming home from my station in the West Indies. I'd been away nearly three years but my boy knew me, all right. He was swinging on the front gate and saw me approaching about a hundred yards away. He came running down the street as fast as his little six-year-old legs would carry him. It was in the early summer and my wife had moved. We were in our own house at last. That is, we had started to purchase the house under a pay-as-you-go scheme. The family was nicely settled in and delighted about it all after living in rented rooms for so long. However, when I arrived there was much to be done, especially outdoors. We had a patch of lawn at the back and a little border garden. There was a garage, too, awaiting the day when we could bear the expense of a car. And so, during my leave, I got busy outdoors, with the boy beside me every spare moment he had. It got so that I used to become impatient waiting for him to come home from school. Then he would arrive, and except for half an hour at tea he would be with me all evening. He learned how to use a paintbrush, screwdriver, and pliers, and soon knew the names of all my tools. If I was weeding the garden he would be beside me, his chubby little fingers busy with what he knew to be weeds. When I mowed the lawn he would be alongside, with one hand helping to push. When bedtime came his mother would take charge of a very happy youngster. Sometimes she would say, 'All right, your dad will put you to bed tonight.' He always needed a bath, so off we'd go. He would walk ahead of me up the stairs and I'd watch his tired little legs climbing. As we reached the bend in the stairway I'd pick him up and carry him the rest of the way. Of course I had to give him swimming lessons in the bath before the more serious business could be attended to. Eventually I would have him nicely dried and his face would be shining like a new pin. As he pulled on his pajama trousers I'd slap his little backside before he could cover it up, and he'd laugh his head off. Then I'd carry him to his own room. It was then that I'd see the effect of his mother's training: Before he would go to bed he'd say, 'Wait a minute, Dad,' and he would kneel beside the bed and pray: 'God bless Mum and Dad, and Agnes and Muriel, and Grandma and Grandad, and Grannie and Grandad in Leeds, and Auntie Evelyn and everybody in the whole world. Amen.' It made me feel very humble—and happy. I'd leave him with only his little face visible outside the bedclothes. As I'd switch off the light he'd say, 'Leave the door open a bit, Dad.' I'd fix the door and say, 'That all right, young fellow?' He'd reply, 'All right, Dad. Good night,' and we would hear no more of him until morning."

Lieutenant Tangry was a good listener. He waited, thinking there was more to come, but Mr. Mayson appeared suddenly to realize that he was a long way from that little patch of lawn. So the younger man took matters in hand.

"Look here, old lad; I'm the chap who's homesick, remember?"

They both laughed. Then came a knock on the door.

"Come in!" called the lieutenant.

An able seaman looked in at the doorway.

"Engineer Officer of the Day, sir, please?"

"Yes," said Mr. Mayson.

"The duty senior officer wishes to speak to you, sir. He's in the wardroom now."

"Right-o. I'll be up in a moment."

The able seaman left and Lieutenant Tangry nodded. "Steaming orders, I expect."

The duty senior officer on board represented Captain Graham in the absence of Commander Sands, who was ashore with the captain.

Mr. Mayson went up to the wardroom. Soon he was back. He looked in on Lieutenant Tangry. "Yes," he said, "we're leaving at five o'clock in the morning. I'd better make out the steaming orders."

"Right-o, Mr. Mayson; want any help?"

"Oh no, thanks. I'll put the watch below at one o'clock. Kelling will be down to help in the middle watch. I'll let him know when he comes off from shore."

After issuing the steaming orders to the duty chief petty officers, who would arrange for the necessary engine room ratings to be below at the required time, Mr. Mayson went back to the cabin flat intending to go to bed, but on seeing a light in Tom's cabin he went over and looked in. "Off early, Tom, aren't you?"

Tom Langley was pushing his letter back into the envelope. He seemed to be unhappy.

"Oh, hello, Harry. Yes, I am. Come in. Have you heard from home?"

"Yes, I had two letters by the same mail that brought yours. The news isn't good from Plymouth."

"No, and it's getting me worried, Harry. Those air-raid warnings are wearing Ethel down. She hasn't been really well since the baby was born and her doctor says all she needs is rest."

"And how's the baby, Tom?"

"She's a healthy little girl, nearly eight months old now. But how can her mother get rest if she has to keep hopping out of bed at night?"

"Well, couldn't she have beds made in the shelter? I was able to fit four narrow bunks in mine. So now when the family has to dive into the shelter they stay there till morning."

"We don't have any backyard shelters in our area yet, Harry, and the nearest large shelter is over a hundred yards away. Ethel has to run carrying the baby, with the boy beside her. She now says she isn't going to get out of bed any more because of air-raid warnings. She's tried to get accommodation elsewhere in Plymouth, but that isn't easy when you have two children."

"Well, don't you think she should try to get out of Plymouth? Obviously Plymouth's going to catch it soon."

"I've told Ethel that, and asked her to leave, but she doesn't want to leave her present doctor, and all her people live within half a mile of her. She says she doesn't want to be alone with the children in a strange place. Her mother offered her accommodation and suggested that she store our furniture. The trouble is that her mother's home is rather crowded as it is, and they have no air-raid shelter, either."

"Then there doesn't seem to be anything you can do, Tom."

"No, and I feel so helpless about it. I can picture the boy asleep in his room, and his mother and the baby in the adjoining room. We have a flat one floor up, so it seems that if they stay in bed they have little chance of survival from a bomb anywhere nearby."

"By gosh, Tom, I'm sorry to hear this. Is there anything we can do? Mrs. Mayson would be happy to help in any way."

"Yes I know, but it's a good two miles from your house to mine, and there's your own family to be looked after. So don't you worry, and thanks for offering."

With that Tom Langley opened a drawer in his desk and dropped the letter in. He sat still for a moment, looking into the drawer, then closed it with a slight snap and turned to meet the other's eyes. It was a gesture that seemed to say, "All right, that's that. So what next?"

Harry Mayson noted the action and smiled sympathetically. "By the way, Tom, how are things ashore after the bombing last night?"

"Oh, just about what you'd expect. Alice was telling me this evening of some conversation she heard in Arabic. The general gist of it was that they'd like the British to leave

Alexandria. The bombs in the native quarter killed over a hundred people and wounded many more."

"Not so good, eh?"

"No, but Alice was saying what she heard in her hotel, and in the street rail cars, and it doesn't necessarily reflect the attitude of all the people, or of the government. All the same I wonder what they think would happen if the British did get out.

"I had a little experience of my own, too," Tom went on. "It happened in the bus between the gate and Ramleh Station. I sat beside a chappie in a beautiful white uniform and a red fez. He said he belonged to the Egyptian secret police. He kept looking at me sideways, and after a while he turned and said, 'Are you not affright?' I said, 'No, of course not. What is there to be afraid of?' He patted his chest and said, 'I am much affright—in here. The bombs kill many people.' "

Harry Mayson smiled. "Getting in a flat spin already!"

"Yes, and I felt like kicking him in the arse; but I suppose the poor blighter couldn't help it."

"No, I suppose not. Anyhow, it's time you kicked me out of your cabin. We both need to go to bed."

"Right-o, old chap, but you'll only get about an hour. Send up and have me called at twenty to four. I have the morning watch."

"All right, Tom. Good night."

"Good night, Harry."

CHAPTER 11

At twenty minutes to four Sublieutenant Kelling was a tired young man. There was no great pleasure in raising steam in all boilers. The task entailed climbing up and down the hot steel ladders of one boiler room after another and checking that the correct steam and exhaust valves were open. Kelling had become proficient in this work, and Mr. Mayson was thankful to have the young fellow in his watch to undertake this duty. Mr. Mayson himself had attended to the starting of the auxiliary machinery in the engine rooms, and the preparing of the main engines for use. Lieutenant Leyton was kept busy in the machinery control room where he was able, by means of instruments, to keep a check on the whole operation and to log the sequence of events in the rough engine room register.

Mr. Mayson had checked with the sublieutenant on what had been carried out in the boiler rooms and engine rooms and had then gone to the machinery control room to spend the last twenty minutes of the watch with Lieutenant Leyton.

Young Kelling leaned against a lathe in the workshop and breathed deeply. The workshop was situated on the deck above the control room. It was a cool, well-ventilated compartment, but it would be some time before the young officer fully appreciated this fact. His brown overall suit was unbuttoned all the way down, and his underwear clung damply to his body. His service cap, with his gloves and torch inside, had been dumped on the head of the lathe. His mouth hung slightly open and his fair hair had fallen in a rough parting and plastered itself to the sides of his head.

At ten minutes to four he heard the sound of feet on the steel ladder between the workshop and the deck above. The sound was made by a stoker who had been sent up from the control room to call the morning watch. The man failed to see the sublieutenant, for most of the lights in the workshop were out and a large milling machine partially obstructed the view. Kelling, however, could see the stoker, for a light had been left on above the ladder. The man sat on the bottom step taking a breather before going down the hatch of the machinery control room a few feet away. Kelling was trying to remember the man's name, and suddenly it came: Hicks. Yes, that was it; a young chap, he'd just been rated stoker first class.

Hicks stood up and was about to go below when another stoker clattered his way down the ladder. Hicks turned and recognized his relief, an older man named Smithers.

Smithers spoke with the sleep still in his voice: "Morning. What's doing?"

Before Hicks could reply, feet sounded again on the ladder, and the warrant engineer of the morning watch, Mr. Langley, appeared. He trotted lightly down the ladder, passed the two stokers, and promptly disappeared into the control room to relieve Mr. Mayson. Hicks watched him go before speaking to Smithers.

"Nothing much doing," he said. "We've been busy all the middle watch, but there's only this left now," and he handed a paper to Stoker Smithers.

Smithers held the paper to the light and read aloud: "Call the senior engineer at oh-four-fifteen. Call the commander (E) at oh-four-forty-five, and a good shake, with cocoa."

Then the sleepy voice of Smithers became abusive.

" 'Oo the 'ell does 'e think's going to give 'im cocoa? Let 'im buy 'is own bloody cocoa. One day I'll put a dose of jalap in it for 'im."

Smithers turned away, still muttering, and his words could only just be heard: "Descended from a long line of bachelors, that's wot 'e is—and fat ones at that."

Sublieutenant Kelling could hardly believe his ears. He heard young Hicks laugh and pass up the ladder while Smithers clumped his disgruntled way down into the heat of the control room. The young officer felt that he had been disloyal to the head of his department in not reprimanding Smithers at once. It had been a shock to know that a junior rating could speak so of an officer. But there hadn't been much time to do anything about it. Kelling realized that the psychological moment for action on his part had passed. He found himself wondering what the other officers would have done had they been in his place: the senior for instance—or Mr. Mayson. Yes, what would Mr. Mayson have done? He felt that something should be done about it. A man like Smithers obviously was a menace to the ship, in light of the fact that there were many young stokers living with him on the same mess deck.

Mr. Mayson came up from the control room. He was in little better shape than Kelling.

"Hello, Sub," he said, seeing the young fellow approaching. "You didn't need to wait for me." And he started off up the ladder.

Kelling followed him up and Mr. Mayson waited at the top.

"I want to talk to you about a serious matter," said Kelling.

"Oh! Come into the bathroom while I get out of this wet clothing."

Kelling soon had the story off his chest. During the telling of it Mr. Mayson was glad that the untieing of bootlaces and the removal of clothing allowed him to hide his face. As he struggled out of his wet undervest he sat down for a moment as though needing a rest before making the final effort to free his head.

"The point is," said Kelling, "what should I have done about it?"

Mr. Mayson jerked his head free, and Kelling was surprised to see that he was smiling. The young fellow smiled himself, involuntarily.

"Of all things, don't rebuke yourself about it," said Mr. Mayson. "Remember, it wasn't intended for you to hear, and you didn't have much chance to do anything."

"But what would you have done?"

"Well if I'd been quick enough I'd have called him back, and Hicks, too. I'd have given Smithers a darn good blast and pointed out the seriousness of his offence. Then if his demeanour showed that he realized the seriousness of it I would have let him go, with a caution."

"I see, but what about now, when nothing has been done."

"Well, just send for him after he comes off the morning watch and talk to him in your cabin. Of course he can deny it then and I don't think Hicks would let him down, but I know Smithers. What you have to say will have its effect. He's in my division, and as far as work is concerned he is one of the best stokers in the ship."

The sublieutenant felt greatly relieved. "All right, Mr. Mayson, I'll do that early in the forenoon. And thanks for carrying me around again." He moved into the adjoining bathroom but Mr. Mayson's voice followed him.

"What do you mean, carrying you around? You were carrying me around when you were connecting up those boilers, weren't you?"

The two men were soon in and out of their respective

baths. They were soon in and out of their beds, too, for the break of dawn found them at their action stations, there to remain until the growing light dispelled the danger of a surprise attack.

A new day. There would be several like it before the fleet made its way back to Alexandria. The same fleet—less one cruiser—with the same gallant little destroyers steaming in V formation.

CHAPTER 12

Mr. Mayson opened the watertight door and passed through it on to the quarterdeck, closing the door and clipping it tight shut behind him. Some inherent unease had set him wandering aft, checking on the watertight subdivision of the ship. An almost jubilant atmosphere existed in the warrant officers' mess. It was a mood that Mayson could not share: Things had been too easy.

Now after a series of successful operations the fleet was steaming eastward, returning to harbour. The engineer walked out under a starlit sky, and the ship's stern vibrated as the rumbling propeller shafts thrashed out a wash made beautiful by millions of phosphorescent specks dancing in the turbulent water.

He was alone except for the alert, silent lookouts, one on each side of the deck. Their presence was a reminder of how quickly the scene could change: the sudden swish of a torpedo as it raced out of the night; the jolting crack of the explosion as it struck home and erupted under the stern. Then in his mind's eye he was between decks near the damage. He saw the struggles of the damage-control parties to prevent the spread of water, the shoring of bulkheads, the handling of portable pumps, the rigging of emergency lighting, counterflooding or pumping to correct list; the first-aid parties at work. He took a deep breath of fresh air and turned his mind off it. Tomorrow, all being well, the fleet would be back in Alexandria.

During the nine days at sea the fleet had covered convoys to Greece, Crete, and Malta, steaming continuously except for one day anchored in Suda Bay in Crete. One enemy reconnaissance plane trying to shadow the fleet had been shot down by the ship's Fulmar fighters—young Bowman again. On the run east from Malta, the Swordfish planes dropped the new mines at the entrance to Benghazi harbour, to the great satisfaction of Torps. No planes were lost, and photographs taken the next morning showed one destroyer and two large cargo vessels sunk across the entrance, as well as several ships anchored outside, unable to enter.

That night twenty Swordfish were loaded up with bombs. They flew off to attack the harbour works at Tripoli. All planes returned safely, and the flight observers reported that antiaircraft fire almost ceased after the first bombs were dropped.

The following morning one of four reconnaissance planes reported an enemy convoy of three heavily laden vessels escorted by two torpedo boats, or destroyers, sneaking along close inshore, heading in the direction of Tripoli. Some fast work was carried out by the flight personnel. Six Swordfish planes were revved up and fitted with torpedoes, and off they went. They were back again in time for lunch, and the pilots reported that the job of sinking the convoy had been surprisingly easy. The biggest ship in the convoy must have been carrying ammunition, for it blew up when a torpedo hit. One of the escort vessels steamed away at high speed. The other fired one round from its foremost gun before speeding away.

When Mr. Mayson got back to the cabin flat he found Tom Langley looking for him.

"Harry!" he said. "I missed you after dinner. How about that crib game we arranged?"

"Oh, Tom, I'm sorry. I got an itch to look around aft; had an uneasy feeling about how safe we were back there. Come in and take a seat."

Tom walked in with a pack of cards and dropped them on the desk. "Harry, old chap, I think you take too much on yourself aboard here. With your seniority you could have my job, or Kirklane's—both easier going than yours."

"I know, Tom, but when you stand by a ship like this building for a year, sort of watch it grow up, you almost become part of it. I can sense this same attitude in the senior. He joined her a month before I did, and there isn't much he doesn't know about her."

"How about the chief?"

"Well, he joined her when the original commander (E) fell sick, just before we sailed."

"In that case he can't know much about it, seeing he rarely moves far from his cabin or the wardroom."

"Now you see it, Tom. He hasn't a clue. He doesn't even bother to look over ship's drawings. The average commander (E) spends his first month or two in an overall suit, looking around, studying the ship, and usually, having long experience behind him, he soon knows enough to be able to take control from the office. Then when you bring something to his notice he knows what you are talking about, and can make sound decisions. But with this chief—his decisions are based on nothing."

Tom Langley smiled. It wasn't often that Harry Mayson opened up like this.

"Well you know *he* doesn't need to bother his head, Harry. He's rolling in money, so why should he?"

"Oh! I didn't know that."

"Didn't you? You've heard of Brumpting-Shard's preserves?"

"Yes, of course. Why? Is he connected there?"

"Oh, yes. The firm gets its name from him, or rather from his father, who died a few years ago."

"Well I'm hanged! But what's he doing in the navy when he owns a show like that?"

"That's what I'd like to know. Anyhow, when you think over these last few days, we're doing very well even with him on board."

"I know, Tom, but this is bound to bring repercussions from the enemy, and I hope we aren't getting careless."

"So do I. Still, I think the best thing to do is keep walloping the Italians till we knock them out of the war. They're not happy in it."

"That's so, but if we'd shown our teeth a bit sooner Musso might have known better than get into this. Instead we just encouraged him. We let him send an army through the Suez Canal to overrun Abyssinia. The timid-old-women types, the ones who were running our government then, backed away from the showdown.

"After that, Musso went merrily on. Remember Spain? Hitler and Musso's training ground? You were there, Tom. You saw Majorca overrun by Italian airmen, saw their bombers going over to attack Barcelona. There were many Germans there, too. A leading British newspaper published the names of many senior German and Italian officers and gave the name of the hotels in which they were staying, and still our Government bleated about nonintervention in Spain. I know it's useless howling now; let's just be thankful we've lost the timid old women at last."

"Too bad we didn't lose 'em sooner, Harry. Remember Hitler's joyride into Czechoslovakia? I listened to our Prime Minister's speech after Munich and all our ship's officers were present. Dead silence followed the speech, and my own heart sank, too, for I realized we'd been sold again. Later I found the general feeling was one of relief. Relief, mind you! We should have been hanging our heads in shame. I couldn't believe they were sincere. Maybe they were just unable to relinquish their faith in leaders they had supported for so long. I suppose folks could say all this is hindsight. Anybody can be wise after the event. But there was one great man who was wise before all the events that led to this mess; which reminds me of a remark you made the other day: 'Thank God for Winston Churchill.' "

Harry Mayson slid the crib board along the desk. "You make me happy, Tom. Deal the cards."

The ship entered harbour in the morning and the engineering staff were surprised when the senior engineer told them to get busy on certain repairs. Tom Langley, who was on duty on board for the day, reminded the senior that some repairs in the engine room, once started, might take three days to complete.

The senior was unusually relaxed. "I'm told we're going to be in harbour for a few days, Mr. Langley, so let the duty watch open things up as soon as your machinery cools down, but don't let them work late. Let them get all night in their hammocks. Lieutenant Leyton will be in charge of the men in the boiler room."

All-night leave was piped for men of the port watch, and after tea the first liberty boat left the ship packed with men off duty.

Soon afterwards an officers' boat left for shore, with Torps, Harry Mayson, and Jim Kirklane as passengers. Torps had arranged by shore telephone with Mary Thompson for an evening's entertainment at the Femina with their friends from the hospital. This would be a party of only six, for Kelling's partner, Agnes Andrewes, and Tim Brinn's partner, Josie Weir, were on night duty.

When, in the early hours of the morning, the three officers boarded a felucca to return to the ship, they were in a thoughtful mood. They had danced and they'd seen a very good floor show at the Femina, but the nurses had been quite subdued. Even the merry little Eileen Hall had been quieter than usual.

When Torps questioned Mary Thompson about it her answer surprised him.

"Well, Torps, from the news we get of the fleet's operations we know the navy's on top in the Med; but what happens if the enemy gets through to the Suez Canal?"

"But why do you ask this now?"

"Well, you only need to see today's papers. Again we have withdrawn a little, this time in order to straighten out the line. Every time I see that I feel like singing, 'Tell me the old, old story.'"

Torps looked to the other two nurses, and Susie spoke up.

"She's right, Torps. All we seem to be doing in the Western Desert is withdrawing. It is worded in different ways: 'We are shortening our lines,' one hears, or, 'We are moving to more prepared positions.' We heard it all before in France. Things moved faster then, of course."

Jim Kirklane nodded. He'd heard it before.

"Well, Susie," said Harry Mayson, "from what I read of the evacuation, you only just got out of France in time."

"Yes, that's so; and whether it was by accident or design I don't know, but some German bombers thought the Red Cross made a good target."

"Well," said Torps, "I don't think the enemy will break through. We are interfering and chopping down Italian supplies and that's bound to have its effect. Let's wait and see and not get downhearted."

However, the three officers had little to say on their way back to the ship.

By 9:00 A.M. the engineers' office was a hive of industry as engineers clad in brown overalls referred to drawings of machinery under repair.

The commander (E) entered with his usual lively tread and breezy manner, this time dressed in a clean white overall suit, and sat glancing through the latest correspondence from his In basket.

Soon drawings were being replaced and the office cleared except for the chief, the senior, and Heathcote, who was busy with the engine room register. Speedy and one other messenger hung around outside the door.

The senior picked up his hat, gloves, and torch and stood by the chief's desk.

"Do you need me for anything, sir? If not, I'd better check on the work below."

"No. Off you go, Senior. I might be down myself later on."

The senior looked around the three main engine rooms and was briefed on the program of repairs by Mr. Langley. He then left to view the work in the boiler rooms.

Tom Langley took the elevator up to the engineers' workshop. There was a strong, busy drone about the machinery as engine room artificers skimmed valve seats and turned new parts for the machinery below. A grimy stoker, his overall covered in red lead paint, stood at a grindstone sharpening a scraper he'd been using on the engine room bilge plates. The commander (E) came up the ladder from the machinery control room, and his well-tailored white overall suit, surmounted by the shiny gold braid of his service cap, made him look larger than ever; enough to frighten any young stoker who was sharpening his scraper.

The stoker saw the imposing figure out of the corner of his eye, and the scraper he was holding was deflected a little. There followed a loud, harsh grinding noise as the scraper became jammed between the stone and the guard. Showers of sparks flew from the machine and the stoker jumped back. Mr. Langley, who was passing, knocked the motor switch to the stop position. Then the voice of the commander (E) smote his ear.

"Mr. Langley!"

"Yes, sir."

"Who's in charge of this blasted workshop?"

"I am, sir."

"Well, get hold of Mr. Munday and tell him to change over the leads on that motor and make those bloody stones turn the other way." The chief moved off to go up the ladder, and his seemingly tortured soul vented a great grievance: "Why the hell do *I* have to think of these things?"

His huge white bulk and angry voice left little room for anything else in the workshop. The engine room artificers seemed to shrink into nothing, their presence only becoming apparent after the head of their department disappeared up the ladder.

Tom Langley smiled grimly. He restarted the machine after retrieving the scraper, then he called over a junior engine room artificer.

"Sharpen this scraper," he said. Then, to the stoker: "Did you get hurt anywhere?"

"No, sir."

"That's good. Just wait here for your scraper, then carry on below."

Mr. Mayson had been busy arranging for the delivery of oil fuel from a tanker secured alongside. Fuelling had now commenced and his oil fuel party, under supervision of a very able chief stoker, was controlling the input.

The engineer entered the engineer's office and was pleased to find the writer alone.

"Heathcote," he said, "come along to my cabin. I have some news for you."

"Very good, sir."

On reaching his cabin Mr. Mayson closed the door and saw the chief stoker seated, then sat down himself.

"I thought you might like to know, Heathcote, that we have another writer aboard, a stoker petty officer who joined us this morning."

"Oh? What's his name, sir? Perhaps I know him."

"Saunders. He has about two years' seniority."

Heathcote shook his head slowly.

"So you don't know him. Well, like yourself, he is in my division, and I'm thinking of asking the commander (E) to let him help you get the office side straight."

Heathcote was silent for a moment. "I don't think that will be allowed, sir. We are still short of petty officers, unless more joined today."

"No. Saunders came alone. But supposing I can persuade Commander (E) to let him help, what are your views on the matter?"

"Well, sir, I'd appreciate some help to get everything straight, but after that I'd like to leave the office altogether."

The commissioned engineer took in a deep breath of satisfaction. He had scrutinized the chief stoker's service certificates and found them to be the finest set of papers he had ever known to be held by a stoker rating: a record of over twenty years of very good character and superior ability. Many engineer officers in previous ships had written their appreciation of the man in glowing terms. Mayson had noted the strain under which Heathcote had been working; he feared Heathcote might break under it and do something to spoil that record. Now the chief stoker had given the answer Mayson had hoped for.

"I think you would be wise to do that, Heathcote. You will have to put in a formal request to see the commander (E) and that means you will have to give a reason. Have you thought of one?"

"No, sir, except that I feel I need a change."

"But don't forget, you've been a writer for two full commissions in previous ships. Don't you think, seeing you're close to pension, that you need to get familiar with work on machinery again so that your chances of employment outside will be better when you take your pension after the war?"

Heathcote brightened up. "Yes, sir. That's quite true."

As Heathcote was leaving, Mr. Mayson patted his shoulder. "Good luck, Heathcote."

At lunchtime in the mess Tom Langley told the warrant electrician, Mr. Munday, of the commander (E)'s order about the grindstone. Mr Munday had a habit of holding his mouth slightly open when listening. This time he was silent for a minute and his mouth opened more as his face registered a mixture of anger and amazement.

"Why," he burst out, "if I reverse the motion you'll have to stand on your head to sharpen your tools! The guard would be useless, too, and the sparks would fly up in the air!"

"I know," said Langley.

"Another thing," said Mr. Munday, "the lock nuts holding the stones are right- and left-hand threaded, and they'll slack off if I run the motor the other way."

"I know. And the stones may fly off. Somebody could be killed or injured."

"Then what's the good of changing over the leads?"

"None at all, except that the commander (E) has ordered it."

"Oh, to hell with him!" exclaimed the warrant electrician. "He's not the head of my department. I shan't do anything unless I get an order from my side."

Tom eyes gleamed his appreciation. "Good for you! If you do have to change the leads let me know and I'll see that no one uses the machine."

CHAPTER 13

The few days in harbour slipped by rapidly, but they had a great beneficial effect on the ship's company. There was something akin to lightheartedness about the vessel as she steamed westward. In the engine room department conditions had improved, for many of the steam leaks, which previously had caused excessive heat below, had been stopped, and the weather was cooling off. The sea rose to a moderate swell, and the perky little destroyers, steaming in their protective V formation, seemed to gambol with joy as they rode the waves.

The fourth morning broke clear and fine, and after the flying off of the protecting planes, routine work went on aboard the carrier. On the flight deck the gunnery instructors drilled their crews, striving for an extra ounce of efficiency. The men of the guns' crews were eager to beat their previous time records for loading, training, and opening fire.

Mr. Langley, always interested in gunnery, stood by one of the multiple pom-pom guns at the after end of the flight deck and watched the proceedings there. The gunner's mate snapped his short, sharp orders, and the crew carried them out with a precision in keeping with the tone of his voice. Able Seaman Miller sat on a little wooden seat attached to the power-operated gun and worked two handles that trained the gun. This was a different Dusty Miller; he was not playing tombola now. His keen eye was glued to the gun sights, his ears alert, his jaws clamped grimly together. In the hangar below, his old pal Able Seaman Tuckett still smiled as he helped with the ranging of aircraft.

The gunner's mate rested his crew and cleared his throat.

"Now, men," he said, "you all know what we are training for. So far, except for a few torpedo-carrying planes, we haven't had a chance. It's been all high-level bombing and out of our range, but sooner or later we are going to meet dive-bombing, and when we do—if you'll pardon my French—it's up to us to let the bastards have it."

The men of the gun's crew smiled and their eyes lit up with pleasure. They liked this smart young petty officer. He knew his job and saw that they knew theirs.

"All right, men, you all know your numbers." A slight pause followed, then the gunner's mate's voice hardened to something like a metallic bark.

"Gun's crew— Close up!"

Each man jumped to his position at the gun.

Tom Langley smiled and walked away. It was something after his own heart, and as he walked aft he told himself, "That's the stuff to give 'em."

Mr. Mayson had the forenoon watch below. He lingered a little longer than usual in one of the boiler rooms, talking to Chief Stoker Heathcote. A different Heathcote this—a happier man. Already there was a faint sign that his cheeks were filling out, and they had a healthier tinge. He was dressed in a clean blue overall suit, something strange for him after doing a white-collar job for so long.

Mr. Mayson was pleased to note the changes. "How do you like your new job, Heathcote?"

The chief stoker adjusted the valve controlling the boiler air pressure before replying. "Fine, sir—fine, but I wish I could have stayed in the office long enough to help Saunders get it straight. You know it doesn't give him a chance."

Heathcote kept his eyes moving over all the pressure gauges as he spoke. His steam pressure was not allowed to vary much, and he glanced continually at the gauges showing the water level in the boilers. Mr. Mayson was about to speak to him when Heathcote called to one of the stokers, "Switch off that side sprayer, it's dripping a bit. The cone needs cleaning. Put your top centre one on."

Heathcote hadn't forgotten his job down below.

After the sprayers were changed over the engineer spoke again. "Don't be concerned about the office, Heathcote; I don't think Saunders will worry very much. What's your job at action stations now?"

"I'm chief of the after fire party, under Lieutenant Tangry."

"Oh, that's good," and Mr. Mayson went back up the ladder.

Later, while he was in the workshop awaiting Mr. Langley, who would take over the afternoon watch, the call to action stations sounded. It came with rude suddenness after so peaceful a trip.

Blurp! blurp! blurp! Blurp! blurp! blurp! Blurp! blurp! blurp! Blurp! blurp! blurp!

Tom Langley slipped down the ladder at high speed. "All right, Harry, unless there's something unusual to tell me, you go on. I don't like the sound of this."

"Nor do I, Tom. Everything's all right below. I'm off."

There was a good deal of bustle about the ship, during which men between decks were expecting anything; for anything might happen at this stage of the trip.

The fleet lay to the east of Malta. To the south, a few miles away, a convoy steamed westward, due to arrive at Malta in the morning. Here was an ideal opportunity for the Italian fleet, with its numerical superiority, to shatter British hopes in the Mediterranean.

After a few minutes the bustle of preparation died down and the voice of the paymaster came over the broadcasting system:

"Well"—the predictable pause—"unidentified aircraft have been detected—approaching the fleet about fifty miles away. We have three fighters in the air, and three more"—pause—"are taking off."

Through the loudspeakers could be heard the roar of an aeroplane engine, and then the voice of the paymaster again.

"And there goes the first of them—you probably heard it as it passed the bridge. We still have three reconnaissance planes in the air."

Mr. Mayson, having checked his pumping and flooding parties, looked in at damage-control headquarters. There was another small party stationed here under his direction: the oil fuel party. It consisted of one chief stoker, one leading stoker and two ordinary stokers. Their job was to see that the pumps which supplied the ship's boilers with oil fuel were never allowed to lose suction. In the event that damage to the ship altered her heel and trim they were to be ready to transfer oil fuel from tank to tank to correct the error, if possible, and keep the ship upright.

Chief Stoker Lathom, the leader of this party, was a meticulous little man with a background of fifteen years' meritorious service. He knew all there was to know about those intricate pipe systems in the hold of the ship, including the control position of every valve. Mr. Mayson, with his own knowledge of these systems, was able to assess the value of this man, and he placed absolute faith in him.

The commander (E) had decreed that Lathom should be stationed in damage-control headquarters, but, in order to prevent overcrowding of that comfortable spot, the remainder of the oil fuel party were stationed outside the door.

Mr. Mayson opened the door and saw that Lathom was at his station. The commander (E) was there, too. The extension and headrest had been fitted to his easy chair, and he was making full use of it.

As he closed the door and turned away Mr. Mayson felt perturbed about that forsaken second damage-control position; the machinery control room. Obviously the chief never intended to use it, for it was not uncomfortably hot there now. The remainder of the damage-control staff stationed there had almost forgotten why they were there. There was no guiding hand, no organization whereby that vital compartment, with its fine telephone connections, could assume damage control. If enemy action destroyed the first control position there would be no organized damage control, and chaos might ensue.

The paymaster spoke through the microphone again. "Well"—pause—"that aircraft closed in to about twenty miles. Our fighters are up there." Pause. "There is no news from them as yet. It is a fine, clear day and—Just a moment, there is a report coming in."

A brief silence followed. It was broken by a terse, familiar report that never failed to thrill the ship's company.

"Our fighters have sounded the tallyho!"

There was a quiet tenseness between decks; each man was forming his own image of that fight high up in the blue. How many planes were there? Of late the Italians were getting wiser and sending their reconnaissance planes in pairs. Sometimes they used their fastest bombers for this job. Had they not adopted these measures they might not yet know what was happening to their reconnaissance planes. Previously they had been detected and shot down before they sighted the fleet.

The paymaster's voice broke the silence. "A report has just come in. Our fighters have shot down one enemy plane.

There is no sign of any other enemy aircraft."

Men below breathed their satisfaction. So often had they heard the same kind of report, and yet there was always that anxious period of waiting. The uncertainty of war was reflected in the tense silence below during those fights in the air.

At twelve-fifty came the sound of the bos'n's pipe, and the call, "Hands secure from action stations."

After enjoying a refreshing shower, Mr. Mayson entered the warrant officers' mess. Most of his messmates were at lunch, and these he joined, sitting beside Mr. Mills.

"Hello, Harry," said Torps, "did you have a stiff forenoon?"

"Not too bad, Torps. It's much cooler down there now."

An able seaman entered the mess hurriedly and spoke quietly to Mr. Mills. The torpedo gunner listened attentively, then he threw his napkin on the table and pushed back his chair. In double-quick time his heavy form had passed through the door.

His messmates exchanged quick, inquiring glances, and Mr. Prout found his tongue.

"What's the matter with Torps?"

"Don't know," replied Mr. Ganer, "but there's something in the wind."

"There must be," said the bos'n. "It takes a lot to get Torps moving at that speed."

The ship's signal bos'n entered the mess, and from one glance at his weather-beaten face it was obvious that he was bursting with information. Several voices assailed him at once. "What's up?" "What's the panic?" "What's happening, Bo'?"

The signal bos'n held up his hand. "Hold it, chaps! It's only a small flap up topside. Part of the Eyetie fleet's out."

The news alerted every man in the mess, but because of

superior lungpower, and the fact that he had leapt to his feet, Mr. Munday, the warrant electrician, claimed attention.

"Well, by heaven, if they attack now they'll catch us with our pants round our ankles."

The signal bos'n reached for a piece of bread. "They're not strong enough to attack us—only two cruisers and three destroyers. They're steaming parallel with us at the moment, a hundred and twenty miles to the north. Could be they aim to make a fast raid on the convoy. They have the speed."

Up on the bridge Captain Graham and Commander Sands looked down on a scene of great activity. There were five planes ranged at the after end of the flight deck, three of them with their engines running already. Mechanics were busy about the other two. A sixth plane came up on the after lift. The flight deck party quickly removed the chocks from the wheels and ran it forward off the lift. There they unfolded the wings and locked them in the spread position. Other men were moving trolleys into position near a lift at the side of the deck. Soon aerial torpedoes started to come up this lift to be quickly moved aft to the planes by means of the trolleys. The men wore light, rubber-soled shoes, for the greater part of their work was carried out at the run.

Down below in the hangar six more planes were ready to be sent up. Overhead two reconnaissance planes circled the ship, awaiting an opportunity to fly on.

This was a crucial time for the British fleet, which consisted of two battleships, two cruisers, one aircraft carrier, and eleven destroyers. Early morning British reconnaissance flights from Malta had reported a large Italian fleet, including four battleships and several cruisers, anchored and apparently ready for sea in Taranto harbour, three hundred miles north of the convoy route.

The Italians had many options, and in view of their reconnaissance flights they could be considering them.

Would the fast cruisers and destroyers now at sea attempt a sneak raid on the convoy, and so divert the British fleet, while the superior Italian fleet closed in for a night attack? The torpedo-carrying Swordfish planes were being readied to fly off to intercept the cruisers if they moved south. But Captain Graham and the flight commander knew that a low-level attack in daylight against an alerted enemy by planes burdened with torpedoes could be almost a suicide mission. They were sad-faced men as they looked down on the flight deck and watched those young airmen preparing to leave.

Other possibilities were: would the whole Italian fleet make a night attack, selecting the convoy; or would they steam through the night and intercept the British at dawn? They might send in torpedo bombers at dusk, as they had in the attack on HMS *Wexborough*. Maybe the *Wexborough* attack was only a trial, and they had fleets of efficient torpedo bombers ready.

The afternoon wore on and the crew remained at action stations. Several times enemy planes sighted the fleet but were chased away by the ship's Fulmar fighters. As darkness fell every searchlight and every gun in the fleet was manned ready for action. In the destroyers, men listening on antisubmarine devices were relieved every hour.

By dawn it was clear that the enemy had missed their chance. To the north the ship's locating device could detect nothing. To the south the convoy was nearing Malta.

Six Fulmar fighters went up as an umbrella for the fleet, and later, to the astonishment and pleasant surprise of the captain, a reconnaissance plane out of Malta reported that the Italian fleet was still in Taranto harbour and had been joined by the two cruisers and the destroyers sighted the day before.

In the early forenoon the convoy arrived safely at Malta, and Valetta harbour became a hive of industry as cargos, necessary for the survival of the island, were being landed. The fleet had continued westward to meet another vital convoy from England, carrying supplies and war materials for Malta and Alexandria and escorted by one battleship, two cruisers, and six destroyers. This convoy and the reinforced fleet entered Valetta harbour in the afternoon.

With the coastline of Sicily only fifty miles to the north, Valetta harbour was now a prime target for attack from the air; but the Italian air force had, during daylight, a deep respect for half a dozen Spitfire fighters based in Malta, and the unloading of cargos continued.

For the men of the fleet there could be no shore leave. All naval vessels were kept at short notice for steam. The Italian fleet could still make a fast move.

Aboard the aircraft carrier there was a general air of relaxation with the prospect of catching up on lost sleep. In the warrant officers' mess, after dinner, Mr. Prout voiced his opinion of the war situation in the area.

"It seems to me," said Tiny, "the Eyeties have just about given up after the beating they got on our last trip."

There were several officers present, including Mr. Mills. As president of the mess, Torps felt he should offset any overconfidence. This was no time to let the guard down.

"Don't forget," he said, "the attack on the *Wexborough*. The Italians probably have better torpedo bombers just now than we have. Tonight there'll be a waning moon. They could attack this harbour using torpedos just after moonrise and cripple part of the fleet. The Spitfires won't stop them getting through at night."

"And that," said Tom Langley, "could be a real disaster. With their own fleet intact the Italians could isolate Malta. Do you think they'll try it?"

"Well, if they do they'll get a hot reception. Every pom-pom gun in the fleet will be waiting for them."

"It seems that the sooner we get out of here the better," said Harry Mayson.

"That's so," said Torps. "The aim is to get the harbour cleared of ships sometime tomorrow."

Mr. Prout rose to his feet. "It might be a good idea to turn in early." He stretched. "I'm for the bunk."

But the Italians weren't about to let Tiny sleep. Not yet.

Blurp! blurp! blurp! Blurp! blurp! blurp! Blurp! blurp! blurp! With the warning sound assailing their ears the men raced to their action stations. Then the paymaster's voice came through, tinged with excitement.

"A large number of aircraft are approaching! High flying, rapidly from the north!"

A brief silence followed, then the paymaster spoke again, quietly. "The whole harbour is blacked out now. Clear starlit sky overhead. No moon yet."

In a tense waiting period men below were remembering similar calls to action they'd heard while at anchor in Alexandria, but the attacks then were of short duration, and by only two or three planes from the Western Desert. Now while they lay immobile, awaiting a large-scale attack, there was a feeling of vulnerability. With continuing silence the tension increased.

Then came the click of the microphone's shutter followed by the broadcaster's voice.

"Planes are now circling overhead. Searchlights from ships and shore are probing—"

Bang! Bang! Bang! Bang!
Bang! Bang! Bang!
Boom! Boom!

The men between decks were familiar with the sounds: the bang of the antiaircraft guns and the less metallic but heavier boom of exploding bombs.

The paymaster's voice continued, his announcements interspersed with the noises of war: "All our AA guns about the harbour have opened up. Bombs are falling in the harbour and over the city. The planes are very high up."

The steady bang of the antiaircraft guns and the boom of exploding bombs continued. The paymaster was trying to make his voice heard, but the racket over the harbour seemed unceasing; then in a brief pause his excited voice came through.

"There's one plane coming down in flames over the"—Bang! Bang! Bang! *Boom! Boom!* "—and several fires in the city."

Boom!
Boom!
Bang! Bang! Bang! Bang!
Bang!
Bang! Bang!

The ship's guns ceased firing, but other guns, probably shore-based, could be heard through the microphone. The broadcaster's voice came through a background of noise.

"There's another plane gliding down—trailing fire—just over the breakwater—and there it is"—pause—"down in the sea."

For some time, distant AA guns could be heard firing spasmodically, then the paymaster's voice came again.

"Well, the last of the planes are leaving." Pause. "Several bombs have been dropped in the harbour area. We don't know yet the extent of any damage. The raid seems to be over."

To the great surprise of everyone the Italians had made only the one brief attack. The prime targets were the many ships in the harbour, but the bombs were dropped from a great height and fell wide of their marks. Only one ship, a cargo vessel, was damaged by a near-miss bomb. The bow was well down, but the ship was still afloat.

Unloading of cargo continued through the night, and an early morning reconnaissance plane from Malta reported that the Italian fleet was still in Taranto harbour.

Before noon the aircraft carrier, two cruisers, and five destroyers had cleared Valetta harbour and were steaming east-northeast at twenty-five knots. The rest of the fleet, and all the merchant vessels less one, would soon be steaming eastward for Alexandria.

Mr. Mills had been busy in the hangar and was late arriving for lunch. His messmates were full of conjecture about what might be happening next. Mr. Munday made his voice heard. "What's going on, Torps—any idea?"

Torps took his place at the head of the table.

"Well," he said, "I think I can guess what might happen, but we won't know for sure till after dark. We're preparing to use both bombs and torpedoes. It could be that if the Italian fleet stays in harbour we'll attack after moonrise tonight."

Mr. Munday's mouth had been slowly opening, indicating his surprise.

"Do you really mean that we'll be sending planes loaded with torpedoes, flying low to attack battleships? That's a hell of a risk."

"It'll be risky all right," said Torps, "but don't forget, the Italians won't know anything until they hear planes overhead—and bombs dropping, probably in the dockyard area. The Italians don't have our locating device yet."

"I see," said Mr. Munday thoughtfully.

There were six Fulmar fighters in the air. Their object was to prevent any Italian reconnaissance plane from sighting the carrier. This protective screen was maintained during the daylight hours. After darkness fell, with the fighters back on board, the carrier and its escort steamed due north at twenty-eight knots, heading towards the heel of Italy.

Inside the hangar, navy air-arm mechanics were making

final adjustments to the planes and filling the fuel tanks. On the flight deck there was dead silence. The guns' crews stood motionless, ready. Shortly after moonrise the flight deck party was piped to muster on the flight deck.

The twenty planes that would take part in the raid were ranged up at the after end of the flight deck, and the engines were started and thoroughly warmed through, then stopped.

At midnight they were started again and the pilots and observers appeared in their full equipment and boarded the planes. Soon the ship turned stem to the wind, and at a signal from the flight deck officer the first plane raced down the centreline of the flight deck and took to the air. The other planes followed at steady intervals, the whole operation moving smoothly as clockwork.

The aircraft carrier, still escorted by the cruisers and destroyers, altered course and soon was steaming away from the target at twenty-eight knots. And the wash from the ships' sterns, visible in the bright moonlight, formed an arrow pointing away from Italy.

By means of the locating device in the carrier the speed and course of the attacking aircraft could be checked for the early part of the flight. After that, contact would be lost, and forty valiant young men would be out in the sky somewhere. Their training for such an operation had been long and difficult; it had cost the lives of some of their comrades. Now, endangering their own lives, they sought to justify their training.

The excitement engendered by getting the planes in the air was simmering down. Ahead were two hours of waiting for the planes to return.

After watching the flying-off operation the flight commander felt an urge to look around below. He was a quiet, pleasant, sensitive officer in his midthirties. He wandered through the deserted aircraft workshop and gazed pensively through the forward door of the hangar. There were formations of planes—the fighters—at the after end, but the vast, vast empty space midships and forward imbued him with a feeling almost of desolation, as though some great loss were impending. A gamble was being undertaken, and his pilots and observers would need good fortune as well as skill to bring them back safely.

This vague feeling permeated the entire ship. Men standing by at their action stations were subdued—waiting. This was a family affair. From Captain Graham down there was deep concern for those young airmen: How many of them would come back?

Inside damage-control headquarters the atmosphere was one of peace. The chief was comfortably asleep with a library book resting on his knee. Lieutenant Morton was leaning on his desk, trying to stay awake; the steady drone of the machinery below was like a lullaby. Saunders—doing Heathcote's old job—and the master-at-arms were reading and also striving to stay awake. Chief Stoker Lathom sat outside on the ammunition conveyer, studying his oil fuel chart. They all came alert when the bos'n's pipe was heard, followed by a subdued voice calling, "Cocoa is ready for distribution in the galley."

The news produced a brief period of activity among the men at action stations. Lathom sent a member of his oil fuel party off for the cocoa issue, and when it was passed around, even the commander (E) revived for a while. Thereafter the quiet of waiting settled again.

Mr. Mayson was on duty for the middle watch below, and after a routine check on the engine and boiler rooms he went up to contact Lathom regarding the distribution of oil fuel. Lathom was glad to see him. He laid his chart on the conveyer and pointed with his pencil.

"These tanks in use are now down to about three-quarters full, and I thought of changing over to the standbys in a few minutes—at two o'clock."

The engineer glanced at the chart. "The standbys are the last of the full ones, I believe."

"Yes, sir."

"That's good, then. Change over." And Mr. Mayson, content, went back below. Lathom knew his damage control. Fuel tanks with air space above could withstand shock better than full ones.

The paymaster's voice came over the loudspeaker system. "We now have contact with aircraft approaching from the north about fifty miles away."

This was followed immediately by the bos'n's pipe and the voice of the bos'n's mate: "Flight deck party muster on the flight deck."

Up on the bridge the captain and the flight commander looked down on the flight deck. When the faint drone of distant machines could be heard, the flight deck party stood ready to switch on the landing-on lights. These consisted of two rows of pinpoints of light running fore and aft, between which the planes must touch down, and lights so positioned astern as to guide pilots into the correct angle of approach.

Soon the planes were in view. They circled low over the ship in the bright moonlight. The landing-on lights were switched on and the ship turned windward.

The principal medical officer of the ship, Surgeon Commander Amy, stood by with a medical party on the flight deck inside the bridge structure.

The first plane was signalled to land. It came in like a huge, hovering bird. It touched down just forward of the after lift, bounced several times, then caught the arrester wire and came to rest. After a moment's pause the engine roared again and the plane taxied forward to the lift.

The second plane made a smooth landing and was followed steadily by twelve more. When the fifteenth plane approached it was rocking violently. It touched down heavily on the after lift and rebounded high into the air. Again it bounced, and the third time it struck the deck there was a jarring screech as the tail swung to starboard. Once more it left the deck momentarily and ran towards the port side. There was another jarring screech as the tail swung round again, and the plane ended up facing forward, its engine dead, on the very edge of the deck.

The flight deck party ran in and called to the pilot. There was no answer. A mechanic jumped on to the fuselage and flashed an electric torch. The observer was slumped forward, silent and still, his face the ashen grey of death. The pilot lay with his face and his right hand on the instrument panel. His left hand hung limply down; his lifeblood dripped steadily from the fingertips.

Quickly he was removed from the plane and the medical party transferred him to the bridge structure. Another pilot ran the plane to the forward lift.

There were still planes in the air, and on receiving the landing-on signal, three more touched down safely and were run to the forward lift to be lowered to the hangar.

The men between decks waited anxiously for the news. They knew the planes were landing on; now they wondered how many. Soon the paymaster's voice was heard again.

"Well—" He paused. "Eighteen of our planes have returned. There are no signs of the others as yet." Pause. "The ship is back on her course. I will let you know the result"—pause—"of the raid"—pause—"as soon as I get a report."

After the long waiting period and the doubts engendered by the risks involved, the return of eighteen planes out of the twenty was accepted almost with relief. There was still hope that the remaining two would appear or would at least land safely in enemy territory.

In the sick bay a battle was going on to save the life of Sub-lieutenant Blakeney. This quiet, unassuming young man had brought home his flying crate almost shot to pieces, and in his last moments of consciousness he had landed it.

In the air operations room the flight commander, after interviewing the flyers, was checking and summarizing their reports. The Italians had been completely surprised. Eight planes had dropped bombs in the dockyard area, and twelve torpedo bombers had attacked ships in the harbour. At least six naval vessels had been torpedoed and probably sunk.

By daybreak six fighters had been ranged up on the flight deck ready for takeoff, and the ships steamed at high speed to join up with the rest of the fleet and the convoy vessels.

In the afternoon a coded message was received from Malta: Photographs taken of Taranto harbour by reconnaissance planes from the island revealed that three battleships, two cruisers, and two auxiliary vessels had been put out of action.

The menace from the Italian fleet had been effectively reduced.

While this satisfying news was being absorbed, more news was being received over the radio—amazing news, startling in its suddenness.

Mr. Mayson heard it in the warrant officers' mess. He had been relieved from the first dogwatch by Mr. Langley at five minutes to six. Ten minutes later he was back in the workshop, having left a dozen of his messmates in a state of jubilant consternation. He hurried to the hatch of the machinery control room.

"Below there!" he called. "Is Mr. Langley there?"

"Yes, Harry," said Tom, from the bottom of the ladder. "What's the buzz?"

"No buzz, Tom! Our people are wiping up the Italians in the Western Desert!"

"What!" Tom Langley bounded up the ladder.

Inside the machinery control room Lieutenant Stanning looked up suddenly from his register. "What was that? Italians what?"

"It was Mr. Mayson, sir," said one of the stokers excitedly. "He says the Italians are being beaten in the Western Desert."

Lieutenant Stanning leaped to the bottom of the ladder. "Come back and tell me about it, Mr. Langley!" he yelled.

In the workshop Harry Mayson related the news.

"I know it's hard to believe, Tom, but it must be true. The Eyeties are running like hell from Sidi Barrâni. Our people have taken thousands of prisoners. Lots of them are giving themselves up without a fight."

"Well, Harry, I never thought much of the Italian army, but I never expected this until we'd built up our strength out here. We all know they had the advantage in everything: manpower, air power, and tanks. Why, we were expecting *them* to attack!"

"Yes, and that's what's so surprising about it. It looks like a masterstroke to me. General Wavell must have hit them in the right place at the right time."

Mr. Mayson left the workshop, and his messmate disappeared into the machinery control room to spread the news to the watch below.

The fleet steamed eastward, and before it reached Alexandria, Surgeon Commander Amy let it be known that Sublieutenant Blakeney was making a good recovery and would fly again.

Alexandria harbour was buzzing with activity. Merchant ships and small vessels were arriving. They were packed with Italian prisoners, many of them happy men. Destroyers were arriving. They stayed long enough to refuel and take in stores and ammunition before going off along the coast to worry the retreating enemy. As the aircraft carrier made fast to her buoys two small river gunboats steamed out. These gallant little ships, with their shallow draught, were operating close inshore along the coast, sometimes actually entering enemy harbours and shooting up shipping and shore establishments at close range. They hurried out of the harbour like children going to a tea party. Their magazines were stocked with presents for the Italians, in the form of six-inch shells.

The recipients of these unwelcome gifts must have been a little bewildered. Hadn't their strong—if not silent—leader claimed the Mediterranean as his own? Italy had six big battleships, the best in the world, and lots of cruisers and destroyers! And here were two little boats shooting Italians in the backside before they had a chance to run away. Not fair!

Before the carrier entered harbour all her planes had been flown off. Soon they would be operating from shore bases in support of the army.

It was a busy day for the ship's company. The routine fueling, storing, and provisioning had to be carried out. But as usual the men worked with a will. Lighthearted men these, for the success of the army meant much to them. Poor old "Tommy" had been on the sticky end for a long time.

The mail arrived while the men were at tea. The serving out of it created the usual happy bedlam about the mess decks. Afterwards, the last letter having been claimed by eager hands, there was a strange quietness as men sat and read the news from home.

But soon the bos'n's pipe was heard, followed by the voice of the bos'n's mate. "Do you hear there? Leave to the starboard watch from seventeen-thirty until twenty-two-thirty, chiefs and petty officers twenty-three hundred! All leave expires at twenty-three hundred!"

At half past five the first liberty boat left the ship, packed with men of the starboard watch. In the bows of the boat, on the forward thwart, sat the now inseparable three: Dusty

Miller, Smiler Tuckett, and Speedy MacLeod.

Up on the flight deck Tim Brinnell was watching the boat leave when Tom Langley joined him.

"Aren't you going ashore with the gang, Tim?"

"Not tonight, Tom; Josie is on night duty. What about you?"

"No. I'm duty clown tonight. Torps and Harry and Jim and young Kelling are going—heading for the floor show at the Phaleron this time."

They heard a heavy tread behind them, and then the voice of Mr. Prout.

"Did you chaps hear the news just now? We must have scared the pants off the Eyeties. German air units are moving into Italy and Sicily."

"Oh ho," said the bos'n. "Adolf doesn't like that Taranto raid."

"And now we'll have to look out for dive-bombing," said Tom. "What about the war in the desert, Tiny? Anything new?"

"Not much. The Eyeties are still batting it west, and our chaps are giving them hell around Bardia."

"Well they've a devil of a long run before they reach home. Maybe that's why so many of them are slinging their hands in."

"How about the Gyppos?" said Tiny. (He referred to the natives of Egypt.) "I'll bet they think we're fine chaps now."

"They'll be a lot happier, I expect," said Tom. "It will be better for us in harbour, too. The farther astern the Italians go, the more difficult it will be for them to bomb us at night."

"That's so, and we'll get all night in bed more often." Tiny was moving away as he made this happy observation, but on reaching the after ladder he stopped and looked back. "Don't know what you chaps think, but it's getting bloody cold up here now, and I'm for a gin. What about it—coming down?"

The pair looked at each other.

"Good idea," said Tom. "Come on." And all three disappeared down the after ladder.

CHAPTER 14

For several days most of the big ships, including the aircraft carrier, remained in harbour. Meanwhile the destroyers and small craft still played havoc with the Italian positions along the coast. Merchant vessels carried supplies to Empire forces and returned packed with Italian prisoners.

To the crew of the aircraft carrier it was an unexpected pleasure to remain in harbour for so long, especially since there were no night bombing raids to disturb their sleep. All-night leave had not been permitted, and as each day came to a close there was the feeling that morning would find the ship at sea again. Then one evening there were definite signs that the stay in harbour was coming to an end.

Tim Brinnell and Torps, who'd gone ashore together in the early afternoon, became aware of this when they returned at 7:00 P.M. As they stepped off the gangway on to the hangar deck they met Lieutenant Stanning, who had just come down the ladder from the flight deck. Seeing this officer in an overall suit at this time of day in harbour, the pair were naturally curious.

"What's going on in the engine room department," said Torps. "Having trouble?"

"We don't have trouble in my part of it," said the lieutenant. "John Stanning looks out for that. We've checked over the equipment and we're ready to fly on planes as soon as we get to sea. No problems: lift machinery, arrester gear, crash barrier—all serviced and ready."

"Good for you, then, John, but that sounds as though we're going to sea tomorrow."

"And that will put the kybosh on the party," said the bos'n.

"What party's this?" asked the lieutenant.

"It's a sort of 'at home' the nurses are arranging for Saturday—if we're in," said Torps.

"Well, I wish you luck, but I don't know why those nurses want anything to do with that scandalous bunch in your mess."

"Ah, you're jealous," said Torps.

Next morning found the ship at sea, part of a fleet of three battleships and a dozen destroyers, steaming westward at high speed. Commander Sands called in at damage-control headquarters and revealed the object of the trip. A large Italian force had been surrounded along the coast by a much smaller Empire force. It was expected that the Italians would attempt to break out during the day. The main line of their retreat, should they break out, must be by the coast road. This road led away westward over a high shoulder of land. It was intended that one battleship should shell this point, while the other two would bombard enemy positions and troop concentrations. Planes from the carrier would spot and report the fall of shot for all three ships. Meanwhile the army would attack from the south.

As soon as there was sufficient light six Swordfish planes and nine Fulmar fighters appeared over the fleet. Three of the fighters remained in the air while the other planes landed on. They would be retained on board, ready for instant service.

At noon the ship's company went to action stations. By this time all the fighters were in the air, protecting the fleet, and three Swordfish planes were taking up their reconnaissance positions over the targets.

At twelve-thirty the battleships opened fire. For two hours they steamed to and fro along the coast, lobbing fifteen-inch shells at a rapid rate.

Little was known of the results of this bombardment until the spotting aircraft returned to the carrier late in the afternoon. The reports handed in by the observers were interesting. It so happened that the coast road leading over the high ground had been packed tight with slow-moving enemy vehicles when the first salvo from the flagship arrived. After the dust cleared away it had been obvious that the Italians would not get very far on wheels. Subsequent salvos did much towards the levelling off of that particular part of Africa. The shelling from the other two battleships was equally devastating, and no doubt charged many Italians with a strong desire to go elsewhere.

Proof of this wanderlust on the part of the enemy was provided next day as the fleet lay in Alexandria harbour. Vessels of all descriptions were arriving packed with sorry-looking Italians. Most of them had wandered at a goodly pace, with their hands up, in the direction of the Empire forces. They had had enough. Sunny Italy was a nice place, but they no doubt thought themselves better off than hosts of their brethren who were hastening west in the hope of reaching that fair land. British Empire forces were hot on their heels, and, after all, there was something in this British Bulldog business.

CHAPTER 15

Mary Thompson was pleasantly surprised when, in the early afternoon, she was called to the telephone and heard the hearty voice of Torps. She had been told earlier in the day that the carrier had gone to sea, which meant that the party must be called off, for the ship always went away on long trips. Now her mind was back on the party.

"Where are you speaking from?" she asked.

"Same old berth, Mary. We came in early this morning."

"Can you come ashore?"

"Yes, of course; we have the usual leave."

"Then we can throw our party after all?"

"Well, we're all looking forward to it, Mary."

"Oh, good! Can you all get away?"

"Yes, I think so. One of the engineers may be duty officer, but I expect someone will substitute for him. How soon do you want to see us?"

"Right away after supper, Torps. We'll be waiting for you."

Soon after tea the nursing sisters set about altering the arrangement of their sitting room. Furniture not required for the party was shifted to other rooms, a heavy carpet was rolled up and carried away, and extra chairs were brought in. By the time they had finished there was ample room for dancing in the centre of the floor, while around the sides were settees, easy chairs, and small tables. A large sideboard was retained at one end of the room to hold the refreshments, and in one corner stood a radio-gramophone to provide the music. Fresh flowers in vases graced the window ledges on two sides, and each table had a small bowl in which a few young roses had been arranged by someone with the touch of an artist. The lighting was sufficiently subdued to give an air of restfulness to the room. There was only one drawback: The guests might be too comfortable to feel like dancing, but the nurses would remedy that.

Shortly after eight-fifteen the guests started to arrive. They were directed to a cloakroom by Mary Thompson.

As soon as they were comfortably seated, Mary and Eileen Hall each carried in a trayful of glasses. The women had concocted a bright red cocktail. Mary stopped before Harry Mayson.

"Hello!" he said. "Who's responsible for this potent-looking brew?"

"We have Eileen to thank for that," replied Mary. "It's one of her specials."

"It is, eh? Well Eileen ought to be made to tell what she put in it. I'll try anything once, but this looks like a risk to me."

"You'll drink that and like it, Harry Mayson," said Eileen, overhearing him. "If you don't I'll baptise you with a bowlful of it."

"Oh yes? And who'll lift you up?"

Fortunately, Eileen was handicapped by the tray she held, and in any case Harry Mayson had a clear line of retreat, being near the door.

Sublieutenant Kelling and Agnes Andrewes were fussing about the radio-gramophone, selecting records. Soon they found what they were seeking and started to play—a waltz. The sound was of a good, mellow-toned instrument but no one except the sublieutenant and his partner appeared to be taking much notice of it. The record finished and was soon followed by a slow fox-trot. Young Kelling was itching to dance and so was his partner, but they hesitated about being the first to start. Susie had the same inclination.

"Jim," she said, "do you think if we got up to dance someone else might join us on the floor?"

"It's worth trying," replied Jim, standing up.

Susie rose and soon her eyes were shining as Jim swung her through a series of intricate steps in time with the music. Then Tim Brinnell and Josie Weir took the floor and began to show what they could do. They were followed by the sublieutenant and his partner. Before the record finished all were dancing. The party was off to a good start.

It was a happy evening. There was a Paul-Jones early on, which mixed everyone up and caused a good deal of fun. As time wore on, some of them started to sit out more. Torps referred to this as the elimination of the unfit, meaning himself. However, Torps still had a good deal of bounce in him. Seeing Mary Thompson, Eileen Hall, and Harry Mayson sitting out he inquired what they were drinking; then he went away and came back with the drinks on a tray: Tom Collinses for Mary and Eileen, and whisky and soda for Harry Mayson and himself.

Then Sublieutenant Kelling and Agnes Andrewes went out to get some fresh air. They were soon followed by Jim Kirklane and Susie.

There was no moon, but the sky was clear and full of stars. There was a large open lawn beside the building, and Susie and Jim walked slowly away over it, hand in hand.

"We shouldn't be away too long, Jim," said Susie.

"No, let's just wander around awhile and then go back. It's nice out for a change."

"Yes, it is— Are you enjoying yourself, Jim?"

"Of course I am, young lady. You know I always do when I'm with you."

"And I feel the same, Jim. I'm always happy in your company. You give me a feeling of security and peacefulness."

Jim smiled and bent his head towards her. "But you always are happy anyway, Susie. You were born that way."

Susie made no comment, and Jim went on.

"I believe you find pleasure in everything you do. And you really like your work here, don't you?"

"Yes, I do."

They paced on in the stillness of the night. Soon the distant rattle of a streetcar intruded on the silence. They saw the flash of sparks from its trolley. It passed by on the road near the seafront a hundred yards away from them. It was almost out of their range of hearing, on its way to town, when Jim spoke again.

"Well, I wish we men were doing something more useful"; and he added quietly: "I often wonder what you think when you see us as we come back."

Susie turned to ask what he meant but Jim spoke again. "All we're trying to do is kill our fellowman; and if we are successful at it, and lucky enough, we could end up as heroes and return home with our chests sticking out like feather beds. But we could be carried back—pretty flat-chested then—and if we had any brains left, we'd have to admit being thankful there's a source of strength like yours to fall back on."

There was sadness and a hint of bitterness in his tones that almost stopped Susie in her tracks.

"But Jim," she said, "no man needs to be ashamed of fighting for his country, and for the security of his home and family. We must all do the job we are fitted for, and trust that those above us know how to do theirs—and may the Lord guide them."

"Yes, that's it—may He guide them. The idiocy of man brought about this mess. We are working very hard to destroy all the good things put into this world to make life beautiful for us. We have no time to walk into the woodlands and sit under the trees, to take a good look at a leaf or a wildflower and let the wonder of it all sink in. There are thousands of streams making music for us. Millions of birds singing and fluttering their wings in the light and shade. What things we are missing!"

Susie changed her grip on his hand and walked beside him in silence for a few seconds. When she spoke there was a tinge of sadness in her voice.

"Jim, I've noticed you've been very quiet tonight, and I wondered what was on your mind. We all know that war is madness, but it will come to an end, and what we should be thinking about is how we can stop it happening again. Apart from that we have to get on with our jobs and realize that this is only a passing phase in our lives. It might seem little else but gun smoke, sand, and sea to you now, but you'll see those woodlands again, Jim, and enjoy them all the more."

Susie did not see the tender smile suffusing Jim's face, but she heard his reply, though it was only a whisper.

"I'm not so sure."

She stopped at once and pulled his hand so that he stood before her. She peered into his face.

"What do you mean, Jim?"

"I don't know, Susie. It's something I feel, or sense."

"Then you must forget it," she said gently. "You *must*. It means nothing— Promise me!"

He stood looking down into her face. He had an almost overpowering desire to crush her in his arms. Something within was prompting: *This may be good-bye!* She gripped him by the arms, and he knew she was anxious for his reply.

"All right, Susie— I'll try."

She kissed him gently and released her grip. "That's better, Jim."

They were not the last to return, for Tim Brinnell and Josie Weir were behind them as they walked through the hall, and Sublieutenant Kelling and Agnes Andrewes were still taking the air.

Susie entered the room first. The radio-gramophone was silent and everyone had gathered at the end of the room near the door. They stood around chatting and helping themselves to refreshments from the sideboard. The nurses had made a good show of sandwiches, sausage rolls, cakes, and biscuits. Susie and Jim caught the conversation as they entered. Torps was speaking and his voice, as usual, was loud enough for everyone to hear.

"Well, we've had a good run, and we have nothing to grumble about, whatever happens next."

"Yes," agreed Harry Mayson, "the ship's done her stuff, and if she takes a wallop or two now she's justified her existence."

Susie stopped at once as if a barrier stood in her way. Then she took two slow paces to the rear and leaned against the doorpost, and her brow was troubled.

"Are you all right, Susie?" asked Jim.

"Yes, I'm all right, thanks; but what is all this nonsense?"

Before Jim could reply Mary Thompson let herself be heard. "We've had enough of this twaddle. What's got into you men tonight? Anybody would think this was a good-bye party. Somebody put a record on and let's wake up!"

There was some laughter at this, and Mr. Mayson went to start the gramophone.

"Give us a waltz, Harry," called Tim Brinnell. "This is where I take Jim's partner from him. All right, Susie?"

"Of course, Tim," said Susie, smiling.

Tim was very light on his feet and they made a graceful pair as they moved away. Soon there were others on the floor, including young Kelling and his partner. Susie and Tim were silent for a while, then Tim spoke.

"How are you doing, Susie? Having a good time?"

She looked up at him. The music was slow enough for them to converse easily.

"Well I was, Tim, but now it seems there's something in the wind and it bothers me. Perhaps you can help. I have a question to ask, but don't answer if you feel you shouldn't, and I don't need any details: Are you going out on any specially dangerous trip next time?"

Tim looked down in surprise. "Not that I know of, Susie. In any case, none of us ever know where we're going or what we intend to do until we get to sea. Why do you ask?"

"Well, some of your friends, including Jim, seem to feel that something will happen soon. You heard what Mary Thompson said just now?"

"You mean about it looking like a good-bye party?"

"Yes."

"Oh, that's all tosh! There's a certain morbidity that creeps over men sometimes in this kind of life. We think we have some additional sense that warns us of danger. I'm old enough now to put that sort of thing down to indigestion."

"You're a comforting man, Tim."

From then on they concentrated on the dance, and by the time the record finished Susie was enjoying herself again.

At eleven-thirty the taxi arrived, Torps having ordered it earlier, but the guests were loath to leave. They had one more dance, knowing it to be the last, then as they all stood still when the music stopped something seemed to creep over the company: a feeling that now was the time to sing "Auld Lang Syne." Susie sensed it very strongly. She glanced at Tim Brinnell. He was standing sideways to her, silent and tense. The spell was broken by the voice of Torps.

"Come on then, hearties, we'd better look lively!"

To Josie Weir it seemed that Tim was strangely silent as they walked along the hallway. He had on his blue raincoat and was carrying his hat.

"Will you be ashore tomorrow, Tim?"

He did not answer at once. It seemed he had to collect his thoughts. She was wondering if he had not heard her when he replied.

"Why, yes, Josie. Strange to say, I'd taken it for granted that we'd be going to sea tomorrow—don't know why. Shall we go out to dinner?"

"Yes, if you wish, Tim."

When they all reached the taxi, Torps was directing the driver.

"Number Six Gate, Driver. We have to be there by twelve o'clock."

There followed many good nights and thanks during which everyone seemed to be speaking at once. As the taxi moved away Susie and Josie caught a glimpse of the dim interior of the car. Jim Kirklane, in the rear seat nearest to them, appeared to be his old self again. Beside him sat Tim Brinnell, looking ahead, his face still pale and tense. Josie and Susie watched the car until the red taillight vanished into the distance, then they turned away and quietly followed the others indoors.

CHAPTER 16

Under way again, on a Sunday morning. The fleet moved on a northwesterly course, a battleship leading the line of heavy ships, followed by the aircraft carrier, two other battleships, and two heavy cruisers, while fourteen destroyers formed the protecting screen. The fleet covered a large convoy to Crete and Greece and was strong enough to tackle anything Mussolini would put out, though that unhappy man might muster a large number of ships.

Soon after daybreak the remainder of the planes, released from duties in support of the army, had rejoined their base afloat.

The trip had come as a surprise. Following the bombardment of enemy positions along the coast there had been a feeling that, so long as the army was advancing, the fleet would be retained at the eastern end of the Mediterranean to repeat this form of attack if and when required. However, before noon on this Sabbath day, the ship's company became aware that the fleet would be at sea for several days.

For three days there were no signs of the enemy. During this time the ships of the convoy arrived safely at their respective destinations in Crete and Greece, and the fleet bore westward towards Malta. The weather remained fine throughout. On the fourth day, in the forenoon, the crew of the aircraft carrier went to action stations. Unidentified aircraft had been detected approaching from a northerly direction. There were three fighters in the air protecting the fleet, and six were taking off. Three reconnaissance planes were up too, seeking enemy sea forces.

The men between decks waited calmly at their action stations. All damage-control gear had been placed in readiness for instant use. Anything might happen now, for the ship was approaching Malta.

Mr. Mayson entered damage-control headquarters to check with Chief Stoker Lathom on the disposition of oil fuel in the ship. The commander (E) seemed to ignore his entry, so he was able to sit beside Lathom and set to work at once.

The chief looked quite jolly. He lounged comfortably in his easy chair. He wore a brand-new deep blue uniform suit, the three thick, shining gold rings on each sleeve enhancing its beauty. At his elbow, on the control officer's desk, lay a library book, but he had not opened it yet; he seemed to be sufficiently entertained by the activities of the damage-control staff: Lieutenant Morton still working away at the card index scheme; the master-at-arms explaining some of the telephone systems to the new engineers' writer, Saunders; the electrical artificer speaking over the phone to the warrant electrician, who was standing by the switchboard well forward on the deck below; and three messengers sitting around trying to look alert and ready. The chief was a picture of self-confidence—the monarch of all he surveyed. Here in this damage-control nerve centre he could, through these men around him, direct the damage-control parties to deal with any situation that might arise. Everything would be done in a neat and tidy way. *Let's see,* he thought. *A torpedo hit starboard side forward— Right. The message comes through the master-at-arms or Saunders. Then come the more detailed reports: 'So-and-so compartment on fire,' or 'So-and-so compartment flooded,' or 'Number so-and-so bulkhead damaged.' Saunders and the master-at-arms select the correct chits, with the coloured corners—red for fire, black for flood-*

ing, and blue for structural damage— Yes, that's right, my memory's still pretty good. The electrical artificer takes electrical damage reports on his green-cornered chits. They write their reports in duplicate and pass one copy to the damage-control officer, who puts it in the correct coloured clip before him. The second copy of each report goes by messenger to the machinery control room, where somebody puts it on the correct clip. Hmn. Better hustle the messengers about on this job. And then the damage-control officer reports to me what has happened. I tell him to refer to the flooding board and work out how much the ship has gone down by the bows, and how much she's listed to starboard— But wait a minute! The lieutenant hasn't had time to make a study of damage control—been too busy on that card index so far, and he's only a youngster, too. Better keep Mr. Mayson handy. Somebody will have to tell our men forward what to do to keep the ship afloat. As soon as we get their reports on what they're doing we'll have the whole story neatly filed. I can reach over, grab that phone to the bridge, and report to the captain everything that's happening.

The chief could visualize himself giving the orders, getting the results, and then, in secret triumph, telling the captain all about it. It was easy. Everything would go like clockwork. One only needed to pick the right men for the right jobs. He came out of his pleasant daydream to hear the voice of Mr. Mayson.

"That's all right, Lathom, there's only that one point: Put one of the boiler rooms on Number Seventeen Tank for a couple of hours; it's a bit too full for my liking."

"Very good, sir," said the chief stoker.

"What are you up to, Mr. Mayson?" asked the chief.

"Just dealing with a small matter regarding oil fuel, sir; trying to keep all the tanks in the best condition to resist shock."

"Oh, I see." But there was a look of puzzled inquiry in the chief's eyes as he met the steady gaze of the commissioned engineer.

The voice of the paymaster came over the broadcasting system.

"Well"—the characteristic pause—"we have lost contact with that group—or whatever it was—of aircraft. We have nine fighters up now. We shall probably secure from action stations soon. And"—pause—"that's all." Pause. "I'll let you know if I get another report."

The chief's easy chair creaked as he reached to get his library book. Mr. Mayson stood up to leave.

"I wouldn't be surprised if those were German planes."

The chief looked up. His face registered absolute ridicule. He sat upright and looked around the office so that all might see what he thought of such a stupid remark. "Yes, and I suppose they flew all round in a great big circle to find us and then went back again." As he spoke he waved a massive arm around in demonstration of some vague image he had of planes leaving a remote airfield in Germany on a circular tour—of Europe, probably. But the joke must have been weak, for even the stoker messengers failed to laugh. Mr. Mayson was the only one to show any amusement.

"Well," he said quietly, "we know there are German planes based in Sicily, don't we?"

"Yes."

"And I suppose these were enemy planes?"

There was no answer. Silence. The chief looked at Mr. Mayson, his big brown eyes meeting the steel-grey ones just for a moment; then he looked down at his library book and began to read.

This was something new to the damage-control staff. There were quiet smiles now. Never before had anyone taken the chief down in anything. Mr. Mayson picked up his gloves and torch and slid out. As he moved aft he heard the pipe: "Hands secure from action stations."

The day passed without further incident and the fleet

still bore westward. By dawn the next day the island of Malta lay well to the eastward. From the bridge of the carrier the paymaster broadcast the reason for this move so far to the west. A large, valuable convoy was coming through these dangerous waters on its way from England to Malta and the Middle East.

As the paymaster finished giving out this information something happened to take his interest away from the microphone; consequently the men below did not hear of the distracting event till later. In the early morning light the lookouts saw and reported gun flashes to the west. Was this the convoy being shot up by the enemy? In the rapidly increasing visibility it soon became clear what was happening. Two destroyers were racing away northward at very high speed, one well ahead of the other. They were Italian ships and they had, probably by accident, run into the British convoy at the crack of dawn. It was their bad luck, for a British cruiser chased after them. She was a brand-new ship, straight from the hands of skilled British workmen. She opened fire in low visibility. As the visibility increased, so did the range, for the Italian shipbuilders had sacrificed much so that their vessels might have speed. But the British cruiser was out for blood, and she wasn't slow. This was real big-game hunting. There was another flash from the cruiser's forward guns, followed soon after by the flash of shells bursting in the rear destroyer. Then there was an extremely large flash as the unfortunate Italian vessel blew skyward. The leading destroyer got out of range just in time.

The men on deck who saw this action felt very happy about it. The cruiser had proven to the Mediterranean fleet that Britain was still producing the goods. Her firing was surprisingly rapid and accurate. She altered course and steamed towards the fleet like a terrier returning to its master after making a kill. Meanwhile a signalling lantern blinked on her bridge as she exchanged messages with the flagship.

The convoy was away to the southwest and the fleet still bore westward. In the early forenoon the fleet turned about and steamed slowly eastward, maintaining a position between the convoy and Sicily. This convoy must get through and the fleet intended to see that it did.

The sun rose and shone brightly in a sky clear but for a few white clouds high up. As the ships steamed slowly and peacefully eastward one could hardly believe that this was war: such a lovely day, such a calm sea. But Captain Graham knew the danger of the situation, and so did most of his officers. Mr. Mayson voiced his opinion of it to Lieutenant Tangry in the engineers' office shortly after nine o'clock. Little did he know how different the situation would be in a few hours. On his way forward Mr. Mayson, upon seeing the lieutenant in the office, had entered to have a chat.

"Good morning. Doesn't a smart man like you know better than to be here at this time of day?"

"Well, I do, really, Mr. Mayson, but I have to see the senior about a few defect items. In any case, what are you doing here?"

"I came in to talk to you."

The tall young officer stepped back to sit on the edge of a desk. "That's nice of you, old chap. Take a seat and tell me—what's news?"

"I'd say it isn't out yet. Don't you think we're taking a hell of a risk crawling about these waters like this?"

"Yes, I do, but you never know what's behind it all. It may be worth losing a warship or so to get this convoy through."

Lieutenant Tangry would have had more to say, but—

Blurp! blurp! blurp! Blurp! blurp! blurp! Blurp! blurp! blurp!

The short, sharp bustle of preparation for action followed. Unidentified aircraft had been detected to the north. There were six fighters in the air, and in less than half an hour the paymaster was able to broadcast the now-familiar report: One enemy aircraft, which had been shadowing the fleet, had been shot down. Shortly afterwards the call, "Secure from action stations," sounded.

Later in the forenoon the fleet turned into the wind while six more fighters took to the air, and the six already in service landed on to be refuelled and kept in readiness on the flight deck.

Commander Sands had given instructions for all damage-control gear to be kept in the highest state of readiness. The convoy was making good speed, and if it survived this one critical day it would, by morning, be in a much safer position in regard to air attack.

The majority of the ship's company enjoyed the midday meal in comfort. It was usual for the men to go to dinner at eleven-forty-five. In the officers' messes lunch was usually served about twelve, and the meal was in progress when the action alarm came screaming in again.

Blurp! blurp! blurp! Blurp! blurp! blurp! Blurp! blurp! blurp!

It was sensed at once that this was something different. Knives and forks were thrown down, and as the officers hurried away the ammunition conveyers were already working, and damage-control ratings were hastily donning fire-fighting suits.

The chief, Lieutenant Morton, and Mr. Mayson arrived at damage-control headquarters together. No sooner had the chief taken his easy chair than the heavy antiaircraft guns opened fire. The firing was one continuous bedlam; obviously the whole fleet had opened up.

Bang! Bang! Bang! Bang! Bang! Bang! Bang! Bang! Bang! Bang!

The paymaster shouted through the microphone. He could barely be heard.

"The fleet is being attacked by—"

At that point the ship's multiple pom-pom guns opened fire—a nerve-shattering row, a continuous hammering roar. It fluctuated in volume as one or another of the guns ceased fire for a moment. Occasionally the noise was augmented by the heavy *boom* of bombs exploding in the sea close by. One of these must have been very close, for the ship rocked under the force of the explosion.

In damage-control headquarters Mr. Mayson leaned back against a desk. His fingers gripped hard on the woodwork behind him. Then it came. There was no mistaking it. The pom-pom guns were still roaring, but their noise was drowned by the blow struck by the enemy.

There was a heavy, hard, high-pitched cracking report. It seemed as though the massive steel shell of the ship had been shattered—as if it were a huge coconut—by one tremendous blow. The ship shuddered from stem to stern and the lights flickered. Then followed a short period of silence, broken when the pom-pom guns opened up again. A phone buzzed in damage-control headquarters. The buzz was drowned by the noise of the guns, but a round disc of light on the receiver box indicated that someone was calling. The master-at-arms took the message, jammed the receiver back in place and called to the commander (E).

"Number Four Dynamo is off the board and the room is on fire, sir!"

The chief instinctively looked to the commissioned engineer. "Mr. Mayson, go and see what's wrong and let me know!"

Mr. Mayson left the office. No use reminding the chief that there was a party already dealing with the situation. The party had informed damage-control headquarters in accordance with their training. No use reminding the chief that there were three messengers waiting who could collect additional information should it be required. As he hurried forward he met Mr. Langley, who was hurrying aft. No word passed between them. Mr. Mayson went out of his way a little over to the starboard side, where he threw open the lid of a wooden box and lifted out a breathing apparatus. When he arrived at Number Four Dynamo he found the lights had gone out in the room. Smoke poured out of the hatch. A chief engine room artificer emerged with a handkerchief round his nose. A stoker appeared. He held two fire extinguishers. Another stoker dragged a canvas fire hose along. Seeing the engineer, they stood awaiting orders. Mr. Mayson waited until the chief ERA was clear of the ladder, then he went to go below himself, wearing the breathing apparatus. The pom-pom guns were still roaring. The chief ERA removed the handkerchief from his face and called, over the noise of the guns, "It's all right, sir! No need to go down! I've killed the fire and shut the steam off the engine!"

Mr. Mayson looked him straight in the face for a couple of seconds, and then spoke loudly in the man's ear.

"Good man! Come, put this hatch down!" He motioned to the two stokers to help the chief ERA, and they were all bent down tightening the clips of the hatch when—

Crash!

Mr. Mayson staggered under the shock and his head struck the side of an electrical junction box. The two stokers pitched forward on to their hands, while the chief ERA saved himself from falling by grabbing the chains around the hatch. The main lighting went out but the secondary battery lighting was soon brought into use by the nearby fire and repair parties.

"Are you hurt, sir?" asked the chief ERA, but Mr. Mayson was already moving away. He had switched on the electric torch that hung around his neck.

"I'm all right, Chief," he called back.

He was soon back at damage-control headquarters. The guns ceased firing. As he opened the door he heard the commander (E)'s voice raised in anger:

"Damn the bloody chits, man! What do they say? Let's have it!"

"There's a fire in the paint store and the seamen's fore upper mess deck, sir. Sublieutenant Kelling is dealing with it," replied Saunders.

Half the lights were out, and the deck before Saunders and the master-at-arms was littered with little pieces of paper with coloured corners. The chits had overflowed on to the desk. The damage control officer's desk had been swept clear of all signs of the index scheme, and that energetic officer was scribbling reports on a signal pad as fast as he could. The chief caught on to the idea and encouraged it, at the same time shouting with impatience at almost everyone in turn. His shouting had little effect on Mr. Mayson, who went straight to Lieutenant Morton.

"Have you issued any instructions to the pumping parties?" The chief heard him.

"Instructions!" he shouted. "How the hell can we issue instructions? If there's any pumping to do they should get on with it!"

Another telephone buzzed, and the door burst open under the hand of an excited messenger. "There's a big bomb come in aft, sir!" he cried. "It's blown all the inside of the ship about! Nearly everybody's killed or wounded back there!"

Lieutenant Leyton put his head in at the door, and spoke loudly and hurriedly over the head of the messenger. "That last bomb burst in the wardroom flat! There's a terrific fire in there and we've had to shut the armour bulkhead door! We can only get aft by way of the flight deck now!"

Saunders dropped his telephone. "The hangar's on fire, sir, fore and aft!"

The chief looked wildly around, then his eyes rested on the busy pencil of Lieutenant Morton. "Write it down! Write it down!" he shouted.

Mr. Mayson was speaking quietly on the telephone: "One-eight-four, please."

In a few seconds he was through. "Mr. Mayson speaking—that Petty Officer Wright?"

"Yes, sir."

"Well, listen carefully: Check all depth recording instruments for wing watertight compartments in your section. Note them on paper and report the results to damage-control headquarters. Afterwards recheck your readings every twenty minutes."

"Repeat that order."

Mr. Mayson listened to the repetition and replied: "That's it. Good man, Wright!" He pressed down the receiver hook and spoke again. There seemed to be less noise about, and suddenly he realized that there was silence except for the sound of his own voice.

"One-nine-seven, please.

"Mr. Mayson speaking. That you, Davies?"

"Yes, sir."

"Listen carefully: Check all depth recorders for your wing tanks. Be very careful about those on the port side; I believe we've had a near miss there in your section. Note the readings on paper and report back to damage-control headquarters. Afterwards recheck your readings every twenty minutes."

"Repeat that order."

Mr. Mayson listened again and smiled like a proud mother as his order was clearly repeated. "Well done, Davies." And he pressed down the receiver hook once more.

"Two-oh-five, please.

"Hello; Mr. Mayson speaking. That you, Turner?"

"No, sir. Petty Officer Turner has been wounded."

"Oh, has he? Is that Leading Stoker Harris?"

"Yes, sir."

"Are you all right?"

"Yes, sir."

"You know how to check your depth recorders, don't you?"

"Yes, sir."

"Well, listen carefully."

Mr. Mayson gave his instructions. He had just hung up the receiver after hearing Harris repeat his orders when two things happened. The master-at-arms, holding a telephone receiver away from his ear and, quite naturally, speaking to the person who seemed to know something, addressed Mr. Mayson. "Sir," he said to the commissioned engineer, "there's something wrong here. I can't make out what this man is saying."

As Mr. Mayson took the phone the door burst open and an engine room artificer entered. The man looked to the commander (E) and made his report: "Steering gear has broken down, sir, both primary and secondary!" And then Mr. Mayson became aware of an excited voice over the telephone. It was a young voice, and its owner shouted feverishly into the transmitter. "Now then, son," said the engineer, "speak quietly. There's no hurry."

The voice calmed down and the message came through. "From Sublieutenant Kelling, sir—the fire forward is under control. Can you send a breathing apparatus?"

Mr. Mayson repeated the message, and running through his mind was the thought: *Well done the young sub!* He turned to the master-at-arms: "Ring one-eight-one and tell them to take the breathing apparatus from Number Four Dynamo room hatch to Sublieutenant Kelling forward."

The master-at-arms complied at once.

"Mr. Mayson! Mr. Mayson!" called the chief. "We must do something about this steering gear—quickly!"

Mr. Mayson glanced at him sharply. "Just a minute, sir." He reached up to point to the flooding board, placing his hand on Lieutenant Morton's shoulder. "See this?" he said, indicating the plan of the hold. "You heard the instructions I gave to the pumping parties. They're checking all these compartments here within the armour belt. They'll report in to you every twenty minutes. Keep a record, old lad.

"And now, sir—steering gear?"

"Yes," said the chief. "This man says both positions are gone."

"Well, steer by main engines."

"We can't, apparently; they can't get the rudder amidships."

"Well, Mr. Langley is the best man for that. It's time I got about and saw to some pumping. We're listing to starboard."

"Mr. Langley's wounded."

"Right, I'm off!" said Mr. Mayson.

At that moment the pom-pom guns opened up again with their deafening roar. Up on the flight deck the gun's crews, smoke-grimed and sweating, worked like madmen—but with splendid method and timing. German dive-bombers came out of the sky with fanatical daring and skill; wave after wave they came, with all the hate and vicious will of their Führer behind their determination to wipe out this nuisance of an aircraft carrier. The flight deck was a shambles; the after lift wrecked. Smoke came from the gaping hole in huge, belching clouds. Forward of this lift the deck had been pierced by a second heavy bomb, and smoke poured from there, too. There was still evidence of the fire forward. Kelling and his men were fighting it. The hangar was ablaze inside but some survivor of the hangar party had pushed the buttons and pulled the levers that set the hangar's drenching system working. So water poured into the hangar in a deluge, and the ship steamed around like a crippled seabird: She had a fair list to starboard and was well down at the stern. A near-miss bomb had sent splinters flying into the bridge structure, where Captain Graham had stood calmly giving his orders. He had had a miraculous escape, for the steel structure all about him was pierced. Another bomb had scored a direct hit on one of the pom-pom guns, killing the whole gun's crew, including Mr. Rathbone, the commissioned gunner, before the captain's eyes. Back aft in that inferno of smoke and flame, a first-aid party struggled to get the wounded away. Plane after plane still dived at the ship. The rest of the fleet was ignored, and these kept up a heavy fire at the enemy. Occasionally a hoarse, lusty cheer broke from the guns' crews of the carrier as an enemy plane crashed into the sea or caught fire in the air.

And up in the air the fight still raged. The fighters played havoc with the German planes while their ammunition and fuel lasted. Sublieutenant Bowman bagged one bomber before he had to pancake into the sea, short of fuel. A British destroyer picked him up. Two other pilots were forced to come down in the same manner. Others continued to fight throughout the day, landing at Malta for fuel and ammunition and taking off again.

Down below in the boiler rooms a grim struggle was going on. The smoke belching over the flight deck was being caught in the air inlet trunks leading to the boiler room fans. The fans, which supplied air to the oil sprayers, were drawing down the smoke and delivering it into the boiler rooms. Men were working almost blindly, stumbling about and peering with smarting eyes into the face of each important gauge in turn. Conditions were almost unbearable: Some of the men were going into uncontrollable fits of coughing. Mr. Kirklane continually passed from one boiler room to another, letting the men know he was about. He encouraged and advised them. The telegraph from the machinery control room rang frequently, and on each occasion a stoker had to climb on to a boiler water drum to peer into the face of the telegraph and shout its order to the chief stoker of the watch.

In the machinery control room the senior engineer was doing his best to obey the orders from the bridge. Mr. Mayson walked down the ladder and was surprised to find the senior alone except for one stoker at the telephone exchange. He saw the danger again: Suppose that second bomb had dropped a little farther forward; damage control would have been just a farce then. But he had no time except to make his report, and the senior was more than busy. With praiseworthy determination that officer was dealing with the one job that mattered, as far as he was concerned: keeping his engines moving. Mr. Mayson called to him.

"The rudder is amidships now, sir. You can steer by main engines."

"All right, Mr. Mayson," shouted the senior, and he leapt across the room to alter a telegraph.

Mr. Mayson left. That simple message hadn't sounded very important, yet the fact that the rudder had been placed amidships made it possible for the ship to escape. Together with the engine room artificer in charge of steering gear, the commissioned engineer had dealt with a desperate situation. The main steering gear was inaccessible owing to the damage aft, and control of it by telemotor from the bridge had been destroyed. The secondary gear, in the engine room, was capable of moving the rudder, but the pipeline through which the power was transmitted obviously had been damaged—somewhere beneath that fire raging near the stern. The liquid that formed the power medium was disappearing rapidly from its storage tank. In a few minutes the rudder would move no more. The helm indicator wiring had been shot away somewhere between the engine room and the rudder. How then could one tell when the rudder was amidships? Mr. Mayson saw the danger at once and stopped the power unit in order to conserve the liquid remaining. He took the ERA by the arm and pulled him to a sitting position on a steel girder near the unit.

"Come," he said, "sit here with me. We have to think. *Think!*"

The pom-pom guns opened up again with their shattering roar. It drowned the whine of the main turbine gearing. Hell seemed to be let loose and falling about them. Still the pair sat there looking at the complicated unit.

Suddenly the ERA turned to the engineer. "The hunting gear!" he yelled. "There must be a way by that!"

Mr. Mayson jumped to his feet and slapped the ERA on the back. "There is," he yelled. "Well done! Measure the length of travel and call out when the hunting gear is halfway along."

While the ERA took up a steel rule from his tool bag, Mr. Mayson started the power unit. Then, while the guns still roared, he moved the steering wheel slowly, watching closely as the ERA checked the hunting gear travel. Suddenly the man threw up one arm and called. The engineer stopped moving the wheel and shut down the power unit. At that moment the guns ceased firing.

"Is Mr. Langley hurt very badly?" asked the engineer.

"No, I don't think so, sir. He was picked up unconscious, but it was shock, I believe."

"All right, then. Now, you report to damage-control headquarters about the rudder. I'll tell the senior."

After making his report to the senior the commissioned engineer moved aft, avoiding damage-control headquarters. Immediately abaft this office was situated the after medical station, inside which a surgeon lieutenant and the ship's padre, along with their assistants, were busy tending the wounded. More wounded were being brought along by stretcher bearers. In a compartment close by, which served as the ship's chapel, dozens of wounded men lay; they had been dealt with by the first-aid parties and were awaiting further treatment.

As Mr. Mayson entered the narrow passage between the chapel and the medical station, stretcher bearers entered at the other end. He stood aside to allow the stretcher to pass. The wounded man was in a bad way; the blanket that covered him was stained by blood on one side, and only the slow-moving eyelids indicated that he was alive. Mr. Mayson looked him in the eyes and smiled gently. The man smiled weakly in return. His smile was followed by a wince as the leading stretcher bearer came to a rather abrupt halt and called back, "Where shall we take him? Into the chapel?"

Before the other bearer could reply the wounded man spoke. His head moved slightly and he made a great effort. "Chapel my Aunt Fanny!" Then his voice trailed away, but Mr. Mayson heard him. "What the 'ell? I ain't dead yet."

Mr. Mayson took in a deep breath and shook his head slowly in wonder. He moved aft.

Soon he had reached the armour bulkhead. The water-tight doors there, which gave access to the wardroom flat and compartments aft, were closed. Some of the lights were out. Broken glass from the globes littered the deck, mingling with hoses, coils of rope, breather apparatus, piping, and tools. And here and there were patches of blood. Two steam pipes were hanging loose, some of the supporting brackets having broken away from the deck head. A few men stood around, obviously not fully recovered from shock. He felt the steam pipe flanges; they were hot, still under steam pressure. Here was an additional danger to life, for another hit anywhere close by might break those pipes. He provided what the men were waiting for: leadership—just enough direction to get them moving.

"Come on, men!" he called, picking up a length of rope. "Get these pipes secured."

The rope was taken from his hand at once. Willing men lifted up the sagging pipes while others tied them up to other fittings overhead. Seeing the men busy he called a chief stoker to one side.

"What's happening here, Chief?" he asked. "Why are those doors closed?"

"There's fire in there, sir. Commander Sands ordered us to keep them closed."

"Where's Lieutenant Leyton?"

"He's along with Number Three Fire Party dealing with fire on the gallery decks."

"And Lieutenant Tangry?"

An expressive look appeared in the chief stoker's eyes. He nodded towards the closed doors and spoke with quiet sadness. "He's back there, sir."

Mr. Mayson looked round quickly. "Here, you!" he called, pointing to one of the stokers. "And you! Open this door! Quickly!"

The men obeyed at once. First they opened the heavy armour door, then they knocked the clips off the watertight door behind it. As they opened it, smoke poured through and drove them back. Mr. Mayson jumped to the door and pushed it open wide. Smoke enveloped him, and a heavy lick of flame flashed out. He turned his head away just in time and with a quick movement closed the door. Already the flat was full of smoke and men were coughing and groping their way about. It was obvious that the doors would have to be kept closed. Anyone on the other side could not be alive.

"All right, men," said Mr. Mayson, "I'll try to get in from aft."

He went to damage-control headquarters to report. He saw that the electric party had been busy there: All the lights were on again. He reported to Lieutenant Morton on the situation at the position he had just left. The lieutenant had a huge pile of notes before him. The chief had assisted in taking down the reports, and every scrap of information that had reached the office had been timed and noted. It was something the chief had seen done properly so far, whatever his shortcomings in other things might be.

As Lieutenant Morton noted Mr. Mayson's remarks a stoker messenger opened the door and spoke to the commander (E).

"I can't get aft, sir. They won't let me go over the flight deck. There's danger of another attack."

"Oh, damn!" said the chief.

Mr. Mayson spoke to Lieutenant Morton: "How are the wing compartments? Have the pumping and flooding parties kept up their reports?"

"Yes. Here you are, Mr. Mayson—a complete list."

"Good." The commissioned engineer checked the list. "That's fine—we've no water at all anywhere within the armour belt."

"Mr. Mayson," said the chief, "I can't get a report on the situation aft. Go and find out what's happening."

"All right, sir. I was about to go back. I don't know who is doing what back there; Lieutenant Tangry is believed lost. But what about this imbalance? We're listing to starboard. Have you issued any orders about it?"

The chief looked at Mr. Mayson and opened his mouth but gave no answer. Mr. Mayson looked to the damage-control officer. He was still writing furiously. The box holding the index card scheme had been pushed away by his left elbow and lay on the deck. The cards, spread about the floor, were being trampled underfoot by the busy messengers. Over in one corner lay the board with the beautiful coloured clips. Lieutenant Morton in his need for space had thrown it out of his way. The chief still sat in his easy chair, shouting whenever he could find a reason for it. The telephones were buzzing frequently and Saunders, the master-at-arms, and the electrical artificer called the messages as they received them: "From Lieutenant Leyton: Fires in the gallery decks starboard under control." "From number two electrical repair party: Emergency lighting is rigged ready for use forward of the wardroom flat."

Mr. Mayson looked at the chief again. The chief looked back and suddenly remembered something.

"Go on, Mr. Mayson! Get away aft!"

"Yes, sir, I will. But just a minute—

"Lathom! Come here!"

The small chief stoker rose from his desk. Mr. Mayson stood looking at the flooding board, which showed the arrangement of all the hold compartments. "Bring your oil fuel chart, Lathom."

"Here it is, sir."

"Right. Now just a second— Yes, I see. You are on this tank in use, and this one, and this. And these are standby, eh?"

"Yes, sir."

"Good! Now, Lathom, it's dangerous to use your pumping-over line. If the pipes are damaged you might start fires all over the place. So level off through your suction lines. Run down oil from these two tanks on the starboard side to those two nearly empty ones on the port side. That should correct this list."

Mr. Mayson spoke rapidly but the chief stoker followed him. "Yes, sir. I see."

"Good! Now I know the suction line is complicated here, but I can rely on you, Lathom. Make sure of what you need to do before you start."

"Very good, sir."

Telephones were still buzzing. Shouted messages rang out across the office. Mr. Mayson hurried out, glad to be clear of the place. His head was throbbing, his mouth hot dry. He had lost his cap and his hair was plastered to his head with sweat and grime. A dark brown streak clinging to the left side of his face indicated that the wound in his head had dried up.

He made his way up the midship ladders to the flight deck, stepping aside occasionally to allow casualties to pass on their way down. The flight deck appeared to be deserted except for the guns' crews, and smoke still rose through the after lift and the hole forward of it. As he reached the port after ladder a young seaman came up, carrying a limp form over his shoulder. Mr. Mayson noted the two and a half rings, indicating lieutenant commander rank, on the sleeves of the casualty. Obviously he was seriously wounded. He was being sick over the youngster's back.

"Get him on a stretcher, son," said the engineer.

Another young seaman threw a stretcher up the ladder and climbed up after it. "Here you are, sir," he said.

"All right then. You two lads get him on to it and take him forward. I can't stop."

At the bottom of the ladder Mr. Mayson met the warrant shipwright, Mr. Ganer.

"Hello, Chippie," he said.

"Hello, Harry. What are you doing back here?"

"Oh, snooping around, Chippie. Checking on the damage."

"Well, it's pretty grim, Harry"; and Mr. Ganer's eyes met those of his messmate. The engineer was shocked. Something had gone from Mr. Ganer's eyes. They were bleak and dry; the reddened eyelids blinked rarely, and then only slowly, as though with great effort. Though Mr. Mayson did not know it at the time, the warrant shipwright had been working like a hero amidst the carnage aft. A few men in his repair parties had helped him. Together they had hacked and levered a passageway through the twisted metal that had once been the ship's structure. Steel ladders had been torn from their positions, some screwed into spirals as though by the hands of an enraged giant. Decks and bulkheads had been shattered and distorted out of all recognition, cabins wrecked and set on fire. Among it all lay the dead and wounded, and the shipwright party fought on, choked by fumes, scorched by hot steel, and sometimes doused by water being played from hoses on the flight deck down through splinter holes in the lift shaft. The work made the rescue of wounded possible. And now Mr. Ganer felt he had done all he could aft. Those who had been freed were being dealt with by the first-aid parties. So Chippie was going forward to see what needed to be done there.

He was a pleasant man, Chippie—a few years younger than Mr. Mayson, and a little taller, with a fresh, ruddy complexion. He loved his home life—and England. Mr. Mayson gave him a parting glance. It was then that he noticed that Chippie's hands and clothing had been fouled by the miserable wreckage he'd travelled through. The remains of some of his shipmates had strewn the way he had had to go, sometimes on hands and knees.

Mr. Mayson watched him walk up the ladder to the flight deck before moving aft himself. Soon he became aware of another figure emerging from the haze of smoke ahead. It was the slim form of Surgeon Commander Amy, the principal medical officer of the ship, and, in Mr. Mayson's view, a kind, gentle man. He was now a very tired man but also, obviously, a very tough one. At first he had dealt with casualties as they arrived at the medical station forward. Then, as the stream of wounded eased off, he had left the work to a subordinate officer and made his way to the worst scene of damage to help on the spot.

Other officers had made their presence felt back here, too. A young accountant officer had been working unceasingly on first aid since the first bomb struck. Commander Sands and the first lieutenant had been on the scene early. Both these officers had taken their lives in their hands to give morphia to men who were trapped and in great pain. They had moved continually from one point of damage to another, thinking nothing of their own safety and setting examples that encouraged and inspired all the other men.

The surgeon commander halted at the bottom of the ladder, where the air was clearer, and took in deep breaths. Mr. Mayson moved aft, shining his electric torch on the deck. He passed another pair of stretcher bearers in a space where the deck was clear. He knew he was just aft of the after lift; he could look through splinter holes in the bulkheads and see the lift well. He stopped and made a note: "Port side second gallery deck— Deck holed and all bulkheads shattered. No fire. Light fumes."

The holes in the ship's side allowed daylight in. He moved on aft and paused beside a wounded marine lying on a stretcher. A young stoker in a blue overall suit was sitting beside him holding his hand, and at the head end a stoker petty officer was squatting, holding the marine's cap and speaking gently to him. The wounded man's face was ashen grey; he was obviously dying; but the faces of all three radiated an aura of quiet peace. It seemed that despite holocaust and destruction a breath of heaven had reached them all.

The stoker petty officer looked up and spoke. "The surgeon commander asked us to stay with this man, sir."

Mr. Mayson smiled gently and moved on. Soon he found and went down the ladder leading to the first gallery deck. Here conditions were worse. He could see no clear way aft, so he moved over to starboard. He had to tread a wary path, for there were gaping holes in the deck. Many of the dead lay where they had fallen. Others had been laid aside to allow passage through the twisted network of steel. First-aid men were dealing with the last of the wounded. Fumes were thick but not unbearable. He noted the extent of the structural damage and then went down a shaky ladder to the level of the hangar deck.

He moved aft slowly, in a crouching position, shining his torch down and sliding one foot forward to feel a firm support before moving on. Unless debris blocked his way he would emerge on the quarterdeck, a large space extending aft to the stern. The fumes were rising and moving aft; the fire must be lower down. Soon he saw daylight. He hurried out on to the quarterdeck.

Then the heavy antiaircraft guns opened up:
Bang! Bang! Bang!
Bang! Bang! Bang!
Bang!

Every bang seemed to be hitting him on a sore spot in the middle of his head. Perhaps the fumes were getting him, too, for he reeled as he moved aft, but his head cleared when he breathed in comparatively clear air.

He met Heathcote. The chief stoker was playing a fire hose over the port side of the deck. Farther forward on the port side two stoker ratings handled another hose, directing the jet through the port door leading fore abreast the lift shaft. Heathcote was soaked from head to foot but seemed full of energy. The quarterdeck was planked over, and the underside of the timber appeared to be afire. Wherever Heathcote saw a large rising of smoke he played his jet until it subsided, and then he looked for more signs of fire. On seeing the commissioned engineer he smiled in recognition.

Bang! Bang! Bang! Again Mayson heard the AA guns.
"Hello, sir," said Heathcote.
"Hello, Heathcote. Glad to see you're safe."
Still the guns barked.

"Where's Lieutenant Tangry, Heathcote?"

"He's gone, sir."

"Are you sure?"

"Yes, sir." Heathcote's eyes blinked rapidly. "I was with him. We were walking along the first gallery deck by the lift when the bomb came in."

"Good heavens! And you got away with that?"

"Yes, sir. I think we three are the only ones left of the fire and repair parties aft. Lieutenant Tangry was about four feet ahead of me. I saw it in a flash—the ship's side was blasted open and he was blown right through and overboard."

They had to shout over the din of the guns. Mr. Mayson was about to speak again when the pom-pom guns opened up with their terrific hammering roar. The engineer and the chief stoker braced themselves. Leading Stoker Soames and Stoker Smithers, handling the other hose, gripped hard on the nozzle and steadied each other.

"Here the bastards come again," said Soames.

Then—*crash!*

The ship's stern was jolted down and then up again, shaking all four down on to the wet deck.

As Mr. Mayson's head cleared he moved to a sitting position. He heard the voice of Heathcote.

"Are you hurt, sir?"

He moved his arms and legs. "I'm all right, I think." He rose and looked around, trying to grasp what had happened. The ship had listed further over to starboard, and smoke now poured over their heads, streaming from forward. Then Mayson's vision cleared, and Heathcote was surprised to see him smiling.

Mr. Mayson pointed to the port forward corner of the quarterdeck. Leading Stoker Soames was rising from the deck to help Stoker Smithers, who was moving forward dragging the fire hose. The hose had obviously been damaged, for only a pitiful stream came from the nozzle. Heathcote ran to them and brought them aft.

"All right, now," said Mr. Mayson. "Have a breather."

The ship was moving at a fair speed and under control. She had taken another heavy blow close to where she had been hit before; the last bomb had exploded in the lift well. She was paying a tribute to her designers and constructors by staying afloat. She was still steaming!

The bomb killed all the first-aid party aft, including the young accountant officer. The surgeon commander had walked forward a little and up on to the flight deck for a breath of fresh air. The move saved his life, and though he was badly shaken, his first thought was of casualties aft. As he recovered from the shock of the explosion he saw men running towards him from the bridge structure. They carried new lengths of fire hose and tools. This was no prearranged fire party; it consisted of shipwrights, air-arm mechanics, stokers, marines, and seamen, led by the first lieutenant. The surgeon commander asked the first lieutenant for men to assist in first-aid work. These were forthcoming at once, and while a messenger went to the bridge structure to collect medical supplies, the newly formed first-aid party followed the surgeon commander down the ladder. But they found no wounded.

The first lieutenant and his party had work to do on the flight deck. Several long leads of canvas fire hose had been rigged earlier on to deal with fires aft. These had had to be run from well forward, for the pipes supplying water aft had been shot away. Some of the canvas hoses had been damaged and were leaking. Two of the hoses ran aft of the lift and hung over the side. These were the ones Heathcote and his men were handling. Quickly the water was shut off and the damaged hoses replaced by new ones. And all the time the pom-pom guns opened up with intermittent bursts. Down below in the machinery spaces the men remained steadfast at their jobs. Fires were still being fought in the gallery decks on the starboard side. Lieutenant Leyton was now assisted in this work by Sublieutenant Kelling and his men. Mr. Ganer and his men were patching over holes in the deck to render the footing safe as the fire parties advanced, replacing and securing ladders and rigging up temporary wooden ones. The fires still burned in the hangar in spite of the constant downpour of water. Here a few planes had been ready for service with their tanks full of oil and petrol. Many times had Commander Sands and the flight commander opened the hangar doors. Flying officers had entered the hangar wearing breathing apparatus and dragging hoses, attempting to reach the seat of the fire, but on each occasion the admission of air had caused the fire to increase until the doors had to be shut again. Up on the bridge the captain calmly gave his orders. Again the planes dived. The guns' crews were tired, had been for a long time, but with grim eagerness they served, trained, and fired. Still they cheered when they scored a hit. The ship swerved to avoid the bombs as they were released. Observers in other ships saw the aircraft carrier enveloped in a huge column of water as near-miss bombs exploded. The ship rocked and pitched violently and then pushed her nose through the turbulent water to appear before the eyes of the fleet again, still steaming ahead on a blue sea under a blue sky, smoke billowing up from her stern.

The firing ceased. Heathcote and his men had advanced from the quarterdeck into the port side of the lift well. The deck there was badly buckled but not broken, and water from the hoses welled up and overflowed the doorsill to the quarterdeck. It was evident that the seat of the fire was beneath them, for the water swishing at their feet was so hot that they advanced on furnishings taken from the cabins at the ship's side. The deck was littered with suitcases, mattresses, cabin trunks—anything that could keep their feet out of the water. The chief stoker was aiming to reach a hatch farther forward in the hope of partially opening it and directing a spray of water downward.

Mr. Mayson moved forward, going back the way he had come, to try to get lower down on the starboard side and check the extent of the damage there. He was surprised to find the air clearing. Daylight, coming through holes in the ship's side, allowed him to see the deck he was treading on. It was badly buckled and had many splinter holes through which smoke issued and blew away aft. There was much wreckage about; minor bulkheads that had formed the sides of cabins had been so ripped and twisted by the blast that they almost blocked the passageway. The deck overhead was torn; jagged pieces of steel projected downward. Soon he reached the hatchway down which he had come and through which he must return. The ladder had been twisted and torn away, but he knew he could climb to the deck above with the aid of a chair from a nearby cabin.

The guns had stopped firing, and the rumble of the propeller shafts and the swish of water along the ship's side gave an impression of calm. Mr. Mayson became aware of another sound—like a running stream within the ship. He moved forward and looked down an open hatch, and many things became clear to him. The deck below—the level below the hangar—was under about fifteen inches of water flowing rapidly aft. It was obviously the runoff from the doused hangar. The bomb hole in the hangar was near the after end and starboard of midships. The downward blast had pierced through numerous decks below, and flow from the hangar had flooded some compartments above waterline on the starboard side aft, putting the ship down astern and causing the starboard list. The water was now flowing over those flooded areas, but where was it going? He had to find out.

The ladder down to the next deck was still intact, so he went down it and stood in the water. Plenty of light came through holes in the ship's side and he was still above waterline. There was a bulkhead astern of him and the door in it was closed, but water flowed away through large splinter holes in the bulkhead. He could not cross over to the port side until he opened the door, and as he approached it he received a shock.

Mr. Mayson had seen many dead during the day, but this was different. Something became wrapped around his legs. It looked like clothing, and he stooped to unwind it. It was the trousers part of an overall suit, and the legs were still inside—legs broken so badly that they were able to become wrapped around his own. He was trying to clear himself when the dead man's face came to the surface. The water gave a gentle caress to the face while presenting it to his view; the hair had a perfect parting down the centre and was swept back clear of the forehead. The mouth was slightly open and the upper lip drawn back from the teeth. It was the face of Stoker Hicks, and that young man seemed to have smiled a peaceful goodbye to Mr. Mayson, for the legs unwound themselves, the head dipped back under, and the body floated away, farther to starboard.

The engineer knew the service record of Stoker Hicks, having been his divisional officer. He had been so impressed by the ability of the youngster that on one occasion he had sent for him. The memory of it flashed through his mind while the water surged about him. He heard again that timid knock on his cabin door, and his own voice in response: "Come in!"

Back through a haze of time he saw the face of Hicks again as the door curtain was pushed aside. It was a young, intelligent, inquiring face.

"You sent for me, sir?"

"Yes. Come in, Hicks. Tell me, why haven't you passed Education Test Part One?"

"I don't know anything about it, sir."

"But surely you have some knowledge of arithmetic?"

"Oh yes, sir. I always did well in school, but I don't know how I can sit any examinations."

"Oh, I see. There hasn't yet been an exam on board here. But still someone should have told you about it in barracks. What school did you go to?"

"A council school in Liverpool, sir."

"How old were you when you left?"

"Fourteen, sir."

"But why did you leave so soon?"

"Well, sir, my parents wanted me to earn something. You see, I had two brothers and two sisters younger than me, and my father didn't earn much."

"What did your father do?"

"He was a builder's labourer, sir, but there wasn't much work for him then, and he was on the dole most of the time."

"And what work did you do?"

"I couldn't get a proper job, sir. I used to do anything I could, like carrying suitcases for ladies and gentlemen near the station. I tried selling newspapers once, but there were so many already doing that, so I went to help a man chopping wood that he sold for firewood. After that I used to get a job now and then on ships at the docks, cleaning bilges and chipping rust off the plates. But I was on the dole most of the time. Honestly, sir, this job in the navy is the best I've ever had. I'm glad they called me up."

"Well, you'll have a chance now, Hicks. I'll speak to the schoolmaster and he'll let you know when he starts preparing men for the next exam. Would you like to sit for it?"

"Yes, sir. I want to learn all I can."

"That's good. Now off you go, Hicks."

Mr. Mayson, looking over to starboard where the back of a blue overall suit bulged on the surface of the water, felt miserable. The air trapped inside the suit gave buoyancy and kept the body afloat. The corpse moved easily in the slightest swirl or eddy. "Off you go, Hicks."

He knocked the clips off the door and opened it. Water rushed away aft over the sill, and a strong breeze blew from forward to aft, clearing most of the fumes from the starboard side. He looked into a compartment almost as bright as day. The ship's side had been badly damaged, and there were a few smouldering fires away aft. There was a great hole in the centre of the deck abaft the lift machinery space. It was about eight feet in diameter and the water poured through it into the compartment below. The deck head immediately above this hole had once been the bottom of the lift well. It was now practically nonexistent. Over to port, beneath the feet of Heathcote and his men, fire raged in rows of cabins at the ship's side. The breeze blowing from forward through shattered bulkheads kept the fires glowing red.

Mr. Mayson felt all he needed was a look down that hole into which the water was pouring. He moved warily to the after end of the hole to avoid the downpour, and he dropped to his hands and knees. The ship's side of the compartment below was badly holed, and through the holes he could see the waterline. It was about five feet below the deck he was on. All the water running aft from the hangar was now running into the sea. Those holes, caused by the enemy, were well above the ship's normal waterline and were now a blessing in disguise.

The engineer crossed out his notes and started again. Then he moved back the way he had come, and as he climbed the ladder to the deck above he heard a strange sound: a human voice calling his name.

"Mr. Mayson, sir! Are you below?"

Surprise jerked him to a halt, and he shouted in reply, "Yes, here I am!" And with the strangeness of his own voice ringing in his ears he moved forward. There, framed in the hatchway of the deck above, he saw the head and shoulders of Stoker MacLeod, the senior engineer's messenger. There was a look of concern on Speedy's face.

"Are you all right, sir?"

"Yes, Speedy. What are you doing back here?"

"I came to look for you, sir. I heard you were back here when the last bomb burst and I asked the senior to let me come."

"But how did you get over to this side? It was bad enough before. I suppose those gallery decks are blown to pieces by now."

"It is a bit awkward, sir, but if you can get up through this hatch I can show you the way back."

"I've no doubt you can. You must have risked your neck to get here. You shouldn't do that sort of thing all alone."

"Oh, it doesn't matter about me, sir. You see, I'm only an orphan."

The engineer smiled. "God bless you, Speedy. Wait here for me. I'm going aft to see Chief Stoker Heathcote and then I'll come with you."

"Very good, sir."

He found Heathcote and his two men on the quarter-deck. All three were red-eyed and smoke-grimed and gasping for breath. They had reached the hatch they were aiming for and had partially lifted the cover when smoke and flame made them drop it again. Heathcote had blistered his fingers but had seen the hatch clips screwed down before leaving.

"No luck, Heathcote?" asked the engineer.

"No, sir. We'll have to get at it some other way."

"Well, have a breather and I'll show you how. There's no hurry."

"Come on. I'm ready now, sir!" said Heathcote.

"Yes, let's go, sir," said Soames.

"All right, then—but how are you feeling, Smithers?"

"Never better, sir."

Mr. Mayson looked at the three men, ragged as scarecrows, and smiled. Did he but know it, he made a fourth scarecrow himself. "Come then," he said.

They dragged the hoses over to starboard and pushed them down through holes in the deck. Mr. Mayson, Heathcote, and Smithers went below and took the hoses as Soames passed them down. Soon Heathcote and Smithers were enjoying themselves. Dense clouds of steam poured up the lift shaft as they directed the jets of water on to the fire over to port.

"I'm going now, Heathcote," said Mr. Mayson. "Must get back to report. Always work in pairs below here. I'll send help as soon as I can get forward."

"All right, sir."

Speedy led the way back to the flight deck. They moved over to port through an indescribable tangle of wreckage on the gallery decks. And in that tangle, mingled with it, were three human forms. Blue overalls, a marine's cap, a crumpled stretcher—three shipmates had passed on together.

On the flight deck Lieutenant Stanning, with the assistance of two men, was busy ramming a canvas awning into a bomb hole forward of the lift. It was not a very large hole, for the bomb had punched clean through the four-inch flight deck and the deck of the hangar to burst in the wardroom flat below. Lieutenant Stanning hoped by his action to help in smothering the fire in the hangar. He looked round as the smoke stopped rising from the hole and saw the commissioned engineer.

"Hello, old chap," he said, and a look of concern spread over his face. "Are you all right?"

"Yes, thanks. Can't stop, though. Have to go below."

"Well, if you need any help, send for me. There isn't much I can do up here now. Got a good set of pictures though—I think." The lieutenant slapped his hand on a camera hanging at his side. During the attacks he had stood on a platform at the side of the flight deck and had taken photographs of the planes, falling bombs, and near-miss bomb bursts.

Mr. Mayson arrived at damage-control headquarters to find Chief Stoker Lathom standing outside the door. The little man looked anxious. He took a quick step towards the engineer with his right hand partially outstretched, as though reaching out to hold the officer by the coat while he unburdened himself. "I was afraid you were lost, sir. I've kept coming to the door here, hoping to see you. I must speak to you, sir, it's important."

"Just a second then, Lathom, and I'll be with you."

In damage-control headquarters there was little to indicate that the ship had been struck except for a trickle of water coming through a cracked ventilation trunk overhead and slowly filling a bucket on the deck. The desks had been wiped off and the deck swept clear. No one but the damage control officer appeared to be doing anything. He was trying to get all his reports in something resembling order. The chief sat back in comfort. He jerked his head round when the door opened.

"Mr. Mayson!" he said, apparently surprised. "Where have you been?"

"Aft, sir."

"Oh! What's it like back there?"

Mr. Mayson needed to economize in words. His tongue was sticking to the roof of his mouth, and he felt a little sick and dizzy. He walked over and placed his notes on the desk between the damage-control officer and the chief.

"Here's the report," he said.

The damage-control officer read it out. Mr. Mayson knew that it would convey little to the chief. But the chief knew how to take charge.

"That's all right! That's all right! Leave it there!"

Mr. Mayson moved to the other side of the damage-control officer.

"Be careful with that paper," he said, and with a pencil he pointed up to the flooding board. "Look: This compartment is flooded. I believe that one is, too, and that's putting us over to starboard. Here's where the fire is. I don't think the damage extends down to any of these compartments in the hold, but you never know. They may be flooding slowly. So this is important."

He pointed to the ship's profile drawing, which was tacked to the bulkhead behind the damage-control officer. Lieutenant Morton turned round and Mr. Mayson drew a line in pencil. "There," he said, "that's the waterline at One-six-two Station on the starboard side. If you get a similar report from forward you can draw the waterline fore and aft on this profile. We can check again later and get some idea of what's happening as regards flooding.

"Are the wing compartments still all right?"

"Yes. The readings are the same."

"Messenger!" called the chief. "Go and see if the galley is working. And see if you can get me a cup of tea or cocoa."

The commissioned engineer made for the door, and the chief, who had started to flick over the pages of his library book, suddenly looked up.

"Where are you going, Mr. Mayson?"

The commissioned engineer stopped and swallowed hard. His throat was sore and dry and he spoke with difficulty.

"The fire and repair parties aft need reinforcing. There are only three men left out of about twenty-five. As for those parties in the wardroom flat, I don't think there are any survivors at all." He opened the door, but before he closed it behind him he heard the masterly voice of the head of his department: "Better see to that at once!"

Outside the door Lathom was waiting.

"Just a minute, Lathom," said the engineer, and he called to a stoker of the oil fuel party. "Go and find a stoker petty officer and four stokers and tell them to come here. It doesn't matter who they are if they are not already busy."

The stoker went away.

"And now, Lathom, what's the trouble?"

"Well, sir, I haven't been able to run that oil across."

"You haven't! Why?"

"The commander (E) wouldn't let me go. He told me to send someone else to do it."

"Who did you send?"

"The leading stoker, sir, but he must have made a mistake."

"I should think he would. That's one of the most complicated transfer jobs in the ship. I only decided on it because it would have the best correcting effect, and I knew you could do it. Have you told the commander (E)?"

"Yes, sir, and I asked him to let me go away and see to it, but he said, 'No, let it go. You stay here.' So I couldn't do anything else but wait for you, sir; and we've gone farther over to starboard."

"Well, we'll see to that in a minute."

Then Lathom relaxed and became confidential. "You know, sir, I can understand the commander (E) keeping me here. You see, he doesn't know much about the ship and he's afraid somebody might ask him something. He always asks me things when you're not about."

Mr. Mayson smiled. No man could be more loyal than the little chief stoker. He had spoken his thoughts with absolute frankness. And as the engineer remained silent he went on.

"You know, he's not a bad chap, sir. He's just a blusterer, that's all."

Another voice broke in. "You sent for me, sir?"

Mr. Mayson turned to face a tall young stoker petty officer. "Oh, it's you, Johnson. You have four men with you, I see."

"Yes, sir."

"Good! I want you to reinforce the after fire party under Chief Stoker Heathcote. Now listen carefully." Mr. Mayson gave instructions on how to reach the fire aft, and the petty officer led his men away. As they left he leaned back against the bulkhead of damage-control headquarters.

"Are you all right, sir?" asked the chief stoker anxiously.

"Yes, I think so, Lathom— Will you send someone to get me a drink of water?"

"Certainly, sir."

He pulled himself together and walked out into the fore-and-aft passageway. Then he heard the voice of Commander Sands calling his name. Tired as he was, the quality of the voice soothed him. The commander stood in the middle of the passage not three yards away. His face was blackened and his steel helmet had slipped behind his head, the chin strap pulling at his throat. He took out a handkerchief to wipe his eyes, from which tears were streaming, and he spoke again.

"I've just tried to get into the wardroom flat, but it's too bad there yet. Both sets of self-contained breathing apparatus have been destroyed, and if you use the other type with the long air tube you can't close the door behind you, which means that the smoke pours into the flat this side and nobody can see what they're doing. We can't have that, for both our main wireless transmitters are this side."

"Well, sir," said the engineer, "if you've been in there at all the fire must be dying down now. Why not wait a bit. It will smother itself soon."

"That's so," replied the commander, "but there's water pouring into the flat from somewhere."

"That will be through the bomb hole from the hangar, sir. Perhaps we should stop the hangar sprayers."

"I've done that. It's some pipe system leaking."

"All right, sir. We'll have to find it and isolate it."

"That's the spirit, Mr. Mayson, but don't take unnecessary risks. It's pretty bad in there. You mustn't go in alone. I have to go up on deck now, but I'll be back when I can."

"Very good, sir. Leave it to me."

There was still a good deal of smoke in the flat forward of the armour bulkhead when Mr. Mayson reached it. However, there were two supply fans working in the compartment and the air was clearing rapidly. A few men of the fire and repair parties stood about. The engineer called over to the chief stoker he had spoken to before. "Commander Sands tells me there's water still entering the wardroom flat, Chief. Have you isolated the fire-main lines on this bulkhead?"

"Yes, sir."

"And the freshwater supply line?"

"Yes, sir."

"How about the freshwater filling and transfer line, and the evaporator distiller pump discharge system?"

"They're shut off, sir. Every pipe system going through this bulkhead is isolated."

"Well, there's a mystery here. Stand by to open those doors, Chief. I'm going in there."

The chief stoker hesitated. "It's pretty awful in there, sir. You can hardly see anything when you open the door."

"That's all right. Go ahead and open the armour door." The engineer tied his handkerchief over his mouth and nose and tried his electric torch. He was putting on his leather gloves when Sublieutenant Kelling appeared.

"Hello, Mr. Mayson," he said. "Chasing that leak back there?"

"Yes. Are you?"

"Well, I've come to help you. I met Commander Sands in the starboard passage and he asked me to join you."

"Good show! All ready?"

"Rather—come on!"

The armour door had been opened, and soon the clips were knocked off the watertight door. Mr. Mayson stood with his hand on the door handle.

"What we have to look out for, " he said, "is holes in the deck. Better keep our torches shining at our feet. Now—all set?"

Kelling had pulled the edge of his scarf over his nose and mouth. His eyes met Mr. Mayson's and he nodded. Mr. Mayson spoke to the chief stoker. "Once we're inside, close the door and stand by. Don't put any clips on."

"Very good, sir."

With a sudden push they were inside, groping into the unknown. The smoke was hot and thick. Somewhere, a few paces ahead, water was pouring into the compartment. They could not see the deck they were walking on, for the smoke reflected the light from their torches, but they could feel no wetness at their feet. The water must be running through holes to the deck below. They moved cautiously aft. They became entangled in a network of electrical cables, which had been spread about like the branches of a grotesque tree, and they had to back out and find their way around the debris. Conditions were almost unbearable, and they would have turned back, but something happened to help. Two yards ahead of them a great shower of red sparks fell through the bomb hole from the deck above. And in the middle of the shower of sparks was a steady stream of water, which poured through a hole in the deck they were standing on.

Mr. Mayson reached into the murk ahead, his hand cupped, and soon he felt the water slap upon it. He withdrew his hand quickly and tasted the water. Then he turned and pushed. Kelling understood, and together they made a scramble for the door—and fresh air. They reached the door together and pulled. The next moment they fell into the arms of the chief stoker, almost knocking him off his feet. Two stokers closed the door at once.

Kelling snatched the scarf from his face and sank to a sitting position with his back to the bulkhead, his mouth open and his eyes streaming. Mr. Mayson staggered a little and fell to his knees beside the conveyor, his head sideways, supported by his hands, as he gasped for air. While his lungs were clearing, one fact stood out in his mind: *That was fresh water!* At that rate of flow there would soon be no fresh water in the ship. Then what about the wounded? *Got to stop the leak!*

He staggered to his feet. Kelling was beside him at once, a hand on his shoulder. "I'm with you. What next?"

Mr. Mayson's mouth had so dried up that he could barely speak. "Need a drink, but got to stop that leak." Together they walked shakily forward, wiping their faces and coughing.

When he opened the door of damage-control headquarters, Mr. Mayson stood dazed for a moment, then he became aware of the huge blue bulk in the easy chair, for the chief was looking at him and pointing a preemptory finger at the trickle of water falling from overhead.

"Find out where that is coming from!"

The order thundered into Mr. Mayson's brain. He turned about and staggered out, bumping into Kelling. He moved aside and leaned on the bulkhead. Blind anger surged within him, and his lips moved, silently giving it vent. "Oh, that stupid bastard!"

The door opened beside him and Lathom came out with

a jug of water. The engineer was still leaning back against the bulkhead, his eyes closed.

"Here's water, sir," said Lathom.

Mr. Mayson opened his eyes. He took the jug and drank. Then he met Sublieutenant Kelling's eyes and the jug changed hands. "Thank you, Lathom," he said.

Then his mind became startlingly clear. He pushed the door of damage-control headquarters wide open and looked straight at the electrical artificer.

"Get the power taken off the forward freshwater pump at once! It's urgent!" As he slammed the door shut he caught part of the chief's exclamation.

"What the—"

Kelling smiled. "Now what?"

"Come away from here and I'll tell you."

They moved aft together until Mr. Mayson stopped to sit on the ammunition conveyer.

"That's fresh water leaking back there," he said. "That means a water pipe is broken in the hangar. We must have lost nearly all our fresh water by now."

"Well, what can we do?"

"I'm trying to think, and we have to move fast. All the ship's drawings are behind those doors, and there's no diagram of the water system in damage-control headquarters. At one time I knew every pipeline in the ship, but I can't place this one now."

"Shall I try to get the drawings from the office?"

"No. Wait. If you go back there again you may not come out alive." Then Mr. Mayson started to speak his thoughts aloud. "Fresh water to pom-pom guns? No, that line leads to the gallery decks. Fresh water to blacksmith's shop? No, it goes along the second gallery deck, port side. Fresh water to cabins aft? No, that leads along the starboard side of the first gallery deck. But wait— There's a crossover pipe to the port side, and it crosses through the hangar abaft the armour bulkhead. Yes, high underneath the flight deck, right over that hole in the hangar deck!"

He sat for a moment, getting the image of the pipe system clear in mind, then he jumped to his feet.

"Got it!"

"You have?" said Kelling. "Tell me which pipe it is and I'll shut it off."

"It's easy. The valve is on the underside of the forward gravity tank, up in the bridge structure. It's marked, 'Two-inch supply to cabins aft.' "

Kelling patted the commissioned engineer on the back. "I know where it is. You take it easy; I'll shut it off." And away he went, running forward.

With a sigh of contentment Mr. Mayson sat again on the conveyor and idly watched a steward placing a mess kettle on the deck close by.

"Anybody want a drink?" called the steward.

A few men gathered around at once, and the steward unhooked two cups from the little finger of his left hand. Soon the men were drinking in turn. Mr. Mayson caught a faint whiff of what they were drinking. It interested him.

"What is it you men are drinking?"

"It's rum," replied a young stoker as he received the cup from the steward. "Will you have one with me, sir?"

"With pleasure, so long as the steward will give you another one."

They all laughed a little and Mr. Mayson took a good tot of the fiery liquid.

"Thank you," he said, passing back the cup, and he rose to his feet, feeling refreshed and strengthened. Kelling would now have closed that valve. He picked up a nearby telephone receiver and got through immediately, direct to damage-control headquarters.

"Mr. Mayson speaking. Get the power put on the forward fresh water pump."

The electrical artificer repeated the order, and the engineer smiled grimly, thinking of the chief sitting there and overhearing it. He replaced the receiver and picked up the receiver of another phone. This one was connected to the exchange.

"One-eight-four, please."

Soon he was through.

"Mr. Mayson speaking. That Petty Officer Wright?"

"Yes, sir."

"Having any trouble?"

"No, sir. All compartments forward are all right except the paint store, which is damaged above the waterline."

"Good. Now, I want you to leave your leading stoker in charge of the party for a while. You know your oil fuel suction lines forward there?"

"Yes, sir."

"Right. We're going to correct this list to starboard, so listen carefully. I want you to run down oil fuel from the starboard side—ready with your pencil?"

"Yes, sir."

"Well, here goes: Run down oil from tanks R1 and R2 into double-bottom tanks X4, -5, and -6 until R1 and R2 are empty. Got that?"

The petty officer repeated the instructions word for word.

"Good," said Mr. Mayson. "Now there's another thing: that sullage tank on the starboard side—tell your leading stoker to empty it. Pump the stuff overboard."

The petty officer repeated the order. Then Sub-lieutenant Kelling reappeared.

"That valve's shut," he said.

"Oh, good. If we have a couple of tons of fresh water left

in those forward tanks now, we're safe in that respect. We can't get water from aft—the pipes are shot away."

"Well, we'd better sound those forward tanks and get the distilling plants working, too."

"That's part of the trouble, Sub. Mr. Prout had some bad luck with his plants this forenoon, and he's probably still struggling. It's damned hot in those rooms, too. His men had just started changing the coils in one plant when the other broke down. That's why I was so scared of losing fresh water."

"All right, Mr. Mayson. I know you're busy. I'll get those forward tanks sounded."

Just then Chief Stoker Lathom appeared. "That drip from the fan trunk is stopping now, sir. The trunk runs forward and up into the hangar, and water was leaking into it there. I've closed the valve where the trunk goes through the deck head."

Mr. Mayson smiled. "Well done, Lathom." He moved to go forward and suddenly met Mr. Langley again. The warrant engineer had just left the chapel and walked out into the flat. His head was heavily bandaged, but his eyes, nose, and mouth had been left clear. He stood with his hands in his pockets and had the air of a man who was thoroughly disgusted with everything. A faint gleam appeared in his eyes as they met.

"Hello, Harry," he said.

"Hello, Tom. What happened to you?"

"Well, I'm not exactly sure." He nodded toward the armour bulkhead. "I was back there when the bomb came in."

"What! In the wardroom flat?"

"Yes."

"But how did you get out?"

"I must have been blown out, Harry. I hear they picked me up on this side of the bulkhead."

Mr. Mayson stared in amazement. It didn't seem to make

sense; the bomb had burst only a few yards inside the wardroom flat.

"How badly are you hurt, Tom?"

"Not very much. It's only slight burns on the back of my neck and ears where the blast caught me."

"Is that all?"

"Yes, I feel all right otherwise."

Mr. Mayson shook his head slowly. "Well, it beats me. It's almost a miracle! But I suppose you don't remember much about it."

"Yes, I do, up to the time the bomb came in. You remember when we passed each other early on?"

"Yes."

"Well, I was going aft to look at the steering gear. Thought we'd been hit back there. When I stepped into the wardroom flat I saw a man walking towards me wearing only a singlet and a pair of trousers. His arms and face were roasted and his body had been pierced—by bomb splinters, I suppose. There were holes punched in him from his shoulders down to his waist. *And he was still walking!* There were several men about in the wardroom flat and they stood and stared. I made him stop walking. He seemed to understand when I spoke to him. There was a stretcher inside that door, and two men helped me to lay him on it. One of the men took the forward end of the stretcher and I bent down to take the handles at the after end. Then the bomb came in. I remember flying through the air in a sheet of flame, and that's all. The blast must have caught me in the back and lifted me through the door."

"What happened to the other chaps? Have you heard?"

"Well, nobody seems to know. They had to shut the doors at once. A chief steward who was watching us from this side said that two men standing beside him were killed."

There was a pause. The warrant engineer still stood with

his hands in his trouser pockets. He now looked around the flat with an air of wonder, then he stepped back to lean on the bulkhead of the chapel near the door.

"Bit stupid fitting these red lights here," he said. "Don't see any sense in it."

It was Mr. Mayson's turn to look around in wonder. The electric light party had renewed all the broken shades and lamps, but they had fitted the usual type, and the lights shone white and brilliant. The question leapt to his mind: *What red lights?* Then realization dawned upon him. He looked at his messmate and spoke as naturally as he could. "Why didn't you stay in the chapel, Tom?"

"Well, I thought I had better get out of the way. There are a lot of wounded chaps in there."

"Then why not go somewhere and take it easy? Would you like to come down to the double-bottom store? I'll get a camp bed rigged for you."

Mr. Langley looked pained. "No," he said, almost indignantly, "I've been hoping to get around and help when my head clears a bit."

"Have you seen Tim?"

"No, I haven't Tom. If I—"

The roar of the pom-pom guns drowned Mr. Mayson's voice. There'd been no preliminary heavy AA fire, so the shock was all the greater. Everything about them seemed to be dancing in violent little jerks. Mr. Langley squinted. The noise pained his head. The firing continued for several minutes, some of the guns ceasing for short periods and then opening up again to swell the roar to its maximum.

Then everything became still and silent again. Mr. Mayson felt almost lighthearted. "That attack failed," he said. He was about to move forward when a crackling noise from a loudspeaker drew his attention. The speaker was high up on the bulkhead at the side of the flat, and several men soon gathered beneath it. It was only then that Mr. Mayson realized the broadcasting system had been out of action. Someone had repaired it. It was not functioning properly but among the crackling noises a voice could just be heard. The two engineers walked over together. As they joined the group a leading stoker spoke softly to Mr. Mayson. "The captain speaking, sir."

The men were straining their ears, trying to catch every word. The two engineers settled quietly and listened carefully. Soon they were catching the gist of the speech.

"——deeply impressed by the conduct of the whole ship's compan——a time of trial you————your duties————you would——always been proud of you. Now, words fail me——————a little longer——— ——getting quite dark now————air attack————last attack by torpedo bombers————feeble———think they may have had enough——————to arrive in Malta————three hours at——speed—————— and God be with you."

The noise from the speaker ceased and the men dispersed. Mr. Mayson looked at his messmate and spoke with some surprise. "Getting dark! Why, I thought it was about half past three."

"That's because you've been busy, Harry."

"I suppose it is, and I've lost my watch off my wrist. Anyhow, I'd better get moving. You be careful, Tom. You've had a bad shock."

Mr. Mayson moved forward. He felt elated. Darkness meant so much. Now it was only a matter of keeping the ship steaming for three hours—and then Malta. With lightened step he made for the chief petty officers' washstand and helped himself to a towel and soap Lathom had left ready for him.

Inside damage-control headquarters the staff had heard

parts of the captain's speech. Everyone was taking it easy; even the damage-control officer was idling his time away, smoking a cigarette and chatting quietly with the electrical artificer. The master-at-arms was telling some yarn about the peacetime navy to two interested messengers. Saunders had followed the example of the commander (E) and sat reading a novel. The commander (E) lounged comfortably in the easy chair, his legs crossed and his library book resting on his upthrust knee. He read rapidly, turning the pages over with a noisy flip. He was no longer concerned about a leak from a ventilation trunk; in fact, he didn't appear to be concerned about anything.

There was some indefinable quality here that must have had its effect on the damage-control staff in spite of the chief's shortcomings in other things. Here he had remained all afternoon and evening through the long hours of peril. There was death and destruction fore and aft, and though he had seen nothing of it he had received the ill tidings from different parts of the ship. The noises of war had beaten about him, and still he had kept his chair and maintained his blustering command. If his heart quailed he had never showed it. His lack of knowledge of the ship might have been to his advantage here. It is strange that a light steel bulkhead can give a man confidence under fire. The chief knew he was within the armour belt. The belt would stop anything in the way of bomb splinters and blast at the ship's side. Of course that would give him a feeling of security. But did he know that the decks above him were no stronger than those over the wardroom flat? If he did he was a brave man. Had that bomb dropped a few yards farther forward, inside the armour belt, it would have taken the rescue party some time to decide where damage-control headquarters used to be. The explosion would have made pretty configurations out of those steel bulkheads as it swept them away.

Darkness was closing in. Heathcote and his reinforced

team played their hoses over fires, which now were only smouldering. They used electric torches to light their way. Lieutenant Leyton, Sublieutenant Kelling, and their men had earlier extinguished the fires in the starboard gallery decks and had opened the way through to aft along that side. The fire was out in the hangar. Mr. Prout's staff had started both distilling plants and there was no longer danger from loss of water.

Mr. Mayson felt refreshed after his wash. He went down to the double-bottom store, a compartment on the next deck down beside the workshop, and checked the heel of the ship: three and a half degrees to starboard—proof that the forward pumping party were doing their oil transfer job. He went back up the ladder and ran into Mr. Mills.

"Hello, Torps," he said. "Glad to see you got away with it."

Torps was uninjured but he looked tired and unhappy. "Thanks, Harry," he said. "Glad to see you're all right, too. We've lost a couple of our messmates. Did you know?"

"No. I've only heard about Ted Rathbone. Who's the other one?"

Torps's reply was little more than a whisper. "Tim's gone."

A look of infinite sadness crept over Harry Mayson's face. He thought of Tom Langley at once. Between Tom and Tim had existed a friendship that was rare and fine. Tom had had one shock today; soon he must receive another.

Torps stood still, his head slightly bowed. The engineer spoke. "How was it, Torps?"

"Pretty sudden, I think, Harry. When that first bomb came in it started fires at the after end of the hangar. Tim went with two able seamen to remove the bombs from the planes we had ready back there. They were still in there working when the second bomb set the whole hangar on fire. I should think he was killed by the explosion."

There was silence again while Torps shuffled his feet. "I'd

better get for'ard," he said. "There are lots of rounds of live ammunition lying about. They ought to be restowed in the magazines."

Mr. Mayson moved aft, and as he reached damage-control headquarters, Mr. Ganer was just entering the place. The warrant shipwright was tired and anxious, and the sight of the damage-control staff sitting around in comfort, doing nothing, annoyed him. He looked at the commander (E) and spoke with some heat. "When are we going to do something about this water coming in aft? As far as I can see we're sinking ourselves."

"What water?" asked the chief.

"That's what I'd like to know," said Mr. Ganer. "Some of your pumps are delivering water into the ship back there, right at the after end. You can see it running from forward."

Mr. Mayson moved to the ship's profile drawing. Lieutenant Morton had drawn the waterline on it.

"You mean under the lift well, Chippie?"

"Yes."

"Well, I expected that would stop running when they stopped the hangar spray."

"They're using hoses again in the hangar now," said Lieutenant Morton.

"That explains it, then," said Mr. Mayson, "but in any case that water is all levelling off to sea, isn't it, Chippie?"

"I'm not so sure. We seem to be going farther down at the stern."

"Did you check the waterline?"

"Yes."

"Good! Mark it up on this profile, will you?"

Chippie looked the drawing over. "Here we are, at One-five-eight Station on the starboard side"; and he drew a line in pencil. It was above the line drawn fore and aft by Lieutenant Morton.

"You're right, Chippie," said Mr. Mayson. "We're farther down. Some of that water from the hangar has been flowing into compartments perforated from above. We've got to find out which and pump them out."

"Where are the pumps?"

"K pump is back under the wardroom flat, and L pump under the flat farther aft. These two pumps can clear all the hold compartments aft of here. We'll have to use portable pumps to clear flooded spaces above the hold."

There was a look of inquiry in Mr. Ganer's eyes as they met those of the engineer. Mr. Mayson nodded. "We've got to get back there, Chippie."

"That's right, Harry. I'm game. Come on."

The chief looked back at his library book. Lieutenant Morton watched them go. There was nothing he could do. Mr. Mayson motioned by hand for Lathom to follow.

As they approached the armour bulkhead they halted to check that hoses and emergency lighting were ready.

"I opened the doors just now," said Chippie, "and it isn't too bad back there. The fire is in the wardroom pantry on the port side."

When they opened the doors the wardroom flat was still full of smoke, but the smoke was much lighter than when Mr. Mayson had entered the room earlier. The warrant shipwright and the engineer led the way, closely followed by Lathom, two electrical ratings with emergency lighting, and two men of the fire party. The fore-and-aft passage here ran along the centre of the ship, and in the centre of the passage, along the deck, ran the ammunition conveyor which served the heavy AA guns on the afterdeck. Mr. Mayson and Lathom advanced along the starboard side between the conveyor and the warrant officers' mess, while the warrant shipwright moved along the port side. With the aid of the emergency lighting they were able to see their way through the twisted network of electric cables that almost blocked their way. There was much coughing about the flat as the men advanced, and the two officers could barely see each other. Suddenly Mr. Ganer called, "Switch on!" The men following called the order behind them, and Mr. Ganer's hose came alive. Mr. Mayson heard the swoosh of water as the jet hit the wardroom pantry. Then he moved aft, his torch shining at his feet, and Lathom followed. As they moved cautiously round the bomb hole in the deck they realized that the smoke was clearing. They had to step over many dead before they reached the hatch leading down to K pump. Using flashlights they moved down by vertical ladders through three decks and found the pump room dry. Mr. Mayson tried the electric starter for the pump, and to his surprise and joy the pump started. The power lines, running low in the ship, were still intact.

Lathom opened the suction valve to one of the hold compartments.

"Go ahead, Lathom," said the engineer. "Try the pump on all compartments. I'll station a man at the top hatch. Yell if you need assistance."

Back on the wardroom flat he found the electrical parties rigging emergency lighting close by.

The fire in the wardroom pantry was out, and Mr. Ganer's men were covering the bomb hole in the deck.

Mr. Mayson, moving aft, shone his torch into the wardroom and gazed on devastation: Upended tables, books, papers, broken glass, cutlery, ship's-side lagging, rugs, and electric wiring had all been mixed up, most of it scorched or partially burnt away, and amongst it all lay several dead officers, mutilated by the bomb blast.

The engineer entered, shining his torch to take it all in. Against the after bulkhead stood an upright piano, its woodwork scorched and blackened. His gaze shifted outboard and he noted two large picture frames hanging side by side. They were in perfect alignment and the area around them had not been scorched. He wiped a light film of grey dust from the glass of each, the Queen's picture first, then the King's. Then he wondered: Should he have let even Their Majesties' portraits view such an unhappy scene?

He left and continued aft to the next bulkhead, where he opened the port door and was surprised to find the flat behind it comparatively clean and tidy. Farther aft again he opened the port door in the next bulkhead and walked through the passage beside the cabins where Heathcote had advanced over the hot deck. When he reached the quarter-deck he saw a few flashes of electric torches near the stern and called to whoever was back there: "Keep your lights shaded as much as you can, men."

He heard the voice of Heathcote calling back: "Is that Mr. Mayson, sir?"

"Yes. How's it going, Heathcote?"

"All finished, sir. The fires are all out."

"Oh, good man!"

Mr. Mayson's eyes became more accustomed to the dark and he walked on to join the chief stoker. There were several men standing together: Heathcote and his reinforced fire party.

"Well done, all of you," he said. "You can pack it up now. I've just heard something about refreshments in the servery flat, and you can get through to forward on this deck now. So off you go."

As he followed the men going forward he met Lathom, who was standing by the pump room hatch. The little man was beaming.

"All eight of those compartments are clear of water, sir."

"Good. Does Mr. Ganer know?"

"Yes, sir, and he's checked the waterline, and it's steady."

"Now we're winning, Lathom. Tomorrow we'll get down to L pump and check the hold compartments under the damage aft. Let's take it easy now."

The servery flat was situated forward of the boiler rooms. It was here, at a long table, that the men normally came to collect the dishes of food for their messes. There was plenty of room about the flat, for it also served as the work area where the ammunition parties handled the supplies for the forward guns. Just now it was crowded. The ship's stewards had prepared sandwiches and cocoa, which they served from a long table. Men stood about the flat enjoying the refreshments.

Heathcote and his men were chewing away and swapping information with men who had been on the flight deck during the action.

Speedy, the senior's messenger, was pushing his way about, looking for his friends, Dusty Miller and Smiler Tuckett. He could see neither, so he started to make inquiries. "Anybody seen Dusty Miller?" he called.

Eventually he had a reply from a bedraggled-looking able seaman. "Yes, Dusty is still up on the gun—cleaning up around it. I've just left there."

"Have you seen Smiler?"

"No. Not since dinnertime."

"Thanks," said Speedy, and he hurried away. He had a torch slung around his neck so he soon found his way up the ladders. On reaching the flight deck he switched off the torch and moved cautiously towards the afterdeck pom-pom gun. There was no moon, but by the starlight he could see the men standing silently about the gun.

Speedy was reluctant to break the silence, but after a moment's hesitation he spoke softly. "Is Dusty Miller there?"

A figure moved towards him. "Yes, it that Speedy? How are you?"

Speedy closed in and the pair shook hands. "I'm fine," said Speedy. "How are you?"

"Not too bad. Have you seen Smiler?"

"No. Nobody seems to have seen him. Would he have been working in the hangar?"

"Yes, very likely. Either there or in the aircraft workshop."

They gazed at each other for half a minute in silence, and there was a note of alarm in Dusty's voice when he spoke again.

"Were there many blokes killed down there, Speedy?"

"I don't know. I'll go down and see if they'll let me in."

"Well, I'll be down soon. See if you can find him. He may be in the mess, or up the galley or somewhere. I'll meet you in the servery flat."

Speedy hurried away, fearing what he might find. He went down the midship ladders through the two gallery decks to the port door of the hangar. Through the open door he saw men at the after end working with emergency lighting, and he hurried towards them. Many times he nearly vomited at what he saw. The blast had had free play in the hangar; it had swept fore and aft treating men and planes alike: wrecking them and breaking them up into pieces. In spite of his nausea Speedy examined everything recognizable. As he reached the after lift without finding what he dreaded to see, he turned and hurried back to search the forward part of the hangar. And the farther forward he went the worse was the carnage, for at the after end the downward rush of water had partially cleared the steel deck. It was near the forward lift that he found Smiler. The only light there, apart from his torch, was that given by the emergency lighting so far astern. As he shone his torch down he heard Dusty calling.

"Speedy! Have you seen him?"

Speedy did not answer at once. He switched off his torch. He could see Dusty silhouetted against the light, but the able seaman could not see Speedy. He walked aft a few paces and called, "Here I am, Dusty."

The able seaman turned and hurried forward. In his anxiety he had forgotten to hitch up his trousers, and the bell bottoms were sweeping the unclean deck. His voice betrayed his anxiety. "Have you found him, Speedy?"

The stoker moved aft to meet the able seaman. He stopped him, grasping his friend's arms. "Go easy, Dusty. You'll have a shock."

"Is he gone then, Speedy?" Dusty freed his arms. "Let me see."

Speedy shone his torch down and they went forward together. Able Seaman Tuckett lay as a man who slept—face downwards, his head slightly turned as though to allow himself to breathe. One arm lay straight beside his body, palm upwards; the other arm was bent, with the hand resting lightly on the deck near his head. He had been caught in the back by the blast. Above his waist the clothing had been driven into his flesh and there were deep holes where splinters and fragments of steel had pierced him.

Dusty bent over his chum and lifted his shoulder gently in order to see his face. Smiler was still smiling, this time with a look of utter peace. It seemed that a protective shield had been held over his face so that the smile should remain. His mop of sandy hair mingled with drying blood on the deck, the blood of many of his shipmates who lay in unrecognizable pieces around him.

Dusty lingered awhile, bent down and holding his chum's shoulder. Two pearly drops flashed down in the gloom, and he hastily brushed his free arm across his eyes and stood up.

Speedy switched off his torch and a brooding silence fell over the pair. Did they feel Smiler's presence, or was he really gone?

In this universal game of tombola it seemed that Smiler had heard again a number he was waiting for, and had called again, this time triumphantly: "*Here you are!*"

Dusty Miller turned away. "Come on, Speedy. Let's get a stretcher and take him away from here."

At the after end of the hangar the flight commander and the first lieutenant were checking on the damage and seeing that all the fires were out. The captain and Commander Sands were busy on the bridge; the ship was approaching Malta. The senior engineer was still on his feet below, controlling machinery, calling upon that abundance of energy. He would remain there until the captain rang down, "Finished with main engines."

Mr. Kirklane and Mr. Prout sat together on the ammunition conveyor in the servery flat. Conditions in their machinery spaces were back to normal, and they were thankful to get away for a short spell. The continuous strain of keeping machinery going under difficult conditions had taken its toll.

When Mr. Mayson entered the servery flat, Torps walked over to join him.

"Well, Harry, we found Tim."

"Oh— Then there's no doubt now?"

"No. It's an awful shambles, but I found his identity disc, and part of his coat, including one sleeve with the thin gold ring."

"Does Tom know?"

"Not from me. Harry—will you see him? It might be better coming from you."

Harry Mayson nodded. "I'll see him, Torps."

He went to join Mr. Prout and Mr. Kirklane. The pair were somewhat refreshed and about to go below again when the voice of Commander Sands came over the broadcasting system, which had been fully repaired.

"Do you hear me there? We have our lines across now and will be securing alongside soon. Immediately we get our gangways out I want to land the wounded. Ambulances are waiting. Any volunteers to transfer the wounded, muster in the servery flat. That's all, men."

Mr. Mayson was amazed. "Alongside already!"

"Why, Harry," said Jim Kirklane, "didn't you know we were so close to Malta?"

"Yes, I did, but it seems only about half an hour since the captain said we'd be three hours getting here."

Soon the three officers realized that the servery flat was becoming crowded. Men were packing the place. They moved in almost silently and then stood waiting. They were the volunteers.

Mr. Kirklane jumped to his feet. "I'd better get below. We'll be shutting down boilers soon."

"Yes, I'll come along, too," said Mr. Prout, "and see how my chaps are doing."

Mr. Mayson had to find Tom Langley, for he would be leaving for hospital soon. When he stood up to look over the crowded flat he saw Tom's bandaged head entering the forward door and went to meet him. Mr. Mayson saw the pain in Tom's eyes as he spoke to him.

"I've been wanting to see you, Tom. Come and take a seat on the conveyor till it's time to go. Is your head paining you?"

"Not too badly, Harry, but I'm not seeing very well. It's a damned nuisance. Have you seen Tim around?"

"No, Tom, I haven't, and that's what I wanted to talk to you about."

Tom Langley stiffened and turned his head slowly. "Go on, Harry. I'm listening."

"Well, Tim was in the hangar when the bombs fell. It was Torps who found him. He's gone, Tom."

Tom Langley rose and spoke calmly. "Is he still in the hangar?"

Harry Mayson stood up and placed his hand on his friend's shoulder. "He is, Tom, but Torps only knew him by his identity disc."

"Oh— I see"; and Tom Langley sat down.

In less than an hour all the wounded had been transferred to hospital ashore. Mr. Langley was in the last ambulance, and no sooner had it left the jetty than Commander Sands spoke through the microphone again. About the ship men listened with bowed heads.

"Now, men, I need volunteers for another job. It isn't going to be a pleasant task, but we must remove our dead. I would like officers to supervise in this work insofar as their direction is necessary. All volunteers muster in the servery flat."

Immediately men moved from all parts of the ship. Very soon they were crowding into the servery flat. Silent, steadfast men.

It was a long night for the ship's padre, who was already a tired man. All day since the air attacks started he had tended wounded in the chapel and the nearby medical station, offering his services wherever and however needed. Like the surgeon commander and the surgeon lieutenant stationed there, he'd had his hands and clothing stained by blood. Now he was on shore, having arranged with the shore authorities for the transportation and reception of his dead shipmates.

The work went on well into the night. The pumping parties removed a good deal of water from the compartments above the waterline that had been partially flooded through the use of fire hoses. This facilitated access to these compartments for the removal of the dead and also brought up the stern of the ship a little.

By 2:00 A.M. most of the work on board was complete, and

Commander Sands called a halt. He spoke through the microphone again. He knew that too many words at this time would be out of place. "All work is to cease now, except for the necessary watch-keeping. I am very pleased with you, men. I'm proud of you all. You must rest now; there will be plenty to do in the morning. The hands will be called at six o'clock."

Mr. Mayson told his pumping parties to go to bed and then went forward to damage-control headquarters to report. Arriving there he found Chief Stoker Lathom sitting on the conveyor writing in a notebook. Seeing the engineer, Lathom stood up.

"Don't go in there, sir," he said. "The commander (E) is asleep."

"Asleep! Lathom—what's he sleeping on?"

"A camp bed, sir. He sent the messengers somewhere for it."

"Hasn't he ever left the place?"

"Oh yes, sir, he did—once, to my knowledge—but he was soon back again. I suppose he just slipped across to the heads."

"Naturally, he'd have to some time. All right, Lathom. And now you'd better go away and turn in."

"Yes, sir, I'm going in a minute, but what about you? All the officers' quarters are badly damaged."

"I'll be all right. The cushions in our mess are not damaged. I'll take a couple down to the double-bottom store. Call me when they call the hands in the morning."

"Very good, sir, but let me help you."

They picked two long, dry cushions from the warrant officers' mess and laid them on the steel deck in the store below. Lathom produced two heavy watch coats from somewhere and gave them to the engineer.

"I'll be sleeping in my hammock above here, sir. I'll call you in the morning."

"Thank you, Lathom." And before the chief stoker had unlashed his hammock the engineer was asleep.

CHAPTER 17

After an early breakfast the ship's company fell in on the flight deck. This was part of Commander Sands's organization, and as usual he had planned ahead. It had shortened his night's sleep, but he had come up with a routine for the day that would have things running smoothly. It would keep his men busy and they'd do the most important things first. The commander, like the captain, had slept on board in a sea cabin in the bridge structure. A few other officers had slept on board but the majority had stayed in hotels on shore.

The first part of the day's routine was a mustering of messes. Numbers were chalked on the flight deck about ten yards apart, the series running from forward to aft. The most senior rating known to be alive in each mess was given a list of names of the men who had lived with him before the action and was told to stand on deck beside the number that represented his living quarters. When these men had taken up their positions Commander Sands spoke through the microphone to the remainder of the ship's company, telling them to dismiss and fall in again by messes. After each man had found his mess group the senior ratings started their roll calls. It was a sad business. Some of the groups were woefully small. However, it was soon over and the lists were collected. After comparison with the list of men taken to hospital it would be known who had yet to be identified or searched for among the wreckage.

And in Britain there would be many with anxious minds and aching hearts. Those on home turf would be wondering how loved ones afar had fared, for the enemy had lost no time in broadcasting his news. A sneering voice told the world that Britain's great new ship had been blasted into a useless hulk.

The ship now lay alongside the wharf with small craft ahead and astern. On the wharf across the rail tracks ran a long line of storehouses, and behind them towered cliffs of yellow sandstone into which the busy Maltese had, through the centuries, cut many tunnels. Those tunnels were to be useful as air-raid shelters.

On the top of the cliffs and on other high spots around the harbour, antiaircraft guns had been well positioned. The gunnery defence was good, but there were very few fighter planes to oppose the enemy.

The enemy would know that the ship might still be afloat, and it would not be long before their reconnaissance planes sighted her flat top. She was well within range of enemy bombers based in Sicily, bombers that could come escorted by swarms of fighters. It was an urgent matter that temporary repairs should be carried out to enable the ship to steam out of range and on to a safe harbour.

With this in view, Captain Graham was very early on shore arranging for cooperation between the dockyard authorities and the ship's staff; and early in the day dockyard workmen were on board to size up the damage. It was clear that the first necessity was the removal of water from the ship. Many spaces aft had been flooded by downward flow from the hangar spray and from fire hoses. It only required portable pumps to get these places dry.

Mr. Ganer and Mr. Mayson viewed the damage aft together. They stood on the deck beneath the after lift, beside the large hole through which water from the hangar had been flowing and levelling off to sea. Mr. Ganer stretched himself on the deck and looked down into the compartment below. He saw the large holes in the ship's side and, through them, the waterline, still a few feet below the deck he was on.

A large cabin flat just forward of them, where the ship's side was sound, had been flooded well above the waterline by the downward flow from the hangar.

The warrant shipwright stood up. "That's it, Harry. If we pump out the large cabin flat just forward of here these holes will come up above the waterline and we can weld the patches on. The portable pumps are on the way down from the dockyard now."

"Are the pumps heavy?"

"Yes, but the dockyard crane alongside can plumb the lift shaft and drop them down. We'll have to burn away some of the wreckage plugging the bomb hole in the lift well above here, but the burners are already on board."

"Very good, Chippie. I'll go forward now and get the ship's pumps going on the compartments under the wardroom flat. One oil tank is damaged from above. It's holding a mixture of oil and water. We need to pump out our cabin flat, too."

As the forenoon wore on, dockyard workmen appeared in increasing numbers, busy little Maltese workmen in clean white canvas suits. They set about their work methodically: Some took measurements and made templates so that new pipes and fittings could be made in the workshops ashore; others rigged up welding and burning apparatus on board. The foremen busied themselves in the engineers' office, studying the ship's drawings and keeping the senior engineer and the office staff busy answering their queries.

The commander (E) still found work to do in damage-control headquarters. He had been fortunate in that his cabin was one of the dry ones. So he now wore his clean white overall suit and sat at the desk. He busied himself with telling

Lieutenant Morton how to produce the whole official record from the pile of notes that had accumulated.

The chief, in company with all the other officers who had slept on board, had eaten a good breakfast. The food was served in the warrant officers' mess, which, in some seemingly magic way, had been cleaned up well enough to be used as a dining room. This had been organized by the paymaster. That officer had then gone a step further and acquired the use of the premises of a dockyard club, which was situated near the ship and had a dining hall large enough to seat all the ship's officers. The ship's stewards and cooks were installed, and in the early forenoon they were busy in the kitchen, preparing the midday meal.

Commander Sands and the first lieutenant were busy all the forenoon directing the cleaning of the ship. The men worked with a will, and the constant presence of the two officers encouraged them. The commander had emphasized, in a short speech, the necessity of getting the ship clean as soon as possible. It was a mighty task, but it was being tackled with a will.

The electrical staff soon had emergency lighting rigged throughout the damaged parts of the ship that were accessible.

Other important work keeping men busy was the removal of damaged fittings: twisted steel ladders and doors, shattered pipes, broken electrical cables, parts of steel bulkheads, and ventilation trunks. These things were blocking gangways.

Lieutenants Stanning and Leyton and Sublieutenant Kelling busied themselves on this work. Early in the forenoon Kelling had acquired the appearance of a busy coal heaver. He had little respect for himself or his clothing when he wanted to get something out of his way.

When Mr. Mayson and Mr. Kirklane went over to the club

premises ashore for lunch, they found Mr. Ganer waiting for them, and obviously he was worried.

"How is your pumping going, Harry?"

"Very well, Chippie. We should have the wardroom flat fairly dry in the afternoon. Have your pumps arrived?"

"Pumps!" said Chippie in disgust. "I've been hanging around all the forenoon waiting for them."

"Well, that's a poor start," said Mr. Mayson. "Damn it, we haven't any time to lose! Have you shaken anybody up about it?"

"I saw the dockyard foreman who ordered the pumps, and he said they should be here on the wharf. He went away and phoned somebody and was told that an engineer from the ship had cancelled the order."

"An engineer from the ship! Why, that's nonsense. All the engineers know we need the pumps. Furthermore, I don't suppose any of them knew you had made the order."

"Oh yes, some of them did, Harry. It was in the engineers' office that I asked the foreman for them. There were several engineers present, including the commander (E)."

"Well, it sounds damned queer to me, Chippie. Let's get our lunch and then look into it."

Mr. Kirklane moved into the dining hall with them. "What's the situation now, Chippie?" he asked. "Are you getting the pumps?"

"Yes, Jim. The foreman said he would see to it personally and have them here by one o'clock."

All three sat down at the table, and there was silence until the steward removed their soup plates. Mr. Ganer still had the matter of the pumps on his mind.

"Actually, we may not have lost any time," he said. "There's a lot of metal to be burned away before we can get those pumps into position. Still, I could have been checking on the hose connections and measuring the pumps so that I'd know how much wreckage needs moving before we can drop them down."

"Well," said Mr. Mayson, "let's forget it till one o'clock."

Soon they had every encouragement to forget it. The paymaster's organization was working very well, and an excellent hot meal had been provided. There were four long tables and nearly every seat was occupied. Though there was little conversation about the hall there was an air of comradeship throughout. All had something in common: They had survived.

On returning to the ship Mr. Ganer found that the dockyard foreman had kept his word. In fact he had done better, for beside the two large pumps lying on the jetty were two smaller, air-driven pumps. These were valuable, for they could be carried by one man to positions inaccesible to the larger pumps, but Chippie was due for further disappointment. After crossing the gangway he went over the flight deck to look down into the lift shaft, and for once in his life he cursed heartily. The work of burning away metal had not been started. Something had gone wrong and he intended to find out what, but first he arranged with his chief shipwright and staff to get the two small pumps working. Then he went back on to the flight deck to contact the Maltese workmen who were returning from lunch. He recognized one of the burners and called to him.

"Here, José, why haven't you started burning?"

José was a short, squat, light brown–skinned man. Like all Maltese he was proud of his ability and skill, and he could easily be hurt if his efforts were criticized.

"Not my fault, sah," he said. "I wait for de foreman. De engineer stop us working."

"The engineer! What engineer?"

"Engineer from de ship, sah. De big man in white clothes."

"The commander (E)! But why did he stop you?"

"Something 'bout oil, sah. He say we make fire because oil at de bottom."

"Fire, my bloody foot! You'll never set fire to anything down there. The place is soaked in water. In any case it has burnt it itself out once."

"Dat's what de foreman tell him, sah."

"Oh, he did, eh? And what did the commander (E) say?"

"He shout, sah, and make quarrel with de foreman, and de foreman go away over de dockyard."

"Have you seen the foreman since? Is he coming back this afternoon?"

The little man shrugged his shoulders. "Maybe he come back, sah. Maybe not. I see him dinnertime. He say 'All right, de engineer's de boss.' "

Mr. Ganer went below, boiling inwardly. He sought the commander (E) but perhaps it was as well that he didn't find him. In the meantime the pumping was progressing well in the officers' cabin flat beneath the wardroom. There was still oil and water about the floor, but Mr. Mayson went down to seek possible casualties and check on damage. Many of the cabins had been shattered by the blasts; others were intact, though the wooden doors of some had been so swollen by the water that he couldn't open them. These cabins he broke into by knocking in the wooden ventilation slats. He had almost completed his search of the flat when he found one more door he couldn't open. He knocked in the wooden slats and shone his torch into the cabin.

The disc of light settled on one point in the cabin and remained still. It formed a halo around a silver-framed photograph—the smiling girl again!

Many things raced through Mr. Mayson's mind. Everything he saw in that disc of light impressed the tragedy upon him. There was the picture itself. The way it had been secured against the roll of the ship, with the two neat, wooden brackets screwed to the wooden shelf, showed the foresight and thoroughness of Lieutenant Tangry. Then there was the dirty line on the wall behind the photo, which showed the level to which the oil and water had risen. About one inch of the picture frame had been under water. That meant that all Lieutenant Tangry's records had been submerged. Mr. Mayson saw again that fine profile and the dark wavy hair, saw again how the lieutenant had leaned forward listening to the gramophone with the photograph of the girl in Mr. Mayson's line of sight above him.

The girl now smiled on desolation. Soon, somewhere in England, she would know, and the grief would suppress her smile for many a long day. Even the child as yet unborn would suffer the effects of war.

To Mr. Mayson the smile no longer meant what it had. He almost spoke the words aloud:

No, sweet lady. He's no longer yours.

The level of water in the flat had dropped below the coaming of a hatch he wanted to open. While he stood watching his men unscrew the hatch clips he heard Mr. Ganer call from above.

"Seen anything of the commander (E), Harry?"

Mr. Mayson looked up sharply. He sensed something wrong in the tone of voice. "No, I haven't, Chippie, not since lunchtime. Why? What's wrong?"

"Everything," replied Chippie heatedly. "I can't make any headway at all. The silly old—"

He checked himself, looking quickly at the men of the pumping party. He swallowed hard and continued in a quieter tone. "He's stopped the burners from working back there. Says they might cause a fire."

Mr. Mayson considered Chippie's statement. He forgot the presence of the pumping parties. "Well, of all the damned idiots— Which side is he fighting for? We've got to get this ship out of here, and quickly!"

The men about kept a discreet silence.

"I've got to find him, I suppose," said Mr. Ganer. He turned away, speaking to himself, but Mr. Mayson caught the words. "I always did say, 'It's a wise man who can suffer fools gladly.' "

Mr. Mayson turned back to the job at hand. The pumping party had opened the hatch to the deck below, and he shone his torch down. The compartment beneath was a lobby giving access to storerooms, the sides of which were of wire netting. The lobby and storerooms were full of oil fuel. Tanks below had been pierced from the top down and water from the hangar had poured in, bringing the oil up.

It was a depressing sight, but the portable pump was there; there, too, were the men to operate it; and soon the mixture of oil and water was being discharged to the sullage lighter alongside.

The engineer went aft to the warrant officers' cabin flat and was pleased to find it almost dry. Lathom still had the portable pump gathering the last pools of water on the starboard side, and his men were busy operating four hatches leading to storerooms below. They were relieved to find all four compartments dry.

The cabins in the flat were in fair shape. Loose items from desks and some clothing had been shaken to the floor, and the lower parts of the cupboards and some chests of drawers had been submerged. Mr. Mayson called over to Lathom.

"Pack up your pumping parties for tea, Chief. Let the duty watch work for an hour or so after tea to get these lower cabin flats dry, that's all. We have a hard day coming tomorrow. I'm sleeping ashore tonight."

"Very good, sir."

When he reached the dining hall ashore Mr. Mayson sat beside Mr. Ganer and Mr. Kirklane. "Having any luck, Chippie?" he asked.

"Not much, Harry. I've got the two small pumps going, but the others are still on the jetty."

"Have they started burning yet?"

"No." There was a note of sarcasm in his voice. "The dockyard men are still standing around idle waiting for our big engineer to let them start."

"Well, I hear he's at a conference. You can bet he won't be back today. Anyhow, what about you, Chippie? Are you coming to the hotel tonight? You need a rest, you know. Jim and I are going."

"I did intend to sleep ashore, but I need a good scrub first. My chief shipwright very kindly lent me a towel and a clean shift, so I'll go and soak for half an hour."

"That's what we're going to do," said Mr. Kirklane. "I have to collect a couple of towels and some gear from the ERA's mess after tea."

"Well, I'll wait for you, then," said Mr. Ganer. "We can all go ashore together."

"Are you going to keep the two small pumps running?" asked Mr. Mayson.

"Yes. My chief will visit them every hour until bedtime. He'll stop them before he turns in and get one of the shipwrights to start them again early in the morning. I'd keep them running all night but it would be pretty grim for a watchkeeper among that mess aft, and all the men need a night's rest."

Lieutenant Stanning called from across the table. "If you chaps are going ashore you'd better get a move on. There's a duty motorboat leaving at six, and the next one isn't till nine."

They found it strange to be running across the almost deserted harbour in the ship's motorboat. All three had known Malta in peacetime when the harbour buzzed with activity day and night. Gone now were the many gaily coloured *dghaisals* with their Maltese oarsmen standing and plying their oars. For generations many Maltese had earned their livelihood in this way. They were poor enough in peacetime; now the bleak state of the harbour reflected the conditions under which these, and other Maltese as well, must be living. On the narrow harbour front at Valetta there was scarcely a soul in sight. There were no merchant ships to work their noisy winches day and night; and one could look the whole length of the harbour, for there were no warships to fill all those empty berths at the buoys and alongside the dockyard wharves. There were no crowds of sailors to land on the front and flock into those small beer houses that faced the water.

Every Maltese is known to the British sailor as José. It was here on the front that José stood at his door and advertized his wares.

"Here y'are Johnny. Good beer here, chum. Supper and drink, singing and dancing. Come inside."

The music for entertainment varied a little from house to house. Some had a violin and a piano, others a violin and a guitar, a few had only a piano on which many a sailor-pianist tried his hands. The serving girls were happy and willing dancing partners. Some of the houses provided good clean beds at a cheap rate for men who wished to stay the night. A few provided meals at almost any hour. Many a sailor had his first beer of the day here on the front, and often his last one at night before going to bed or going back aboard by *dghaisal.* It was here as the daylight failed that José would switch on the bright lights in his beer house and the whole waterfront would be illuminated. Now, as the ship's motorboat neared the customhouse, there was not one door open on the front; the beer houses were out of business. The once gaily coloured paint on the doors and window shutters was faded and weatherbeaten. Even the customhouse appeared to be deserted except for one small police boat tied to the jetty.

About a dozen officers landed as the boat ran alongside. Mr. Ganer was the last ashore.

"Whither away, chaps?"

"Better call at the hotel first, I suppose," said Mr. Mayson. "I know our rooms are booked for us, but we might as well take a look at them."

Jim Kirklane was carrying a suitcase that held their combined toilet gear. "I'm with you there, Harry—we can drop this case off, but I hear we can get a good supper at the Warrant Officers' Club if we order it early enough. How about calling in there as we pass?"

"Suits me, Jim. How about you, Chippie?"

"All right by me. We might meet a few old friends up there."

They had a climb before them, for the important part of Valetta harbour is surrounded by high ground. They had the alternative of going up by the Baracca Lift, a device that hoisted passengers up the vertical face of a cutting in the rock close by, but the three preferred to walk up by the road and steps. They saw much on their way to remind them that Malta was feeling the effects of war; the shops, which used to be well stocked with merchandise from all over the world, now seemed very short of supplies. At this early stage of the war it was an omen of what the island would have to suffer before the danger was removed from the surrounding waters and ships could once again bring trade and prosperity.

Malta appeared subdued. The streets were almost empty and very few doors were open. It depressed the three friends a little as they made their way slowly up a street of steps.

Later they found the Warrant Officers' Club in keeping with the rest of Malta. The bar was deserted except for one old friend—the manager. He greeted them heartily. Like all

Maltese he had a remarkable memory. He knew each of them and which ship they had served in when they last called at Malta. He was able to tell them when certain friends of theirs had called in last, and where they had come from and gone to. It was a refreshing hour they spent at the bar talking to him. Then, as supper was being laid, Mr. Munday, Torps, and Mr. Prout joined them. These three officers had come ashore by an earlier boat. They all had a good meal, though there was little conversation at the table. Each one had the same idea in mind: a good night's sleep; and soon they were making their way through the dark, deserted streets of Valetta in the direction of the hotel. Their first day in Malta was coming to a close.

CHAPTER 18

The first duty motorboat of the day ran alongside the dockyard wharf and a score or more officers landed. Commander Sands was the first ashore, being the most senior officer in the boat. He was followed by the senior engineer and several lieutenants; then came sublieutenants, followed by the commissioned and warrant officers.

They all trailed along the wharf towards the after gangway, and the warrant officers had almost reached it when Mr. Ganer stopped and called to Mr. Mayson.

"Harry, what's happened to the pumps?"

"I don't know, Chippie. I suppose they've been hoisted in."

"Yes, that's quite likely," said Mr. Kirklane. "Lieutenant Morton may have got something moving last night."

Mr. Ganer looked worried. "Well, I'm going aft to see."

After visiting the lift shaft Mr. Ganer was an angry and frustrated man. As he stormed his way forward towards the engineers' office he was met by Lieutenant Morton and Mr. Kirklane.

"I'm sorry about those pumps, Mr. Ganer," said the lieutenant, "but there was nothing I could do. The commander (E) sent them back."

"Oh, it was him again! I thought so! But why? For heaven's sake, why?"

"That's what puzzles me, Mr. Ganer. He came aboard

after supper and told the dockyard chargeman to take all the pumps back. He said he had told the dockyard before that he didn't need them."

"This is almost sabotage!" said Mr. Ganer. "Can you see any sense in it? Those two small pumps would have lightened the after end a good bit by this morning. Did he know they were working when he ordered them sent back?"

"I don't know, but he went aft to look around."

"A change for him, anyhow, if he went down there," was Mr. Ganer's bitter reply.

The other two had nothing to say, and after a moment of silence, Mr. Ganer turned away. "I'm going to see Commander Sands."

Lieutenant Morton went back to the office, and Mr. Kirklane went down to the double-bottom store to don his working clothes. There he saw Mr. Mayson getting into his overall suit after sending his pumping parties off on the morning's work.

The commissioned engineer looked up and read something in the younger man's face. "What's news, Jim?"

"Only bad news, Harry, I'm sorry to say. The commander (E) has sent all Chippie's portable pumps back to the dockyard."

"He's done it again? He must be out of his mind! The whole stern is weakened where the starboard side is shattered, and we have to bring the after end up so that dockyard men can weld and strengthen it!"

He gazed with unseeing eyes at the heel indicator as he slowly buttoned up his overall suit. Suddenly he grabbed his gloves and torch from the desk. "Where's Chippie now?"

"He's gone forward to see Commander Sands."

"Oh—well, look, Jim. I think I see the answer to this. If we can move one of our pumps back there quickly and run it continuously, it should clear that cabin flat by tomorrow morning, but how can we get the pump into position?"

"Well, do you want to put it back to where Chippie had the small ones?"

"Yes. I thought of moving the pump from our cabin flat, which is dry now, but which way do we go? The best way is over the flight deck and down through the lift shaft, but the burners have been stopped from clearing the way down. The only other way is along the starboard passage, but the area behind the after door is almost plugged."

"Not now, it isn't, Harry. Lieutenant Leyton and Kelling and several men were clearing it yesterday."

"Oh, good. Let's go see."

As they went aft they met Kelling near the engineers' office. "You're just the man I want to see, Sub," said Mr. Mayson.

The young officer stopped and smiled. "All right, Mr. Mayson, here I am. How can I help?"

The commissioned engineer smiled in appreciation of the spontaneous offer. The younger man seemed ready to undertake anything. "How's the wreckage behind that starboard door aft? Any chance of getting a portable pump through there soon?"

"Oh yes. We'll have ERAs with cutting tools helping this morning. Should have it clear before noon."

"Good for you, Sub!"

And the sublieutenant's forecast was proved correct. By noon the pump had been moved aft and put into use, discharging full bore over the side. In the meantime the two large dockyard pumps had arrived back on the dockside, and the small ones were operating again, having been rigged and started by the chief shipwright.

Mr. Ganer was a much calmer man. He had explained the situation aft to Commander Sands and had seen an expression of alarm in that officer's severe, clean-cut face. The commander contacted the dockyard authorities at once and had the pumps brought back. The burners who were to clear the way for the pumps were busy elsewhere in the dockyard, but the foreman in charge, contacted by phone, arranged for their return after lunch.

About the ship seaman ratings were still busy scoring and cleaning. Much was being done in the way of salvage, too. This was very useful work for another reason. Such things as clothing, bedding, curtains, and rugs, which had been washed into flooded compartments, would tend to choke the pump suction pipes. These things were being fished out and set aside on the flight deck.

During the afternoon the burners and many more dockyard workers appeared on board. Some carried lengths of new piping to be installed as temporary fuel, fresh water and sullage systems, which would be necessary during the ship's next voyage. Dockyard electricians were installing a better network of wiring for temporary lighting, and joiners and painters were endeavouring to make the wardroom suitable for use during a short trip.

By late afternoon the two powerful dockyard pumps had been positioned for use.

That night Mr. Mayson was the duty engineer on board. He organized the engine ratings into three watches to keep the pumps going all night. He told the men how important it was to get the water out. At midnight he turned in, sleeping on a camp bed in damage-control headquarters. He was out again at six o'clock. The men had not failed him. He learned that they had experienced increasing trouble with choking suctions, but had pumped the large cabin flat almost dry.

Now they were winning! They would soon have access to the powerful L pump, two decks below, and it had suction lines to all the hold compartments back to the stern.

When the dockyard men appeared, Mr. Ganer arranged with the construction foreman for the patching and strengthening of the shattered ship's side aft, which was now above water.

The rising of the stern had allowed water over the steering compartment to run out through holes in the ship's side, and soon men were clearing the rubble that lay strewn about the deck. It was an unpleasant task, for they also had to remove three of their dead shipmates.

Mr. Mayson was moving forward to arrange for the pumping out of the steering compartment when he met Mr. Ganer.

"I'm glad to see you, Chippie. How long do you think the hull people will be stiffening up the stern?"

"Oh, about forty-eight hours. According to the foreman they could finish it by the time it gets dark the day after tomorrow."

"He thinks so, eh? Well, I think we'll have the steering gear ready by then, and, by gosh, we can steam her out right away."

"That's so, Harry. If it hadn't been for that big interfering sod we could be steaming her out now."

They were standing in the fore-and-aft passage at the after end of the wardroom flat. There were several dockyard men busy about the place, partially blocking the passageway with their tools and gear. Mr. Mayson looked forward at the sound of a voice raised in anger. An elderly dockyard man in a brown overall suit was pushing his way aft. "Come on, men, shift! Let me by."

He walked up to Mr. Mayson, his face flaming red with anger. He wore a collar and a tie and a trilby hat, which told them he was a senior foreman.

"Excuse me," he said, almost shouting, "who's that big fat chap in the white overall suit?"

"You mean the man with the commander's cap on?"

"Yes." The foreman took out a handkerchief and wiped

his face. He had been frothing a little at the mouth.

"That's the commander (E), head of the engineering branch aboard here. Has he been up to his capers again?"

"That he has, and once too bloody often. I'm getting off this ship and I'll damn well stay off. Every job we've started he's come along and stopped! Your other fellow's all right," he went on in a milder tone. "We see him about the drawings and agree about a job and we go ahead with it"—his voice rose again—"until that fat bastard comes and stops us!"

"Now, now, old chap," said Mr. Mayson, "calm down a bit. You're not the only fellow who's being messed around by him."

"I know damn well I'm not! The other foremen are just as fed up as I am! You'll never get this ship out if he keeps interfering!"

"Well, we intend to get this ship out in spite of him; but we need you, so please don't go and leave us. Mr. Ganer here has taken the matter up with Commander Sands, and I'll be adding my weight wherever I can to stop this nonsense."

The foreman turned and moved slowly forward. After a few paces he stopped and looked back. His face was a little less red, his voice a little calmer.

"If he comes messing around again," he said, "I swear I'll hit him with something."

The two officers remained silent. Mr. Mayson felt relieved: The foreman's parting words had implied that he would carry on with his work.

It was then that Mr. Mills joined them. "I've been looking for you chaps," said Torps. "The funeral for our lost shipmates is being held ashore at two o'clock this afternoon. Arrangements have been made for burial at sea afterwards. I'll be going with two or three of our messmates. Tom Langley is well enough now and he'll be there. Commander Sands would prefer you two remain on board—he feels your work is urgent. Guns' crews and some of the damage control staff are to remain on board. If any of your men have lost close friends you can let them go."

"Thank you, Torps," said Harry Mayson. "We'll have a quiet prayer for them all. Just say good-bye to Tim and Ted Rathbone for me."

"And that goes for me, too," said Chippie. "We'll stay and do our best here."

It was nearing the end of a busy day when Mr. Mayson found the senior engineer alone in the office.

"Can I have a quiet word with you, sir?"

"Of course, Mr. Mayson. Sit down and take it easy for awhile."

The commissioned engineer told of his meeting with the dockyard foreman. The senior maintained an unhappy silence throughout and remained gazing straight ahead. Mr. Mayson looked at the rugged profile and spoke with emphasis.

"This could be a matter of life and death to many people, sir. And what about the ship: Are we to abandon her now? Let our country down?"

The senior spread his arms. "What can one do?"

"Well, we don't have a commander (E) worth being loyal to, but we should be loyal to the captain. See him, sir. He doesn't realize what is going on in our department. Mr. Ganer put Commander Sands wise and got immediate action."

"All right, I'll see to it."

"Thank you, sir. I'll go and see to the steering gear."

The senior moved away. Mr. Mayson felt more in sympathy with him. He was a young man in a job that could be tough enough even with a cooperative commander (E).

Lieutenant Stanning was the duty engineer officer on board, and after a talk with Mr. Mayson he arranged for the duty watch to continue pumping operations throughout the night.

By next morning the two storerooms beneath the large cabin flat had been pumped dry. Access had been gained to L pump and Lathom had tried it on all the hold compartments aft to the stern, proving that the ship's bottom was sound back there.

The ship's portable pump had pumped the steering compartment almost empty.

The dockyard men had worked during the night, and there was a vast improvement in the wardroom flat. Patches had been welded over the holes in the deck, the minor bulkheads between the wardroom and the passage had been straightened, and where the plating had been badly shattered it had been replaced by light boarding. A coat of white paint had been applied. Work on the pipe systems was almost complete, and the lighting system had been excellently rigged.

In the early forenoon the senior and Mr. Mayson went aft together to look over the steering compartment. They were peering down the hatch when a familiar voice sounded behind them.

"Well, how's the battle going?"

"Tom!" said Mr. Mayson.

"Hello, Mr. Langley!" said the senior. "How are you?"

Mr. Langley was dressed for work. He wore his brown overall suit and a greasy battered cap with an oily white cap cover. This latter was so characteristic of Tom Langley that he always seemed particularly smart when he changed out of his work clothes and wore a more shapely cap.

"Not too bad, sir—a bit sore round my ears, and I'm to be fitted out with glasses. Can't see very well without them, damn it!"

Jim Kirklane came up the hatch. "Good old Tom! Back again, eh?"

"Yes, Jim, I'm glad to say. It looks as though I've arrived

just in time, too, seeing you've nearly got rid of the water down here."

"It isn't my work, Tom. I'm only helping. Chippie and Harry are the ones who've been doing their stuff."

"You've done your whack, young fellow," said Mr. Mayson, smiling.

The commissioned engineer now felt that success was in sight. With the arrival of Tom Langley he could forget about steering gear. Things were certainly looking up. Tomorrow night should see the ship ready for sea.

And then it happened—The warning system sounded throughout the ship. A temporary lead from the system had been run aft to an electric horn hanging in the compartment above the steering flat. It served to warn men working among the damage. Some time later each of the four officers admitted to the effect it had upon their nerves. Each pulsation swept down through every fibre of their being then rose again with ever-increasing speed to swamp the brain.

Blurp! blurp! blurp! Blurp! blurp! blurp!

For a brief period they stood and looked at each other before starting to move.

Blurp! blurp! blurp! Blurp! blurp! blurp!

As they passed under the electric horn the sound screamed its way in. Each blurp became a pulsing pain that the mind construed as something else.

Crash! fire! flood!—Blurp! Blood! stench! death!—Blurp!

With minds impressed by the possibility of an all-obliterating blow from above, officers and men went to their action stations.

Soon there was silence. Down below in the engine room department watch-keepers maintained the necessary hot and cold water and fire-main services. They tended the steam generators supplying electrical power for lighting and ventilation and for operating all manner of mechanisms, including the guns. The forward ammunition conveyor was in use under the supervision of Mr. Mills, and busy hands passed the ammunition from the end of the conveyor into the lift. In the wings of the flight deck the guns' crews stood silent at their stations. Grim-faced men these. They had learned a lot during those attacks at sea. If "Jerry" was coming again he was due for a hot reception. And up on the bridge surveying them all stood another grim-faced man, Captain Graham.

The dockyard workers had left the ship and taken shelter in those long tunnels in the sandstone close by. The sun shone clear and bright. High up a few white, feathery clouds broke the expanse of blue and a light, cold breeze blew from the starboard bow.

Between decks Commander Sands made his presence felt. In cooperation with the first lieutenant and the engineer officers in charge of fire and repair parties he checked over the fire-fighting equipment. The principal medical officer and his staff prepared, as before, for any eventuality: Mr. Ganer and Mr. Mayson checked over their respective parties; the senior engineer took up his position in the machinery control room; and the commander (E) sat in his easy chair in damage-control headquarters.

When Mr. Mayson reached damage-control headquarters he found quietude. The chief wore his white overall suit and sat still, just looking into space. In fact no one was doing anything except Chief Stoker Lathom, who sat, notebook before him, checking on the oil fuel distribution in the ship.

Mr. Mayson placed a small slip of paper on the desk before Saunders, the engineers' writer, and spoke quietly.

"When we secure from action stations send one of the messengers up to the bridge to get this for me."

Saunders looked down at the paper. "You want the depth

of water here, sir? I'll send up for it now if you like."

"Oh, no. There's no need to worry them up there yet. I fancy these are only reconnaissance planes and we shan't be attacked this time."

The chief had been watching and listening. "What's that got to do with the depth of water here?" he asked.

The tone of voice surprised the commissioned engineer. It sounded like a genuine request for knowledge and didn't carry the inference of ridicule Mr. Mayson had learned to expect. So he replied, "Well, I'd like to know how much water the ship can take in before she rests on the bottom. The depth here possibly can limit the amount of counterflooding we dare undertake. At the same time we must keep the gun platforms horizontal to give the gunners a better chance to repel attacks—"

Mr. Mayson would have had more to say. Indeed, everyone in the office was waiting to hear what was to follow, but he remained silent, looking at the chief, who had dropped his eyes.

The commissioned engineer picked up his gloves and torch and left the office. Outside he stood still, thinking, *So that is our gallant chief—nothing but a big bag of wind!* He had seen a look of stark panic in the chief's eyes, and emanating from such a bullying personality that sort of response disgusted him.

He wandered, a little aimlessly, still thinking of the matter. Soon he found himself in the starboard passage, so he continued forward to the servery flat, which was crowded with men who now had no action stations. Seeing the ship was not steaming, many of the men who kept watches at sea, or worked with the air arm, were now idle. It seemed to Mr. Mayson that here was a mass of human life placed in jeopardy for no reason at all. But someone else had seen that and had taken prompt action about it. The ship's company remained at action stations for a little over half an hour, and when it was over the bos'n's pipe was heard, followed by the call: "Clear lower deck! Hands muster on the flight deck!"

The captain and Commander Sands stood together on the bridge, watching the ship's company assemble. Soon the master-at-arms hurried up the ladders from the flight deck to the bridge and reported to Commander Sands. "Lower deck cleared, sir."

The captain spoke into the microphone at once. "Come closer, men. Gather round."

The ship's company surged forward and formed a thick semicircle before the loudspeaker. The captain waited until the men had shuffled into position.

"Can everyone hear me now? If not, please raise your arm."

There was silence for a brief period while he surveyed his ship's company. He was an unhappy man, but he gave no indication of it as he viewed the upturned faces of his officers and men. His concern was for their lives, and for the life of the fine ship he was so proud to command. Each day in Malta had been a period of anxiety for him, but as one day followed another without interruption from the enemy, the chances of getting the ship clear away had improved, and his hopes had risen. Now, the outlook was gloomy indeed. He adjusted the microphone and began to speak.

"I have brought you up here now on a matter of some importance. You must realize what this air-raid warning means. We know it was enemy aircraft, and that means we have been spotted. I've no doubt that photographs have been taken of the ship, and the chances are that we shall be attacked again soon. Now there are a large number of men about the ship who do not need to be here during action stations, and it is my wish that all those men will take shelter ashore when the warning sounds. Men on watch below, and guns' crews and ammunition parties, are required. Damage control parties are not absolutely necessary, but they should be ready to hurry back to the ship immediately the attacks are over."

The captain stopped and turned to speak to Commander Sands. There was scarcely a movement among those hundreds of men on the flight deck. Soon the captain spoke to them again.

"That's all. I will leave you now. Commander Sands has a few words to say to you."

Commander Sands stepped to the microphone as the captain stood back. His voice rang clear and firm.

"Ship's company! Ship's company, atten*tion!*"

The officers and men stiffened to attention and Commander Sands turned to salute the captain. Captain Graham returned the salute and left the bridge, whereupon the commander spoke into the microphone again.

"Ship's company, stand at ease! Stand easy."

The commander did not intend to waste time. "Now, men, I have little to say. The captain and I believe we can get this ship to sea and away to a safer base where she can be fully repaired and brought into service again. The commendable work by yourselves and the dockyard men have made this possible. However, there's still much to be done, so let's get back on the job."

He raised his voice, and his final words carried enthusiasm. "That's all, men. Just carry on with the good work!"

CHAPTER 19

In the early afternoon Mr. Langley was able to enter the steering compartment. He wore a pair of seaboots for there was still about a foot of water above the deck plates. One man followed him down the ladder: Leading Stoker Soames. This was something Soames had been waiting for. It was here that he kept watch at sea in turn with two other leading stokers. He was seeking something and Mr. Langley was shining his torch on it as Soames dropped down the ladder. It was the body of the man who had relieved Soames from the forenoon watch on the day of action.

"You go up, Soames," said Mr. Langley. "Report to the senior and get hold of something to wrap your friend up in."

The senior engineer came aft and supervised the removal of the last body to be found in the ship.

Soon Mr. Langley knew the extent of the damage to the steering gear, and he was able to assure the senior that it would be ready for use by noon the next day—barring accidents.

At three o'clock in the afternoon the air-raid warning sounded again. By this time there were half a dozen men clearing out the debris that had been washed into the steering flat.

"Come on, you men, get ashore," said Mr. Langley.

They all hurried away, except Soames.

"And you, Soames, come on: Up the ladder!"

Soames stood still, cap in hand, looking very humble. "After you, sir."

Mr. Langley knew Soames. He smiled and climbed the ladder, Soames following behind. Near damage-control headquarters they met Mr. Mayson. "Pretty quiet about now, Harry," said Tom Langley. "Are there any other officers about?"

"Oh, yes. I saw the senior and Kelling just now in the workshop. Chippie is about, too, and Lieutenant Stanning has gone up to the flight deck. Lieutenant Morton is sick on shore. Lost his voice. Could hardly whisper this morning."

"Got a heavy cold, eh?"

"No, Tom. It's reaction to shock. I hear it is affecting quite a number of the ship's company in different ways. Take some time to wear off, I suppose."

Mr. Prout then appeared from forward. As he sighted his messmates he grinned all over his face and walked towards them with his slow heavy tread.

"Did you chaps see the old man going just now? Never saw anything like it in my life!"

"Who do you mean? The commander E?" asked Tom Langley.

"Yes. Who else? He was batting it along the jetty for that long tunnel aft of the ship." Mr. Prout halted awhile to chuckle heavily at the memory. "The old boy was leading the field by a good dozen lengths."

"Hmm," said Mr. Mayson.

"Sorry I missed it," said Tom Langley.

Up on the flight deck the guns' crews scanned the sky, and looking down on them were the captain and Commander Sands. The shore air-raid siren had ceased its wailing and a brooding silence reigned over the whole dockyard. On those high places around the harbour the shore battteries waited for the attack, too, but it was not to come that day. After half an hour the all clear sounded over the island, and the dockyard came to life again.

The day passed without further incident, but not so the next day. At half past ten in the forenoon dozens of German dive-bombers attacked the ship. They came in out of the sun with determination and skill, and they met determined and skillful opposition. This was a day that gave Able Seaman Miller some satisfaction. Never for a moment did he relax as he trained his gun with cool, deadly skill. His whole frame was being shaken by the vibration of the roaring, death-dealing machine, but there was a grim smile at the corners of his mouth as he sat there with his eye clamped to the sights.

Very few German planes returned home that day. Six British fighters rose from Malta and played havoc with the bombers, and with the fighters that formed the escort. The shore batteries and the ship's guns shot down many of the planes as they dived at the ship, but the enemy scored one hit on the target. One bomb—fortunately, a light one—hit the stern.

As the men who had been sheltering ashore made their way back to the ship after the all clear had sounded, they beheld a strange sight. The bomb had come in well aft and had exploded in the gallery decks above the quarterdeck. The downward blast had broken up a large area of the quarterdeck and the timber was on fire. But there was more smoke than flame, for all the woodwork was still wet through. Mr. Mayson, Sublieutenant Kelling, and Mr. Langley were beating out the flames, using wet sheets and pillowcases from a pile stowed near the after gangway and intended for the laundry; while Lieutenant Stanning, assisted by Speedy, was running a fire hose from forward. Soon there was no fire, only steam rising from the hot teak planking of the quarterdeck as the hose cooled the area down.

Then the commander (E) arrived from shore. His clean

white overall suit was as imposing as ever. He stamped about the better part of the deck, surveying the area, and then, apparently satisfied, took off his leather gloves, clasped them in his right hand and tramped breezily forward. His manner seemed to imply: "Well, that's that. Must get forward now and deal with something else."

But it was Mr. Ganer who had to worry about something else. The new damage aft was well above waterline and had let no water into the ship, but the bomb had exploded at the first gallery deck and had blown away some of the ship's frames that supported the heavy flight deck and second gallery deck. It was here that the ship vibrated so much at high speeds. The frames would have to be rebuilt.

Mr. Ganer's heart sank as he viewed the damage. The repairs would take two to three more days.

Down below, Mr. Langley was already at work on the steering gear. He had with him Leading Stoker Soames and the ERA who had helped Mr. Mayson with the gear in action. Mr. Kirklane added his weight, and by nightfall the steering gear had been tried and was ready. Apart from the damage aft the ship was ready to proceed. The damage at the paint store forward, a few holes above waterline, could quickly be patched by welding.

The dockyard pressed on with the work aft during the night, but there was much remaining to be done before the stern would be strengthened enough to permit a voyage at high speed.

Several times during the new day the air-raid alarm sounded. At least half of the working day between dawn and dusk was lost. Each time, the alarm had sounded in response to reconnaissance flights by the enemy.

When the alarm sounded for the first time—early in the forenoon—Mr. Mayson and the warrant shipwright were viewing the situation on the quarterdeck. The dockyard men hurried forward to cross the gangway, and make for the shelters ashore. The two officers started to walk forward, Mr. Mayson leading, when suddenly Mr. Ganer stopped and called out, "Here, Harry! Look at this! Quickly!"

Mr. Ganer had stepped nearer to the ship's side and was looking towards the gangway. Dockyard men and sailors trotted shoreward. Amongst them was a huge figure in white, obviously impatient at the rate of movement and striving with both arms to clear a path through the crowd. Once clear of the gangway he picked up speed. The majority of the sailors were half running, half walking, occasionally stopping to shade their eyes as they looked up into the sky. Not so the commander (E). There was a long tunnel in the rock wall aft of the ship and he was going to get there or burst. With toes turned slightly outward, his fists clenched, his elbows held in, and his head erect, he gave evidence of early athletic training, unsuspected in one so gross.

He was well clear of the stern of the ship and showing the two officers a dusty pair of heels when they heard a voice behind them.

"Go it Brumpting, old boy!"

They turned to find Mr. Langley eyeing the chief's retreating figure and smiling a little grimly. He watched the white form till it made a sharp left turn into the tunnel, then he spoke to his messmates.

"Come on, chaps, it'll be a bit safer forward, don't you think?" And they all moved forward off the quarterdeck.

Later in the day Mr. Mayson was about to enter damage-control headquarters when the warning sounded again. Immediately the door burst open and he had to jump sideways to avoid the huge white bulk of the chief as he tore out, heading for the nearest ladder.

That night the dockyard men worked unceasingly again. The day shift started at eight o'clock in the morning and continued without interruption till noon. Success was in sight.

The topic of discussion at lunch was the possibility of getting the ship away before she was attacked again. Mr. Ganer's spirits were rising. He was full of praise for the dockyard men who were doing the construction repairs. After lunch he had a long conversation with Commander Sands on the progress of the work and learned that the commander was already preparing his organization for leaving harbour.

Mr. Ganer, Mr. Mayson, and Mr. Langley went aboard together. The latter two had little work on hand and intended to check on their cabin accommodations. The mess servants were busy removing wet bedding and attending to their uniforms. Dockyard men were working on the ventilation system, which had been damaged by the blast. The two engineers went below and on the wardroom flat they met Mr. Kirklane, who approached them with a query.

"Did you chaps hear the news at one o'clock?"

"No, why? Have the Germans gobbled up Switzerland for a change?" asked Tom Langley.

"No, Tom. It's a bit nearer home for you, I'm afraid, and for you, too, Harry. The Germans made a heavy raid on Plymouth last night."

The pair looked at each other gravely as they absorbed the war's latest blow. When Tom Langley broke the brief silence there was resignation in his voice.

"I knew it was bound to come."

"Yes," agreed Harry Mayson. "And now we can only hope for the best."

Tom Langley's mind was picturing the scene at home. He saw the ailing woman who was his wife, hurrying wearily yet lagging behind all others as she made for the air-raid shelter. She carried the bassinet that held their daughter, and before she reached the shelter the antiaircraft guns had opened fire. Desperately she tried to hasten her pace. She leaned forward over the child, shielding it from falling fragments of antiaircraft shells. Her mouth gaped open as she fought for breath, and beside her ran their little boy. Anger against the brutal Nazi regime surged through Tom Langley's being and took the last vestige of colour from his face.

To Jim Kirklane neither of his messmates looked very well. Tom Langley could not yet have fully recovered from that shock in action. No one would know how much Tim's death had affected him. As for Mr. Mayson—that stout old warhorse looked strained and tired. The young warrant engineer felt sorry he had spoken about the news broadcast, but even if he hadn't told them they would have heard about what had happened from someone else. He would have tried to change the subject, but suddenly the war at home took a secondary place. War was with them on the spot again.

Blurp! blurp! blurp! Blurp! blurp! blurp! Blurp! blurp! blurp! Blurp! blurp! blurp!

The first high-pitched blurps on the electric horn were nerve shattering. "Damn those bastards," muttered Tom Langley.

The three moved forward at once. By force of habit Mr. Kirklane went to the boiler room in use. Mr. Langley went up to the flight deck. It was his intention to stand by one of the guns, for on the previous day the captain had sent a hand message round asking for one officer to stand by each gun in action. He had foreseen the danger of that speeding white figure. The sight of a fleeing senior officer could shake the nerve of the most steadfast of men when they had been subjected to strain for so long. Whether it did shake their nerves was never known, for the captain's prompt action counterbalanced the effect of the chief's weakness. The hand message never reached Mr. Langley, for more senior officers filled the requirement at each gun. However, the warrant engineer made his way to the flight deck thinking that one or more senior officers might not have been able to get over from the dining hall in time for the attack.

Mr. Mayson went to damage-control headquarters. He sat all alone for a little while, waiting, then suddenly rose to his feet thinking of the watch below: Better let them see an officer about. He went below into the workshop and called down the hatch of the machinery control room:

"Below there!"

"Hello!" came the reply, and the senior engineer appeared at the bottom of the ladder.

"Oh, hello, sir," replied the commissioned engineer. "I'll be here in the workshop if you need me."

He heard the senior's reply, "All right," as he moved away. The more he saw of that officer these days the more he liked and respected him.

There came a rattle of feet on the ladder from above and Sublieutenant Kelling appeared just as the heavy AA guns opened fire. Mr. Mayson looked about him. They were going to be attacked again, and any bombs that struck the ship would come down through and burst inside. If a man were going to be of any further use the main thing was for him to remain alive. The heavy machines in the workshop would serve to stop flying fragments if the bombs didn't burst too close by. He grabbed the handle of a long toolbox and called to the sublieutenant. "Here, Sub, give me a hand."

They shifted the box to a position best sheltered by the heavy machines, and both sat down with their backs against the head support of a large lathe—just as the pom-pom guns opened fire. There was a heavy roar, as though all of the guns had fired together, and almost immediatelly, drowning all other noise, came the sound of explosions somewhere near.

Silence followed while the two officers sat stock-still, waiting. Each had slung his electric torch around his neck. Soon the pom-pom guns opened up again, and that was a clear indication to them of what was happening. The gunners had reached a high peak of efficiency at this game. They had learned to hold their fire, to wait till each diving plane came well within range, then they gave a short burst and saw their own line of fire before the gun smoke became thick enough to obstruct their view. Quickly then, they adjusted their fire and let "Jerry" have it. Their synchronous blast was the one prolonged roar one heard every so often.

Bombs now fell frequently and quite close by, shaking the ship. German planes were disintegrating in the air. The ship's guns, the shore batteries, and the few defending fighters were again making the attack costly for the enemy. At one point, several German planes fell out of the sky together. And still the attack continued. With unsurpassed daring and skill the German pilots dived their planes at the target, but the defence was so magnificent that it was all the more to be regretted when the last bombs to fall caused so much damage to the ship. To the men below decks it seemed the end of everything. First there were two high-pitched cracking explosions, which Mr. Mayson took to be hits either forward or aft. Afterwards he found they were bombs that demolished the whole line of storehouses alongside the wharf. Almost immediately another hard blow shook the ship badly. The vessel was rocking. Gun smoke was finding its way below to mingle with dust being shaken from the decks and bulkheads. The pom-pom guns roared almost incessantly. The lights flickered. The last few planes were diving together. Then, among all the noises of hell carrying the threat of sudden extinction, Sublieutenant Kelling caught another sound. It came from the older man beside him. He was amazed that any man could so behave under such conditions. Mr. Mayson was singing, and the younger man caught on to the last words of the song and joined in.

Oh my, I don't want to die,
I want to go home!

The deck of the workshop was shaking, the guns still roaring. And then it came: the heaviest blow of all. It was an explosion that almost blacked out their senses. They were thrown off the toolbox to fall on hands and knees on the workshop plates. The ship rolled and pitched as though battered by the worst Atlantic gale. Then she started to settle. They learned afterwards that one or more heavy bombs had barely missed the port side of the ship and had exploded underwater.

The guns ceased firing. Slowly the vessel tipped precariously, heeling to port. Mr. Mayson rose and faced forward. He braced his legs wide apart. At a rough guess the ship was fifteen degrees or more over when she came gently to rest. An infinite sadness crept over him and made him sick at heart. In silence, it seemed, she had said good-bye to any hopes of leaving Malta. He knew that a large part of the ship's port side must have been severely damaged and several compartments flooded to cause such a list, and the terrific jolt she had received may have damaged the main and auxiliary machinery beyond the repair capabilities of the dockyard crew. Through his mind flashed the whole sorry story of wasted time caused by the cowardly delaying tactics of a high-ranking officer, one who'd obviously been born to be elevated to a position far beyond his blustering incompetence.

Sublieutenant Kelling stood beside Mr. Mayson and his voice seemed strange to the older man. "We'd better get up the ladder, don't you think?"

"Yes, let's go," was the sad reply.

As they moved up the tilted ladder a desperate battle was being fought in the boiler room. The last violent explosion had broken an oil fuel supply column on the boiler front. Mr.

Kirklane and the two men on watch had been thrown to the floor plates and almost knocked unconscious. When they rose to their feet, hot oil fuel sprayed over them and over the boiler. Soon the heat of the boiler plating began to transform the oil into a dangerous explosive substance, and the fires in the boiler were still alight.

"Stop the oil pump!" yelled Mr. Kirklane. "Shut off the sprayers."

The petty officer of the watch rushed towards the oil pump but fell on the slippery, inclined deck, and rolled over on the oily plates. Mr. Kirklane slid down the sloping surface on his feet like a child on a slide. They could barely see each other for the blinding spray of oil. Both reached the oil pump at the same time, and Mr. Kirklane felt the petty officer's hand on the steam valve.

"Go ahead!" he yelled. "Shut it off!"

He moved aside and swung open the steam valve to the forced-draught fan that supplied air to the boiler room. The stoker had shut off the oil sprayers. As the fan increased its speed he called to the man again.

"Open all your flaps!"

Soon the fumes were clearing, being blown into the furnace, but the boiler steam pressure was dropping back. In a short while the pressure would be too low for the electrical generators, and they supplied energy for the lighting—and the power for the guns.

What to do? Time was short. Mr. Kirklane examined the fractured oil column. His heart gave a joyful leap when he saw that the column was broken on the outlet side of the supply valve. He shut off the valve at once and called to the petty officer:

"Get your oil pump going!"

At the other side of the boiler was another supply column, the one that distributed oil to half the sprayers on the boiler. That would be enough for present requirements.

"Switch on your sprayers from that side," he said to the stoker.

In a few minutes the steam pressure was up to normal and Mr. Kirklane prepared to leave the boiler room.

"Keep away from the boiler front now with your oily clothing," he said. "As soon as I can find reliefs for you I'll send them down. Don't forget that you have two fire extinguishers down here."

He climbed the ladders, leaving behind two men who were, like himself, covered in oil from head to foot.

Mr. Mayson soon found out the extent of the damage to the hull. He hurried to the double-bottom store and checked the heel indicator: eighteen degrees to port, but no further movement. Sublieutenant Kelling had followed him down. "Come," he said to the young engineer, "let's find out what's happened."

They went over to the port side. In five separate compartments on the port side were indicators showing the depth of the water in the hold compartments below. They had checked the after two and were moving to the third when they met Commander Sands. He was hurrying aft but stopped at once on meeting them.

"How are the compartments below, Mr. Mayson?" he asked.

"I'm just checking, sir. It seems we have been seriously damaged, but I'll soon know the extent of the flooding."

"All right, Mr. Mayson. Will you report to the captain when you know? He will be waiting on the bridge."

"I will, sir, as soon as I can."

The two engineers hurried forward. They found most of the hold compartments on the port side flooded. In addition, many oil fuel tanks had been badly damaged and the oil forced upwards into the compartments that held the depth-recording instruments. As they moved aft again they left a trail of oil fuel—it dripped from their trouser legs. The all clear had not yet been sounded so they found damage-control headquarters still deserted. Mr. Mayson indicated on the flooding board which compartments had been flooded. Quickly then, from figures supplied by the shipbuilders, he checked the effect this flooding should have had regarding the degree of the ship's list. The figure he arrived at was very close to that recorded on the heel indicator. It confirmed, near enough, that he knew the extent of the flooding. They were about to leave when Mr. Langley opened the door. "Ah! There you are, Harry. Do you need any help?"

"Yes, Tom. Will you and the sub wait for me in the double-bottom store? I have to report to the captain."

When he reached the bridge he found Captain Graham alone, and grimly unhappy. He saluted and made his report.

"We've taken in about five hundred tons of water on the port side, sir. Certain side compartments amidships are flooded, but the main inner longitudinal bulkhead is holding."

"Does that mean we can still be seaworthy?"

"Yes, sir, and I can bring the ship upright again; but to correct her in the ideal way—by oil transfer—might be risky, and that could take hours. I can correct her quickly by counterflooding."

Then, as the captain hesitated, he added, "I'm thinking of the gun platforms now, sir."

A light kindled in the captain's eyes. "Do it, Mr. Mayson."

The engineer saluted and hurried away to join the other two in the double-bottom store. This compartment held one group of depth-recording instruments for hold compartments on the starboard side. He spoke to the sublieutenant: "Here you are, Sub," and he patted the handwheel of one of the valves. "Open all these valves, but this one first."

The young officer went to work, only too glad to be busy. A good deal of energy was needed, for the valves were operated through long rod gearings.

"Now, Tom," said the commissioned engineer, pulling out his notebook and taking a seat, "will you go down to Number Five Working Space and open T seacock first? There are three other valves there, marked T1, T2, and T3. Open them all wide. Check your depth recorders, and when the mercury in the instruments stops rising you'll know your compartments are full to sea level. Shut all the valves then. I'm staying here to watch this heel indicator."

In less than half an hour the ship was upright and all the valves were closed. Mr. Mayson left to go to damage-control headquarters to record the extent of counterflooding on the flooding board. There were far more men about the decks, but he had reached damage-control headquarters before he realized that the all clear must have sounded. He was about to open the door when he heard the voice of Commander Sands.

"How seriously are we damaged, Mr. Mayson?"

He turned to face the commander. "It's pretty bad along the port side, sir, but I don't think it's vital. Will you come in? I'll show you."

He pushed open the door for the commander and then followed him in. The chief was there, sitting at the damage-control officer's desk, making a note on a signal pad. He looked round quickly as they entered, and glanced at Mr. Mayson's oily boots and trouser legs.

"Don't bring that blasted oil in here!" he shouted. "Go on! Get out!"

There was no doubt that Mr. Mayson had made a mess on the deck. On his previous visit he had spread oil all about. Instinctively he stopped before the large furious figure, then he looked to Commander Sands. "Here you are, sir," and he pointed to the flooding board.

The commander walked over and Mr. Mayson continued: "All these compartments here are flooded, sir. These three oil fuel tanks, and probably these two as well, are open to sea. I have brought the ship upright by flooding these two groups on the starboard side."

The chief sank back into a petulant silence, imposed by his ignorance and the presence of Commander Sands.

"How does this affect our prospects of leaving here?" asked the commander.

"I don't know yet, sir. I'd say the whole ship's side amidships is badly damaged, but this longitudinal bulkhead"—he pointed to the flooding board again—"should hold for a sea voyage. I want to get down with Mr. Ganer as soon as I can and examine the whole inboard side of it. Apart from that, the machinery below will have been badly shaken."

Commander Sands walked slowly to the door, where he paused for a moment to look back at the flooding board. "All right, Mr. Mayson," he said. "Thank you."

The commissioned engineer followed him out and had started to move aft when, Blurp! blurp! blurp! Blurp! blurp! blurp! Blurp! blurp! blurp!

As he turned back towards damage-control headquarters he saw that the chief was already halfway up the nearest ladder. Lieutenant Stanning, who had had to jump out of his way, called after him. The chief shouted his reply from the top of the ladder. "I'm more use alive than dead!"

Lieutenant Stanning stood looking up the ladderway. He wore a steel helmet, for he had taken over the job of standing by at one of the guns. Mr. Mayson spoke into his ear. "Yes," he said, "I know what you're thinking: There's some doubt about that, eh?"

The lieutenant looked round and smiled, then he hurried off to the flight deck.

Mr. Mayson went down to the workshop and was soon

joined by Sublieutenant Kelling. As they stood there waiting for the guns to open up, the chief stoker in charge of the watch below came up from the machinery control room. There was doubt and hesitation in his manner. The watch below had recently come through a nerve-shattering experience. Was he to be left all alone in charge this time?

Then feet appeared on the ladder and the senior engineer came down. The chief stoker turned at once and went below. The senior glanced at the other two officers but said nothing. His face was grim and grey. He followed the chief stoker into the machinery control room.

Mr. Mayson sat on the tool box with Kelling. His heart warmed towards the senior. He wondered if his own face were registering the strain he himself was feeling. He glanced at the silent young man at his side and knew he was in good company. The tough calibre of young Kelling might not have been apparent to many, but Mr. Mayson had already sensed it.

To the surprise of everyone the expected attack did not come. The all clear sounded and the work on repairs was resumed and continued for the rest of the day.

During the night the tenacious dockyard men finished the repairs to the stern. But another task faced the day shift. Careful examination by engineer officers and ratings revealed that the main engines and certain auxiliary machines had been damaged by shock. It was Mr. Langley who reported the state of the main engines to the senior. Certain large important castings had been broken and would require temporary repair before the engines could be moved. And in the boiler rooms the broken oil fuel column was not the only repair job. Mr. Kirklane found certain other castings broken on auxiliary machinery. There was also damage to the refrigerating machinery: Some gas pipe joints had been shaken loose and the gas charge lost.

The senior engineer collected all the information on damage in the early forenoon and took it to the commander (E), who was waiting for it in damage-control headquarters. After about twenty minutes he returned to the engineers' office to find Lieutenant Stanning, Mr. Mayson, and Mr. Langley discussing the situation. He walked straight to his own desk and sat down, obviously deep in thought. After a few minutes he swung his chair round, and the others then saw how sorely perturbed he was.

"Mr. Mayson," he said, "what's your opinion of the damage to the port side? Do you think we can steam with it?"

"Yes, sir, we can steam with it providing everything else is all right."

"That's what I thought, but the chief seems to think we're finished."

"Why? Because of the structural damage?"

"Yes, that and all the other damage, I suppose. He's gone up to see the captain now."

"Well," said Mr. Langley, "the main engines won't stop us. The foreman fitter produced the answer to that damage in less than half an hour." He put on his new eyeglasses and laid a sheet of paper with a pencilled sketch before the senior. "See here, sir; this is the proposed repair." He pointed with a pencil. "These are the fractured castings. They'll drill and tap holes here and here and fit a patch over the crack, then they'll fit angle irons here as stiffeners. They'll shore this part down from the deck head, using timber, and that part from the frames at the side of the engine room. As a temporary repair it couldn't be better; it even allows for expansion of the parts under steam."

The senior took up the sketch and studied it for a minute before handing it back. "I think that's excellent, Mr. Langley. Did the foreman say how long it would take?"

"He said about forty-eight hours if they could work night

and day without interference from air raids."

Lieutenant Stanning chipped in. "If they can repair the main engines, the damage to the auxiliaries won't hold them up."

The senior looked up as Mr. Ganer entered the office. "You're just the man I want to see, Chippie. Any signs of the divers yet?"

"Yes, sir, they're just getting their gear along now, but I don't think they'll be able to tell us much. It's pretty clear to me that the whole side is pushed in abreast those flooded compartments."

"Do you think it would be dangerous to steam with it?"

"No, sir. That longitudinal bulkhead will take any pressure you are likely to get at sea."

"Well, the commander (E) says it's too dangerous. In fact he thinks the ship is in a pretty hopeless state. He was talking about docking her just now."

"Docking her!" said Mr. Ganer bitterly. "What will happen if they dock her? She'll make a better target than ever then! Some use docking her! The hull damage she took yesterday will put her out of active service for the better part of a year!"

"He's right," said Mr. Mayson.

"Well—what are we going to do about it?" asked the senior, looking at them all.

Mr. Mayson caught and held the senior's eyes. "Get the ship out! Your own officers and men are keen to get on with it!"

The senior dropped his eyes. The other officers glanced sharply at Mr. Mayson. The significance of his words—"Your own officers and men"—had struck home to them as it had to the senior. Somehow the chief had to be got out of the way.

Lieutenant Stanning broke the short period of silence. "What Mr. Mayson says is right: The engine room ratings are as keen as we are to see the ship moving. We know you've approached the captain before, sir, about these delaying tactics, but all he could do was balance your report against what the chief had to say, and the chief can be very impressive. I know the captain had a high opinion of his chief engineer—but surely, now that he's seen him beating everyone to the shelter, he'll know who he can rely on and what is best to do to get the ship out."

The senior turned to his desk and picked up his gloves and torch. Without a word he strode away, a man with a purpose.

Repair work had already started in the boiler rooms. Mr. Kirklane's men were busy removing small broken castings to be sent to the dockyard for repair. There was activity in the refrigerating machinery room, too. An ERA, with the help of Stoker Smithers, was checking on the extent of the damage.

The forenoon passed without interruption from the enemy. The senior had not been seen about the ship again after he left to see the captain. He was late arriving for lunch, and as he entered the dining hall he met Lieutenant Stanning, who was leaving.

"Oh, Stanning," he said, "will you tell all the other engineer officers I want to see them in the office after lunch."

"I will, sir. What time?"

The senior was already moving away. He called back, "In about twenty minutes."

He must have hurried over his lunch for he arrived at the office well ahead of time. He spoke to his messenger as he entered. "Close the door, Speedy, and stand outside. Let nobody in."

The engineers were waiting. The senior walked quickly to his own desk and leaned against it. "Well," he said, "there's been a conference this morning. The dockyard men say they can get the ship out, and they want all the help we can give them. They don't intend to dock her.

"There's another thing, and you should keep it to yourselves: We are running short of ammunition and there isn't any more available for our calibre guns. We have enough on board to repel one attack, that's all. The captain and Commander Sands think we should keep what we have in case we need it at sea when we'll have no fighter protection. So now, if the air-raid warning goes we have to evacuate the ship and leave the defence to the shore batteries."

"You mean there'll be nobody left on board at all, sir?" asked Lieutenant Leyton.

"Not a soul. It's intended to make the ship look deserted."

"Then we'll have to shut down the boiler every time, sir," said Mr. Kirklane.

"Yes, and that's why we're here together. We shan't have much time. Let us compare views on the matter."

"Well, the quickest way," said Mr. Langley, "is to shut off the oil sprayers, let the steam pressure drop a little in the boiler, then shut the auxiliary stop valve. The steam in the lines will then run out in the auxiliary machinery."

"That means every man on watch below should have an electric torch in case the lighting goes as he is coming up," observed Mr. Mayson.

"Yes," agreed the senior, "that's one thing. Is there anything else? I have to see Commander Sands. He's waiting to broadcast to the ship's company about it."

"I should think that's all, sir," said Lieutenant Stanning. "There might be a few minor snags we will learn about later on."

"All right, I'd better be off then."

Commander Sands lost no time in broadcasting his instructions for the evacuation of the ship in the event of air-raid alarms. He impressed on all the necessity of getting under cover quickly. Previously many officers and men had scorned the idea of running for it. They had trotted slowly, or walked along. Some had waited in large groups near the entrance to shelters, watching the attacks develop before they sought cover. The commandeer aimed to avoid this: Large groups of men could be spotted on aerial photographs.

It was not long before the organization was tried out. At half past three the alarm sounded, and many of the ship's company went to the tunnels on shore for the first time. Mr. Langley was duty engineer officer for the day and he remained to see the watch below clear after shutting down the boiler. He then made for the nearest shelter. It was a small tunnel that ran straight in at right angles to the cliff face for about ten yards. As he entered it he saw Mr. Mayson and Mr. Kirklane sitting on the floor together on one side. Several officers and men squatted on stones and rubble on the other side. He was unaware that there was a turn in the tunnel. He saw a large candle burning just above Mr. Mayson's head, and he had almost joined his two messmates when he voiced his sentiments: "Hell of a fine place to die in, chaps!"

He was surprised at the men's stony silence. When he saw the turn in the tunnel he knew the reason why. There were two candles burning there, with a crucifix between them. The tunnel curved for about six yards, but the roof had caved in and a pile of rubble sloped down almost to his feet. He could see little of the rubble, for it was covered by brown-skinned men in white canvas suits, some standing, some sitting. All held their caps in their hands. One man stood with his back to Mr. Langley, holding a book so that the light from the candles shone upon it. He was the prayer leader. He spoke a few words and the others repeated in very low voices. Mr. Langley removed his service cap and sat down.

There was no attack that day, just a reconnaissance flight by the enemy. Captain Graham and Commander Sands were glad that there had been enough time to make the flight deck look worse than it really was. "Jerry" would be waiting eagerly to hear that the carrier was definitely knocked out. He would need that news to soften the blow of the previous day, when very few of his planes had returned. The men in those planes must have seen so many bombs bursting—apparently on the target—that they would have been correspondingly bursting with good news when they arrived at their home base.

Before noon on the following day the enemy appeared to be happy about the results of his attacks. A sneering voice broadcast to the world that Malta had now become the graveyard of Britain's proud new ship. The gallant Luftwaffe had gone in to attack and had come away leaving the ship resting on the harbour bottom, a shattered and useless wreck. Nothing was said about German losses.

While the enemy was broadcasting his news, the so-called shattered wreck looked more like a beehive.

After arranging with the dockyard workmen for the repair of the damage to the paint store, Mr. Ganer and Mr. Mayson went over to lunch. Most of the officers had finished their meal and were resting in the lounge. The two latecomers were not to dine in comfort. The main course had just appeared before them when the air-raid siren sounded. Officers and stewards started to move at once.

Mr. Mayson looked to his messmate. "Well," he said, "I'm damned if I'm going to let this go cold." He stood up, placed his bread plate over the lunch, and carried it away; and Mr. Ganer followed suit.

They were now nearest to the deep tunnel frequented by the commander (E), so they hurried towards it. Before entering the dark passage they took one last look at the sky. It appeared to be clear of planes. Mr. Mayson then led the way underground, using his torch, for the lighting system had been put out of action when a heavy bomb struck the top of the cliff. After advancing about fifty yards they reached a cross passage running at right angles to the main tunnel. "Ah, here we are, Chippie," said Mr. Mayson.

A faint glimmer of light shone in the passage to the left, and they found it coming from a large storeroom inside which several of the ship's officers were sitting on packing cases. Among these were the first lieutenant, the senior engineer, Mr. Prout, and Mr. Langley, whose torch supplied what light there was in the room. The senior moved over to allow Mr. Mayson to sit beside him, while Mr. Ganer joined Mr. Langley. There was little conversation; all were just waiting.

The two newcomers soon resumed eating; their torches hung around their necks and shone down on the plates. For a time there was no sound save the click of knives and forks. Then the first lieutenant spoke. He had been getting some quiet amusement from watching the two.

"Damned bad manners on the part of the enemy to interfere with your lunch like this," he said.

Mr. Mayson looked up with a smile. "Yes, they might have waited ten minutes or so."

It was then, as he finished speaking, that he became aware of a figure sitting apart from all others. It was crouching in a corner of the room. Had it not been such a bulky figure, and had that figure not been dressed in white, he would not have seen it in the gloom. As it was, the sight startled an exclamation from him.

"What the—"

"Sh-h-h," said the senior engineer.

Mr. Mayson went on eating. In that silent room he felt as if he were in the presence of something foul. He did not quite finish his lunch, for his appetite flagged as his mind turned the situation over. The commander (E) might be suffering from stark, panicky fear, but he had used his brains in his selection of that corner of the room. Any bomb blast finding its way along the tunnel would need to make one extra turn at right angles to get near him.

Soon the all clear sounded, and it brought relief to Captain Graham and Commander Sands, who had taken shelter in a tunnel nearer the ship. The prospects of getting the vessel away were improving. If the enemy did not see through their bluff and attack again within a day or two, the German reconnaissance planes would come over to seek in vain.

The dockyard men were progressing favourably with their repairs to the main engines, and many defects in auxiliary machines had already been completed. All the officers and men of the engine room department were now eagerly seeking damage and carrying out any repairs the resources of the ship allowed them to take on. Mr. Mayson interested himself in the repairs of the refrigerating machinery. By coincidence he had just left the machinery room when Commander Sands stopped him.

"Do you know anything about the damage to the refrigeration, Mr. Mayson?"

The comissioned engineer smiled. "Well, strangely enough, sir, I've just left there."

"Are there any hopes of getting it going?"

"I think so, sir, but we have to stop leaks in the gas circuit and test the system before trying the machine."

"Can you get it going by four o'clock, do you think? You see, the paymaster says the commander (E) has told him we shall have to land the meat. The point is that suitable transportation for the job will be available only at about four o'clock today, and I must decide by then what to do."

"But the room temperatures are still well below freezing, sir, and the removal of the meat will be a big job. There are several tons on board."

"I know the job will take time we can ill afford; that's why

I want to avoid it. Will you let me know the situation at four o'clock?"

"Yes, sir, I will."

Mr. Mayson went back to the refrigerating machinery room. An engine room artificer was busy tightening up the flanges of the gas circuit piping, and Stoker Smithers was setting a gas flask into position, preparing to recharge the system. The engineer spoke to the ERA: "Has the commander (E) been down here?"

A smile wreathed the ERA's face. "Oh no, sir. He never comes down here, but I saw him once today. I was on the wharf when the alarm sounded and I made for the tunnel. Then I heard him shout behind me: 'Come out of there! That's for officers only!' "

Mr. Mayson couldn't withhold a smile. "Well, if you meet no further snags can you get this machine running by four o'clock?"

"We can run it before then, sir. These are the last two joints to make good and then we'll be ready for charging."

At that the paymaster entered the room. "Why," he said looking at the gauges for the cold and cool rooms, "the temperatures are quite low!"

"They are, sir," said the engineer, "and they will stay below freezing point for days with all those frozen carcases in there."

"Then there's no need to land the meat. Why would commander (E) even suggest it?"

Mr. Mayson knew the reason. The commander (E) was concerned only with keeping *his* hide remote from danger. Why risk *his* neck steaming her out?

"We expect to have the machine running soon, sir," said the engineer.

"All is well then," said the paymaster, and off he went.

Mr. Mayson left the room, and on his way aft he met the

senior's messenger. "Can you come to the office, sir?" said Speedy. "The senior wants to see you."

He found the senior alone in the office. "Hello, sir, did you want me?"

The senior rose from his chair. "Well, I did, but it's Mr. Ganer who really wants you. The commander (E) has stopped the men from working on the paint store. He says the bows will have to come up higher before it's safe to weld the patches on, and that the anchors and cable gear will have to come out to lighten the ship for'ard."

"Oh, hell! Here we go again! Where's Mr. Ganer, sir?"

"He's gone to see Commander Sands. He says it will take two or three days to get the cable out and back."

"Yes, sir, and we can produce the same effect by transferring oil fuel."

"Do you think we need to lighten the ship for'ard?"

"No, sir. The holes are well above waterline."

"That's what Mr. Ganer says, and he can't see what the chief is concerned about."

"Can't he?" said Mr. Mayson fiercely. "We should all be able to see it by now. Excuse me!" He grabbed his cap from the desk and tore out of the office.

He found the warrant shipwright talking to Commander Sands. The two were walking slowly along the wharf towards the bow of the ship. The commander moved with long slow strides; his head hung down, and he nodded occasionally to show that he was listening. As the commissioned engineer joined them Mr. Ganer spoke up.

"Here's Mr. Mayson, sir. Perhaps he can offer some suggestion."

"Perhaps he can," said the commander, looking up. "How about it, Mr. Mayson: Do we need to take the chain and cable out in order to bring the bow up?"

"Definitely not, sir. We can bring the bow up quickly, if necessary, by transferring oil fuel."

"Well, come along. We'll take a look at this job."

When they reached the dockyard lighter secured at the port side of the bow, several Maltese workmen there rose to their feet. Near the ship's side were two sets of welding apparatus and several pieces of sheet steel, cut to size to cover holes in the ship's plating. The largest hole was eighteen inches in diameter and two feet above the waterline, with several smaller holes above it.

The chargeman of welders had drawn near as the commander inspected the job. Commander Sands turned to him. "Are you in charge here?"

"Yes, sah."

"Do you think there is any danger in welding these patches on?"

"No sah, but de engineer stop us. If you tell me to work, soon we finish."

The commander turned to Mr. Ganer. "What about the danger of fire? The commander (E) says the oils and paints will be set alight."

"The store has been cleared of everything, sir. There's nothing anywhere near that can burn. We have two fire extinguishers here that we won't need."

Commander Sands spoke to the chargeman. "Go ahead, finish the job."

When Mr. Mayson returned on board he found the refrigeration plant running while the system was being charged with gas, and soon the plant was operating satisfactorily on the cold and cool rooms. He spoke to the ERA and Smithers as he left the room. "Well done, you two. Commander Sands will be glad to know about this."

Commander Sands was not in his cabin or his office, so Mr. Mayson went to the engineers' office intending to send a note by messenger; but that was not necessary, for the commander was there, and so was Captain Graham. They appeared to be discussing some important matter with the senior engineer. The writer and the messengers stood outside the door. Mr. Mayson was about to leave when Commander Sands called to him.

"Yes, Mr. Mayson. Did you want me?"

"Only to report that the refrigerating plant is working now."

"Oh, splendid! Will you let the paymaster know?"

"I will, sir."

Later that day Mr. Mayson saw the significance of that conversation in the engineers' office. He was standing at the bar in the hotel on shore, enjoying a nightcap with Mr. Langley and Mr. Kirklane. All three were about to retire when Lieutenant Stanning joined them.

"Have you chaps heard the latest?"

"No, what about?" asked Mr. Langley.

"About our chief engineer himself. The surgeon commander has put him sick on shore. The captain has had enough of him."

CHAPTER 20

After breakfast all officers left the hotel with their baggage and returned on board, for the dockyard night shift had completed the repairs to the after part of the ship, and the officers' messes, galley, pantries, and cabins were ready for use.

The only dockyard men now on board were those working on the main engine repairs. They were working against time, yet too much haste could be expensive in just that commodity: time.

For Captain Graham the daylight period crept slowly by; these were hours of extreme danger, and he knew he must endure another full day of anxiety before the vessel could make her bid for safety.

He stood on the bridge and watched the sun set, and he stayed there till darkness fell. The whole day had passed and the dread sound of the air-raid siren had not assailed his ears. He went to his sea cabin somewhat lighter at heart.

By early morning the work below was finished. All the machinery was tried with success. The main engines could only be moved a few revolutions each way, for there was danger of putting too great a strain on the wires holding the ship to the wharf.

With the start of the new day there was little to do but wait. When Captain Graham rose from his bed there were twelve more dangerous daylight hours to be lived through.

Each hour was to seem longer than the one before, so that the short twilight period seemed an age.

During the forenoon the ship's company was allowed to know that the vessel was to leave when darkness fell. More frequently now, men looked at the sky. The day was ideal for a bombing attack. Again there were a few white clouds high above, but the sun shone warm and clear. The captain himself was seen to walk to the side of the bridge and take a long look at the sky. He knew, as did the ship's company, that the locating device would detect approaching aircraft long before they could be seen, and yet—up there the danger lay; he must look in that direction. If only the day had been different. Had there been rough weather and low visibility, or heavy rain, how much anxiety it would have saved him. There was probably only one officer in the ship who was content about the weather; that was Mr. Ganer. He was anxious about the stern of the ship. He was not sure that it would stand up to high speeds in bad weather.

Lunchtime came without incident, and the topic of conversation at the table was the forthcoming trip. The officers were more aware than the men of how risky it would be. Now, with the sun high overhead and the vessel alongside the wharf, she made a good target, but at sea, she would make a better one. There would be no shore defences to meet the attacking planes, nor would there be fighter planes to protect the ship, for she was no longer able to operate as a carrier. She carried only enough ammunition to repel one attack; thereafter she would have to rely on evasion, and on the antiaircraft fire of her escort. It seemed that if the enemy should spot her at sea she would be doomed to a sudden, watery grave.

Lieutenant Stanning made out the steaming orders before lunch. The watch was due to go below, to the engine and boiler rooms, at two o'clock. Mr. Mayson was on watch duty, and after lunch he went once more to damage-control headquarters to check the flooding board. He wanted to know what the balance of oil fuel and water was. He was about to leave when Lieutenant Stanning looked in.

"Hello. What's doing old chap?"

The lieutenant walked in and sat on one of the desks with the air of a man who wants to chat.

"Not much," said Mr. Mayson. "Doing the best we can to keep her afloat if she gets walloped again."

"Well, as I see it, if we don't get spotted at sea we'll get away, providing the engines stick it. If we do get spotted we might as well call it a day and apply for a harp apiece."

"That may be so if we meet another heavy air attack, but can the Germans deliver one after their losses?"

"That's it—can they? And can they do it in time? I'm glad they haven't yet developed a locating device like ours. From what I hear, the enemy has to sight us before four o'clock tomorrow afternoon. If he does, the reconnaissance report can be made and the bombers can leave their bases to overtake us before dark. If he doesn't sight us by that time we should get clear; that is, if we can maintain a speed of twenty-four knots."

"Well, in that case I think we have a fair chance of getting away, but if a reconnaissance plane comes over the harbour here early tomorrow and finds the bird has flown, the Germans will track us down with everything they can put in the air. It's a role of the dice—the luck of the draw."

The watch below had a difficult task to perform. Steam had to be raised in all boilers, but the boilers had to be kept from emitting smoke. In the event of an air-raid alarm it would take some time to shut down all the boilers and machinery required for steaming the ship. If an enemy plane sighted smoke in the vicinity of the ship's funnel the game would be up. But the watch below raised steam without generating smoke, and the afternoon went by while the sun crept slowly down.

About the ship there was no excitement. Two more hours to go before darkness. Success was so near, but no man dared show too much cheer about it. Death and destruction could yet strike suddenly from the blue and put an end to any foolish counting of chickens. Men looked at each other quietly now, and those who felt the tension keenest breathed less deeply than normal. The men in the machinery spaces felt it least, for they were too busy; they were remote from that still, glaring daylight above. Captain Graham must have felt it most. He stood and watched the flaming ball in the sky creep slowly down. After a long, long, weary time, it seemed, it dipped down behind the rooftops of buildings on the high ground to the west. Little time left now—but enough—for the enemy to strike his blow. The captain waited, and he waited, until at long last in the gathering gloom he turned from the bridge to go to his sea cabin. Then he heard the voice of the senior engineer, and the words charmed his ears like sweet music.

"Main engines and steering gear ready, sir."

Now there was a change about the ship. Men talked and bustled about. Here was action; one could now sing and laugh and let go. A huge store of energy had been released. Gangways were lifted on to the wharf, berthing wires were hauled inboard with great zeal, and lines were taken from the two tugs, which were to pull the ship clear of the wharfside.

Soon the great vessel was moving under her own power. Slowly she went astern and at the same time turned her bows toward the harbour entrance. There was a brief pause while the engines were stopped, and then she was off. Gradually she gained speed. The dim form of the customhouse slipped by astern, and throughout the ship men's hearts were singing: *We're off, chaps! We're moving!*

After a few minutes the vessel made the turn at the

breakwater and entered the open sea. At once the captain gave the order for half speed ahead. Below in the engine room the ERAs swung open on the great manoeuvring valves and the whine of the engine gearing increased. Now was the testing time. Anxious engineers and engine room ratings hurried around the machinery, checking on pressure gauges, feeling bearings, seeking trouble yet hoping not to find it. The slightest unusual noise gave cause for anxiety. When the revolution telegraph first moved men started at the sound.

Ding, ding, ding, ding, ding!

Up crept the pointer in short, equally spaced jerks, and with each movement the bell of the instrument rang, calling attention to the dial.

Ding, ding, ding, ding, ding, ding, ding!

On and on crept the pointer: One-thirty revolutions. One-forty. One-fifty. The men on the manoeuvring valves opened up steam to the engines and checked the turbometers which recorded the speed of the shafts.

Ding, ding, ding, ding, ding, ding, ding, ding!

One-sixty, one-seventy, one-eighty revolutions. The noise of the gearing altered; it became louder and higher pitched; it mingled with the hiss of steam at the turbine glands and with the low hum of the many auxiliary engines. The ERAs on the manoeuvring valves opened up, increasing the speed slowly, and before they had reached the required one hundred and eighty revolutions the telegraph rang again:

Ding, ding, ding, ding, ding!

One-ninety revolutions. Two hundred. Two-ten.

Now can she take it? the men wondered. *There are no unusual noises. A little vibration has set in. How about those temporary repairs? those shores? and that weakened stern?*

Time went by. Up and up crept the speed. All bearings

were checked, right through to the stern glands aft. *No trouble! She's sticking it!*

Ding, ding, ding, ding!

Two-twenty, two-thirty, two-thirty-four revolutions.

The senior engineer stood in the machinery control room and watched the speed indicators for each shaft. Slowly the pointers crept up. Behind him stood Lieutenant Leyton casting a roving eye over all the other instruments. Occasionally the senior moved one or another of the boiler room telegraphs calling for more oil pressure or more sprayers on each boiler in the compartment concerned. Several minutes went by before the pointers of the speed indicators reached the two-thirty-four mark. There they stopped, wavering slightly.

"That's it," said the senior. He stepped back. "We're making about twenty-six knots. The captain won't put her up any higher." He walked behind a small desk in the centre of the room and sat down where he could see all the pressure gauges. He sat down in an easy chair, the one the chief had used in damage-control headquarters. That chair was to serve some useful purpose after all; even the headrest was to justify its existence, for the senior was to spend many, many long hours before he felt free to leave the machinery control room.

The sight of the senior in that particular chair brought forth a remark from Lieutenant Leyton.

"I wonder how the chief is tonight. He has some sweet young nurse to look after him, I suppose."

The senior looked up in surprise. "Oh, no," he said, "he's still in the hotel. Someone in the wardroom—I forget who—was saying that he called in there for a drink last night, and the chief was at the bar yarning away quite happily to some of the officers from the shore base."

"Oh. I thought he was sick in the hospital."

There came the sound of feet on the ladder; a pair of

brown overall trouser legs appeared and Mr. Kirklane entered the room. He looked to the senior.

"Everything's all right below, sir. There's a good deal of vibration back in the steering flat, but nothing to worry about. Mr. Ganer is back there and he seems happy about the stern, so long as we don't get bad weather."

"Thank you, Mr. Kirklane. We're off to a good start now."

Yes, the ship was off to a good start. The captain was trying to get her as far away as possible during those precious hours of darkness, but he was using discretion. The vessel was steaming well. She might do more speed, but better let well enough alone.

About the ship damage-control equipment had been placed in readiness for instant use, but the captain and Commander Sands had decided to let the men off watch sleep during the night: Tomorrow might be the hardest day of all. Mr. Mayson thought it better to sleep in damage-control headquarters, so he had a camp bed rigged there. He had the middle watch to keep—midnight till four in the morning—but he intended to get an hour or so of sleep before going below. As he walked forward from the mess, soon after ten o'clock, he lent his ears to the sound of the propeller shafts beneath; the healthy rumble made him think hopefully of that little home of his in Plymouth. He felt in his heart that his home had escaped the blitz. *Bound to get home after this*, he thought. *The ship will need a big refit.* He thought tenderly of that patient woman, his wife, who would quietly and unobtrusively make a fuss over him. For days before he reached home she would be preparing for his arrival: airing his civilian clothes, cleaning his shoes, doing his laundry all over again herself. The most comfortable chair beside the fire would be for him, his slippers beside it. How grand it would be! He felt tired, so tired, but happy in his thoughts. The boy was growing up; there would be grand times to be had with him outdoors.

And how nice it would be to listen to the chatter of the two girls!

He reached damage-control headquarters in a happy frame of mind and was soon undressed and into his pajamas. He placed his life belt, gloves, and electric torch beside his shoes. These he might need in a hurry. He stepped over to switch off the lights; then Fate played an old trick of hers: the trick that shatters rosy dreams.

The door burst open and a stoker messenger called excitedly: "Mr. Mayson, sir! The senior wants you at once! We're getting water in the oil fuel!"

"Right. Tell him I'm coming."

The commissioned engineer moved rapidly. He pulled on his socks and tucked the bottom of his pajama legs inside them. He put on his overall suit, his cap and shoes, and without lacing up the latter ran below carrying his torch and gloves; his life belt was forgotten. When he reached the machinery control room the senior was hopping about, altering the boiler room telegraphs. The boiler steam pressure had fallen a little and the speed of the ship was reduced.

"Where's Lathom, sir? Have you sent for him?" asked Mr. Mayson.

"He's forward somewhere. I believe this happened since he tried to change over tanks. He told me he was going to."

The senior was calling his replies as he leapt about, still altering the telegraphs. Mr. Mayson moved up the ladder at once, calling back, "I'll see him, sir!"

He hurried forward. He knew the tanks Lathom had in use at the start were situated beneath the servery flat. He reached the flat just as Lathom came up from below, followed by two of his oil fuel party.

"They'll be all right for a while now, sir," said Lathom. "I've changed back to the tanks under here."

Mr. Mayson relaxed. Lathom had done the right thing.

The little man always changed over from tanks in use while he still had a reserve of oil in them. Now he was back on them and working on that reserve.

"How long will these tanks keep us going?" asked the engineer.

"About three hours, sir, at this speed."

"Good. We have time to think. Bring your oil fuel chart along to damage-control headquarters."

Lathom hurried away to the double-bottom store to get the chart, and a few minutes later he joined Mr. Mayson, who had pushed his camp bed aside and was waiting.

"Here you are, sir," said the chief stoker, "these are the tanks in use. I had these other three back here as standby tanks, but now there's water coming from all of them."

"But you tested them for water only the other day."

"I tested all the tanks, sir, the day after the last attack. Look"; and he pointed with a pencil to the chart. "These three standby tanks under the engine rooms and these starboard wing tanks were clear of water. Then when we tested these four double-bottom tanks and found them clear of water we knew we had enough oil to get us to Alexandria."

"Yes, that's so, Lathom. And now—are these readings on the chart the ones you took when you tested for water?"

"Yes, sir."

"Right. Now there are two things I want you to do. First, put reliable men to check the depth readings on the standby tanks again. I know the ship is rolling slightly, but they must try to sound the tanks as she reaches even keel. I want you, personally, to sound the starboard wing tanks again. They don't hold much, but I expect they will be clear of water. Using them may give us the time to find more oil."

"All right, sir."

While Lathom was away on the job Mr. Mayson went to the machinery control room to brief the senior engineer on the problem so that he could meet inquiries from the captain. While the ship steamed steadily on, he laid a drawing on the desk before the senior, who had a good knowledge of the intricate system of pipes. He saw the problem, and the gravity of it, and was well satisfied with the steps taken by the oil fuel party.

The commissioned engineer went back to damage-control headquarters and pored over the drawings. He must prevent water from entering the tanks in use. At the same time certain parts of the system, now isolated by closed valves, must be used when oil was to be transferred from other tanks.

Time was precious. He felt sure those starboard wing tanks were clear of water. They were the most remote from the bomb damage. There was one lead of suction pipe along the starboard side. It curved over forward and joined the suction pipe from the tanks in use. The chances were that this pipe was undamaged, and since the oil level in the wing tanks was above that in the tanks in use, it would only be a matter of running the oil down. The important thing was to see that oil was allowed to run down into only one of the tanks in use, so that if there was water present only one of the boiler rooms would be out of action. He checked the system again, carefully noting the valves to be opened and those to be kept shut. If Lathom came back and said that those starboard tanks had gained considerably, he would have to think again, and he had only three hours to find good oil. He might have to ask the senior to ease down speed to conserve fuel.

Lathom returned carrying an oil fuel measuring tape and placed his notebook on the desk. There was a touch of eagerness in his voice. "Here you are, sir; there's hardly any difference in the readings. Not more than two inches in any of the tanks."

"Two inches!" Mr. Mayson was smiling with relief. With the slight roll of the ship, and allowing for expansion of oil owing to the heat of the boiler rooms and engine rooms, the readings were excellent.

"Well done, Lathom," he said. "If there's any water in them, it isn't enough to worry about."

"No, sir, but we'll have to be careful when we transfer the oil, and we should sound those four double-bottom tanks aft again."

"Yes, as soon as we can. And now let's see how long this oil in the wing tanks will last." He made a rapid calculation and scribbled a figure at the bottom of the page. "About six hours. Do you agree?"

Lathom picked up the book and ran his pencil over the figures.

"Yes, sir; about right at this speed."

"Good. Now, let's see."

For several minutes they pored over the drawing of the oil fuel suction system. It was decided to run down oil from the forward starboard wing tank into the tank supplying the adjacent boiler room. Mr. Mayson would go to that boiler room and check on the burning of the oil fuel. If the oil sprayers continued to burn for fifteen minutes after the running down started, they could assume no water was present. They could then open the necessary valves to allow oil to run down into the tanks supplying the other boiler rooms. They went away to start the job and twenty minutes later Lathom joined Mr. Mayson in the boiler room.

"All right, sir," he said. "I started running down at five minutes to twelve."

"That's fine. What time is it now by your watch?"

Lathom pushed back his overall cuff. "Six minutes past twelve, sir."

Mr. Mayson waited for a further ten minutes while the fires still burned brightly.

"Well, I think we're winning, Lathom."

They left the boiler room together. Mr. Mayson told Lathom to call the remainder of the oil fuel party and to employ them on the job of running down the oil from each of the starboard wing tanks in turn, using the same precautions each time. Soon Lathom had three men trained to carry out the work correctly, and he then rejoined Mr. Mayson in damage-control headquarters.

They had to find a way to pump the good oil from the three standby tanks under the engine rooms before seven-thirty in the morning or the ship would stop at sea, and they knew that the suction lines must be damaged somewhere and letting water in. They worked together over the chart of that intricate suction pipe system, seeking a way to draw oil from a given tank; shutting this bulkhead valve, opening the cross connection and that bypass; opening this suction valve and closing that isolating valve; trying to pump oil from one standby tank to one boiler room.

And they did try one tank on one boiler room after another with no success. It was necessary to arrange that, should the fires go out in the boiler room under trial, the other two boiler rooms would be ready to meet the increased demand on them for steam. Hours slipped by while Lathom and his men, under the direction of the engineer, used different routes through the suction system. Time after time they went to one or another of the boiler rooms with hope in their hearts. And each time the fires would burn steadily for a few minutes, then, when it seemed they were getting good oil, the flames would disappear and a loud hissing noise would indicate that water was entering the now-lifeless boiler fronts. Lathom would change back to the original oil suction line, and after several minutes the oil sprays would burn again, ignited by the mass of red-hot brickwork in the furnaces.

By 5:00 A.M. the men of the oil fuel party were tired and

discouraged. The continuous climbing up and down vertical ladders through several decks had made them leg weary. Mr. Mayson, tired at the start, was dragging his feet. The oil in the tanks in use was dangerously low, and it seemed that when full daylight spread over the sea the great ship would lie powerless, unable even to fire her guns.

But the commissioned engineer and Lathom still had a glimmer of hope. They had not tried everything yet.

Once more they pored over the oil fuel drawing. The plan now seemed to be covered with ticks and crosses. Methodically they had ascertained, as a result of trial, which pipes were letting in water and which were not.

"Here we are then, Lathom," said the engineer. "We know this centreline suction pipe is good to here, because we can pump oil from the forward tanks now in use."

"Yes, sir."

"And there are three good tanks back here?"

"Yes, sir, but when we open the centreline to any one of them we get water."

"That's so, and here's where we are getting somewhere." Mr. Mayson placed his forefingers a few inches apart on the drawing. "Between here and here the centreline is low down in the bilges and passes over flooded double-bottom tanks."

The little chief stoker looked down in silence. His active mind was working fast. "Could one of the suction valves to the flooded tanks be leaking, sir? I know they're all closed tight."

"It could possibly be a broken casting as the valve seat within the valve box, but more likely the suction pipe is damaged and letting bilge water in. The same jolt that damaged the machinery would cause that. Can we bypass that section of the line?"

"We can keep that bulkhead valve shut, sir, and shut this after one to isolate the flooded section. Then open this cross connection to starboard and—"

"That's it, Lathom. Go down the centreline aft to here, then over to starboard, and aft along the starboard line, back to centre, and then aft on the centreline. All around the garden, so to speak. We've got it! How's the time?"

"Five to six, sir."

The engineer jumped to his feet. New hope filled him with new energy. "Go on, Lathom. Get started. I have to speak to the senior."

Many times during the night the senior had sent down a messenger with a note asking Mr. Mayson how the work was proceeding. After the first good news of the oil supply from the starboard tanks Mr. Mayson's replies had been less and less encouraging. The captain knew of the situation and was awaiting advice from the senior as to whether he should reduce speed. Mr. Mayson went to make the situation clear to the senior. It now seemed certain that the oil in those tanks could be brought into use.

When the senior knew of the situation he informed the captain by telephone.

It was nearly six-thirty when Mr. Mayson stood once again on the boiler room plates and watched the steady flames at the oil sprayers. Lathom kept referring to his watch. It seemed that the battle was won.

And then the dread result came: The sprayers flickered and went out. From the dark boiler fronts came the loud hissing noise of water in the sprayer cones.

Up on the bridge in the early morning light the captain, Commander Sands, and the officer of the watch gazed in dismay at the steady outpouring of white smoke telling of distress below and advertising the ship's presence in dangerous waters. Any enemy aircraft would spot them from a great distance as the day brightened.

In the boiler room Mr. Mayson and Lathom gazed on in

silence. Lathom's heart was in his boots; Mr. Mayson suddenly felt old and weary.

Was this the end? The engineer had expected some water from certain parts of the pipe system, parts that were intact but through which water had been drawn on previous trials; but now water was entering the furnace in a steady stream. His mind's eye could see that smoke pouring from the funnel. They may already have been spotted from the air. Soon now there would be no steam power—or power of any kind—in the ship, and she would lie idle on the sea, a sitting duck, awaiting annihilation. This—after all the blood, toil, sweat—yes, and the tears! A sneering voice would broadcast it to world, and "How now, Britannia?"

Anger surged in the breast of the engineer, reviving his flagging strength. By God, he would not give in yet! He looked over at Lathom. The little chief stoker leaned on a vice bench, tired mentally and physically, gazing at the dark, lifeless fronts of the boilers. Perhaps he felt the eyes of the engineer upon him, for he turned his drooping head and met Mr. Mayson's gaze for a moment before looking wearily down. The engineer had started to cross the floor plates to speak to him when a muffled bump, accompanied by a flicker of flame at one of the sprayers, jerked them both to attention. The chief stoker of the watch hurried to the boiler fronts. "They're coming on again, sir!" he shouted, moving the air flaps to adjust the air supply.

Lathom was transformed at once into an energetic individual. As the sprayers flickered and came on one after the other, he hurried about helping the chief stoker of the watch to adjust the air supply. Soon the boiler was operating normally and the little man turned to the engineer, his face alight with pleasure. Mr. Mayson smiled in return and sat down on a tool box while the cloud vanished. He remained there for a moment, relaxed and at peace, before rising to speak over the telephone to the senior engineer.

The three standby tanks were now available for use, and they contained enough oil to last eight hours. The battle was not yet won: Those four tanks aft of the standbys had to be brought into use if the ship was to reach Alexandria.

In damage-control headquarters Lathom sat with the oil fuel chart before him. "We'd better sound those four tanks again, sir, before we try the pump on them."

Mr. Mayson nodded. "Yes, Lathom, as soon as we can. Those tanks are near the damaged area." Then he did a strange thing: With several chairs nearby, he sat on the deck with his back to the bulkhead and took off his shoes. He turned his socks inside out then put them and his shoes back on his feet.

Lathom answered a knock at the door, and when he turned back into the room he was smiling and carrying two cups of cocoa. "Here you are, sir. The leading stoker made this for us."

"God bless him," said the engineer, lifting a grimy hand to take the cup.

When Lathom returned to damage-control headquarters after sounding the four tanks, he spoke with some alarm. "There's water at the bottom of all those tanks, sir. Look at the soundings!"

The engineer checked the two sets of figures. One sounding had increased six inches, another four and a half, and the other two five inches each. He stood deep in thought, and Lathom spoke again. He was surprised that the engineer was taking it calmly.

"It *is* water, sir. I tested it with water-finding paste on the sounding tape."

Mr. Mayson nodded pensively. "I'm glad you did. Obviously that water is leaking in slowly through rivets shaken loose in the ship's bottom; and here's what we can do about it: The bilge pump suction to each tank is well below the oil pump suction. Put the engine room bilge pump on the tank that had gained the least water and discharge the water overboard. When we've lowered the level enough in the tank we'll try it on one boiler room. If we get good oil at the burner we'll transfer the oil through the filling system to those good starboard wing tanks we've emptied, and we'll have enough oil to last until well after dark tonight."

Lathom's eyes lit up. "Yes, sir. If we lower the level by seven inches, would that do?"

"It might, but with this slight roll on the ship there could be quite a mixture of oil and water low in the tank. If she smokes, we'll have to pump more overboard and try again."

CHAPTER 21

The sun rose in a clear sky, turning the sea into a vast sheet of beautiful blue. Down on that sheet four objects were moving, one large and three small, behind which white extensions tailed away, widening and becoming less white until they merged with the blue sea. The large object was rectangular in shape. It moved in the centre of a triangle formed by the other three, which were sharp pointed and had rounded sterns. The large rectangular form was the target, the aircraft carrier; the other three were the escorting destroyers, gallant little ships shepherding the wounded giant to safety.

There was no doubt that the giant was wounded. It advertised its presence by belching up smoke occasionally. The smoke would pour out for several minutes, changing colour from white to brown, then to jet black and back to white. From the bridge Captain Graham watched each outpour with anxious eyes. It was a reminder to him of the struggle going on below, and a menace to a small fleet hoping to avoid detection from the air.

Below in the machinery control room the senior engineer moved slowly about, keeping himself awake. Overnight he had rested his limbs in the easy chair, but not once had he rested his eyes. And farther below, the oil fuel party still fought the battle.

It seemed to Mr. Mayson that the forenoon was well

along before one of the leaky tanks had been successfully put into use supplying one boiler room. There'd be no more smoke again in daylight. He heaved a great sigh of relief. He then took stock of his manpower and sent half of the oil fuel party, including Lathom, to get some sleep.

It was at this stage that Mr. Kirklane began to ease the strain on the commissioned engineer. He dogged the older man's footsteps, relieved him of tools, took directions and instructions from him, and, after grasping their significance, saw them carried out by the oil fuel party.

Mr. Mayson felt he could rest awhile. He sat on a valve wheel, watching the stroke of the bilge pump Mr. Kirklane had left running pumping water from an oil tank. He felt pleasantly at peace. The steady drone of the main turbine engine was lulling him to sleep.

Then something jerked him to his feet. It registered as a shrieking voice of doom.

Blurp! blurp! blurp! Crash! fire! floods!—Blurp! Blood! stench! death!—Blurp! Blurp! blurp! blurp!

He moved to go up the after ladder, then saw feet coming down and Mr. Kirklane joined him. As they stood facing each other Mr. Mayson spoke, but his voice was hoarse and could barely be heard.

"Well, Jim, this must be it. We've got it coming. Anyway, we did our best."

There was a puzzled look on the younger man's face. "How do you mean, Harry?"

"How do I mean! Why, didn't you hear action stations sounding just now?"

"Yes, I did—but didn't you hear the pipe from the bridge before that?"

"Afraid not. I must have dozed off."

"Well, that pipe told us we would go to action stations for exercise at eleven o'clock."

"For exercise!" Mr. Mayson gave a short, gasping laugh of relief and sat down again on the valve wheel.

At noon Lathom reappeared. The little man had spent two hours lying on the floor in the double-bottom store—two hours of solid sleep, he said. He had washed his face and hands and claimed to be feeling as fresh as a daisy. Mr. Mayson explained to him the progress made on the job and then both of them took half an hour off for the midday meal. In the afternoon the other half of the oil fuel party rested while those who had slept in the forenoon came back on job.

Darkness fell long before Mr. Mayson knew of it so he didn't realize that the most perilous part of the voyage was over. In need of refreshment, he appeared at the door of the mess—a grimy, unshaven creature—and asked the steward for a whisky. He was surprised to find the place almost deserted, for he thought it must be about suppertime. He stood at the door and drank his whisky, and then he saw the clock in the mess: five minutes to ten!

"Gosh!" he said, "is that the time?"

"Yes," replied the steward. "That clock's right, sir."

The steward made a sandwich for him and he went away eating it.

It was nearing midnight when the struggle was over. There was enough oil available to last for sixteen hours, and the ship was due to arrive in Alexandria the following forenoon. He went to the machinery control room to report to the senior. That officer looked a little brighter. With the steadily improving situation he had relaxed in the easy chair and fallen asleep occasionally for short periods when another engineer was present. Now he was a happy man. Mr. Mayson had rung up from the boiler room to tell him the good news, and that news had already been passed to the captain.

The commissioned engineer handed the senior a sheet

of paper showing the tanks in use, the ones available, and the order in which they would be used.

"Thank you," said the senior.

Footsteps sounded on the ladder and Lathom came halfway down. "Will you want me again, sir?" he asked Mr. Mayson.

"No, Lathom. You go off to bed. Have you packed up the others?"

"Yes, sir."

A voice called from the top of the ladder. Lathom looked up and then moved quickly down into the control room: Commander Sands was coming down.

This was an unusual thing—for an executive officer to walk into the engine room department alone. But these were unusual times, and the commander came with a definite purpose. He reached the foot of the ladder and looked about at the unfamiliar surroundings. He was bursting with enthusiasm. His eyes rested on the commissioned engineer. He stepped quickly over and patted that tired officer on the back. "Well done, Mr. Mayson!" he cried. He caught the senior's eye. "Well done, senior!" He looked about and saw Lathom and walked over and rested a hand on the little man's shoulder and looked straight into his face. "Well done, Lathom. It's been a damned good show!"

Commander Sands put a glow into the hearts of three tired men. Those other tired men who belonged to Lathom's party were already on their way to bed, happy in their knowledge of a job well done, and with a few quiet words of appreciation from the commissioned engineer fresh in their minds.

In the workshop above Mr. Langley was preparing to take over charge of the watch below from Mr. Kirklane. Both knew of the success with the oil fuel supply, and, seeing Mr. Mayson come up the ladder from the machinery control room, Tom Langley called, "Good old Harry!"

The older man stopped. He had not seen the men until he heard Tom's voice. He spoke in reply, but his husky voice could scarcely be heard. "Oh, hello, chaps."

"Going to bed now?" asked Jim Kirklane.

"Yes, as soon as I've had a bath. Good night."

"Good night, Harry," called the two warrant engineers in unison. In silence they watched the older man slowly climb the ladder to the deck above.

CHAPTER 22

There was an unexpected thrill about the arrival in Alexandria harbour. The ship moved slowly along the entrance channel under her own power, and the men not required for duty were fallen in two deep on the weather decks and flight deck in accordance with the usual custom. Ahead, just inside the harbour, could be seen the upper works of the French battleship. Quite recently she had been given a bright new coat of light grey paint, but little of that paint could be seen now, for it seemed as if every man of her ship's company was taking the day off and was sitting or standing about enjoying the bright sunshine. As the harbour was entered and the French ship came full into view, there were signs of activity among her ship's company. Suddenly a loud, wild cheer broke over the harbour. The French sailors, to a man, stood up and gave full vent to their feelings while the British ship steamed slowly by. They were still cheering and waving their caps as the carrier slipped away and drew nearer to a British battleship. The hearty cheers of the British sailors then drowned those coming from the now more-distant French. Soon cheers were coming from every ship in the harbour—ships of several different nationalities; big ones and small ones; warships, auxiliaries, and merchant vessels. To the enthusiastic onlookers the carrier appeared to be undamaged. She steamed on at an even keel and did not appear to be low in the water. It was hard to believe after the terrific beating she had received. Like a phoenix, it seemed, she had risen from the ashes.

The vessel continued on her course across the harbour while her welcome still rang out on all sides. Her special sea-duty men were busy making her fast to the buoys before the cheering died down.

In the machinery control room the senior engineer and Lieutenant Stanning waited. They sensed that the last movement of the main engines had been made and the ship was being secured. During the whole dangerous passage the senior had remained in this nerve centre of the engine room department, so that the captain might, at any time, have instant contact with him. Now, with two days' growth of dark hair about his face, he looked tougher than ever. He knew nothing of the great welcome the ship had received. He had one great desire: to soak in a hot bath.

A high-pitched buzz sounded through the room; it came from the direct telephone to the bridge. Lieutenant Stanning picked up the receiver and took the message.

"Finished with main engines, sir," he said.

"All right, thank you," said the senior. "I'm going up now. I'll leave you to shut down."

He went up the ladder and made his way aft. By sheer force of habit he entered the engineers' office and looked idly down at his desk. One slip of paper caught his eye. It was a chit from the sick bay, officially informing him that Mr. Mayson had, that morning, been placed on the sick list.

Mr. Mayson hadn't intended to be declared ill. After breakfast he had gone to the sick bay to ask one of the sick berth stewards for a gargle mixture. He had not expected any of the ship's doctors to be there at that time, so he was surprised, on opening the door, to find himself face to face with a surgeon lieutenant. That officer became very inquisitive. He took a good look at Mr. Mayson and stuck a thermometer in his mouth. As a result the commissioned engineer was ordered to bed in his cabin. He did not like the idea at first, but as he stretched his legs down between the sheets and rested his head on the pillow, he felt that perhaps the doctor knew best after all.

Before noon the mail arrived on board. Much of it was addressed to men who had been lost in action. This had a sobering effect on those who did the sorting in the mail office. It toned down the boisterous happiness usually prevalent at such times. A good many telegrams had arrived, too, and the majority of these were messages from relatives and friends who had survived heavy air raids in the British Isles. They relieved the anxiety of many of the ship's company.

Leave was piped at midday mealtime: all-night leave for the starboard watch, and leave until 11:00 P.M. for half of the port watch. There would be great doings on shore. Egypt was a land of plenty in comparison with Malta, and after their experiences the men would not miss this chance to let go. The captain and Commander Sands knew that this was the best thing the men could do; it was the reason why only one-quarter of the ship's company were retained on board.

It was late afternoon before Mr. Kirklane and Mr. Langley were free to leave for shore. Mr. Mills had preceded them, going soon after lunch. He had been able to contact Mary Thompson by telephone and had told her of Tim's death, and of how the others had fared. Mary was free for the afternoon, so Torps had gone to meet her.

The two warrant officers sat together in the after cabin of the motorboat.

"Are you going straight to the hospital, Jim?" asked Mr. Langley.

"Yes, of course. Aren't you?"

"Well, I would, just to see Josie Weir; but Torps told me

she's on night duty, so she'll be sleeping now. She'll be some time getting over Tim's passing."

"Oh, I didn't realize— I thought Tim was married."

"He was, Jim, but his wife died in childbirth nearly three years ago, and the baby died, too. He never stopped grieving and blaming himself till he met Josie. Somehow she put him at peace with himself."

Jim Kirklane spoke softly. "And now this. What a shame!"

"Yes, Jim. It's one damned unhappy time. I'm unhappy knowing how this will affect Josie, and I'm wondering what's happening in Plymouth, too. Ethel knows I'm alive if she got my telegram from Malta, but is *she* alive? I'll be sending another telegram from shore here."

"What are you going to do after?"

"Oh, take a walk around somewhere. I feel like a duck out of water today. If you call in at the Grand Trianon later on, you'll probably find me at the bar—knocking a few back."

Jim Kirklane glanced sharply at his companion. "Didn't you get any mail today, Tom?"

"Oh yes, I had two air-mail letters, but they were posted before the blitz in Plymouth. Did you have any?"

"Yes, and mine took over a month to reach me, but I suppose they have been waiting here in Alexandria."

The boat ran alongside and they stepped out. After passing through the dockyard gate they stopped for a moment near the taxi stand.

"Well, I'm going to take a taxi, Tom," said Jim Kirklane. "Jump in and I'll drop you off at the telegraph office."

Tom Langley hesitated. He sensed the sympathy his friend felt for him, and he smiled a little in appreciation. "No, Jim, you go on. A walk will do me good. Give my regards to Susie."

"All right, Tom, I will—but look after yourself."

Tom crossed the road and had a word with the Greek

money changer before setting off at a good pace through the native quarter. He followed the old familiar route towards Mohammed Ali Square, seeing little, but aware of the void at his side that used to be filled by the upright, steadily pacing figure of Tim. When he reached Mohammed Ali Square he was shaken into alertness. He imagined he heard a steady footfall but soon realized it was an illusion. He moved on, hurrying now, and had passed a taxi stand in the centre of the square when he became aware of footsteps again. Those *were* footsteps—padding, hurrying footsteps close behind. A voice was calling excitedly. Tom stopped and swung round.

"Mohammed!"

Two hands met in a firm grip.

"What's-a-matter, Tom?" cried Mohammed. "I see you go by! You look me! You no speak!"

"I'm sorry, Mohammed," said Tom, brightening up, "but where were you?"

"Here—you come look. I show you." Mohammed was excited and almost dancing with joy. He was barefooted but otherwise fairly well dressed in European clothes. He wore no cap or tie; his clean, striped shirt was open at the neck. They had retraced their steps over about ten yards when he stopped and pointed, his dark brown eyes shining with pride as he said, "Mine. I buy him."

Tom Langley looked with some amazement at a fairly well-used taxi. A native, of about Mohammed's age and dressed in the same way, pottered about it with a piece of rag.

"You bought it!" said Tom. "Where did you get the money from?"

"Me! I get plenty money. I go Mersa Matrûh, sell newspaper. Not sell one piastre—sell two piastre, three piastre, sometimes officer give me five piastre." Mohammed was bursting with information, so Tom stood and listened. It was refreshing to hear. "I make thirty pound," Mohammed went on. "Twenty-five pound I buy taxi. But Mersa Matrûh"—he shuddered at the thought—"Mersa Matrûh make me very fright. Plenty bomb come. They say, 'Boom!' My heart go bump-bump. I am much fright. So I speak commander for me leave camp. Commander say, 'No. You stay. Sell newspapers. Not need be fright.' So I stay. But when big battle start all soldier go. I not go. Come back buy taxi."

"And then you learned to drive it, eh?"

Mohammed seemed a little surprised. "No, me not drive. This boy—he drive. I pay him. Me! I am owner."

Tom laughed. Mohammed seemed mystified at first, but the laughter was infectious so he joined in, though he didn't know what it was all about. Tom walked over to inspect the taxi and Mohammed eagerly pointed out its excellent qualities. He threw open the doors and gave the seats a loving pat, told his assistant to start the engine, ran around to the front to open the bonnet and then called to Tom to come and listen. When Tom heard the steady purr of the engine he was able honestly to say that Mohammed had struck a bargain.

Mohammed dropped the bonnet and turned to his friend, patting him lightly on the shoulder. "You come, Tom. I give you coffee. You meet plenty people—over here." He pointed across the square to a small coffee shop. "This place you find me when you come 'shore. All time I come back here. If I go business and you come, you ask. They tell you what time I come back." He started to move away.

"No, wait a minute, Mohammed," called Tom. "I have to send a telegram first."

Mohammed hurried back and opened the door of the taxi. "Come," he said eagerly, "we take you."

"All right, but you'll have to let me pay you."

Mohammed ignored the remark and bustled his driver about. When the engine started he pressed Tom into the rear seat and followed closely behind to sit proudly with his friend.

The taxi moved away and Tom Langley felt lighter in heart than he had all day.

In the meantime Jim Kirklane had arrived at the hospital. He stood near the door in the library at one end of a long reading desk, idly turning over the pages of a magazine. The hall porter had gone away to tell Sister Brown that someone had called to see her. Jim was alone. He felt strangely elated. His surroundings were extremely soothing and peaceful after the violence of the last two weeks. Here was the calm one finds in a village church—in the evening, when the sun has set, and the first bell has not yet rung to call the people to prayer. Jim looked up and around at the bookshelves and panelled walls of light oak. He was marvelling, as he had on other occasions, at the splendid system of indirect lighting when he heard a light step at the door. There was a pleasant tingling sensation at the roots of his hair as he turned. He had a fleeting glimpse of Susie, more beautiful than ever. Without a sound save the swift rustle of her dress she was in his arms. When Jim looked back on it afterwards he realized that the opening of his arms to gather in Susie was the most natural thing he had ever done. She clasped him around the waist, holding him firmly and burrowing her face into his shoulder. He held her closely, saying nothing, while the wonder of it thrilled his being. He pressed his face into her hair and, after a little while, turned his head slightly and spoke softly to himself. It was barely a whisper: "My lovely Susie!"

Susie heard him and moved slightly. She leaned back a little and looked up at him with the light of heaven on her face, utterly unashamed of two shining jewels of tears which welled up and broke free over the corners of her eyes. Swiftly and instinctively Jim placed one hand gently behind her head and kissed the tears away. She sighed and freed her arms to put them around his neck, and she kissed him tenderly. At that moment Jim Kirklane knew what real happiness could be. She clung to him for a little while. He crushed her to his breast and whispered into her ear: "This is the happiest day of my life."

Her reply came, also a whisper. "Oh, Jim, it's been awful. I didn't know until today whether—" She shuddered and nestled closer. He kissed her somewhere below the left ear, and they swayed together in ecstasy.

Afterwards, when Jim released her, they leaned against the reading desk and he told her about Tom. "I feel I owe Tom so much," he said. "It was through him that I met you, Susie."

Susie smiled. "And it was here at this spot that I first met him. Your ship had just come out from England, and he looked so fresh and strong—full of confidence."

"Yes, that's always been an outstanding thing about Tom—his confidence in himself—but he is a worried man now. He is greatly concerned about his family in Plymouth, and of course he's missing Tim."

"Well, it isn't a good time for him to be alone. Shouldn't we go into town and see if we can meet with him?"

"Yes, I think we should, but if he isn't in the Grand Trianon it won't be much use looking for him; he knows Alexandria inside out and might be anywhere. Can you come right away, Susie?"

"Yes—or in a minute or two, when I get my hat and things." She was moving away as she spoke, but Jim caught her hand and pulled her back. She laughed and let him hold her, and he kissed her many times before letting her go.

There was no point in hurrying. Tom probably would be tramping around somewhere. So they walked along the seafront on their way to town, holding hands as children do. The sun was setting while Jim told her about Harry Mayson. She had heard from Torps that the commissioned engineer was ill. "It's just sheer exhaustion, Susie. He put everything he had into saving the ship. If it hadn't been for his knowledge and determination I don't think we would have got away."

When they reached the Grand Trianon they found the bar crowded. Every seat at the tables was taken and the bar stools couldn't be seen for men in uniforms who stood around drinking. Susie waited inside the door while Jim searched the place until he was sure Tom was not there. When he returned he seemed slightly at a loss, but Susie knew what to do.

"He isn't there then, Jim?"

"No."

"Well, come on. We can call back later."

She led the way into the street. Darkness was closing in as they walked away arm in arm, and Jim never for a moment thought to question where they were going. He was concerned about Tom, but his present happiness was so much in contrast to the strain of the recent action that he was slightly bewildered. He could see little of Susie owing to the blackout regulations, and there was silence between them as they walked along, but it was enough for him that she was at his side. Soon he was walking down steps and passing through a blackout screen. And then he stood on a soft carpet and saw Susie again under subdued lighting. Somewhere close by, a band, consisting chiefly of stringed instruments, was playing a familiar tune. Jim passed their coats and his hat to a cloakroom attendant, and a waiter led them into a small restaurant. There was a tiny dance floor in the centre of the room, but no one was dancing. Only a few people sat at the tables. The night was young for this establishment.

They sat at a table near the bar, and the waiter took their order: a red wine for Susie and a beer for Jim. They sat there in quiet content for over an hour, and in the meantime Jim learned how sweet and soothing music could be. And there was something else to be learned. The lesson was there in his own peace of mind, but he couldn't see it at the time. It seeped into his consciousness during the days that followed and, as his mind became readjusted to peace after violence, he saw that Susie had taken him in hand and nursed him. Then he realized how precious the love of a loyal, thoughtful woman could be.

The restaurant slowly filled with people and the little floor in the centre became packed with dancing couples. A waiter hurried along with a tray to serve dinner to a table close by. Jim glanced at his watch and looked up in dismay. "Susie, I'm neglecting you! It's nearly nine o'clock and you've had no dinner yet!"

She smiled. "Neither have you. As a matter of fact I never thought about it. I certainly don't feel very hungry."

"Well, shall we order something now?"

"If you like, Jim, but perhaps we should call back at the Grand Trianon. If Tom is there we could ask him to join us. They serve a nice meal in the restaurant there."

"Oh, yes. That's a good idea."

They found Tom at the bar in the Grand Trianon. The crowd had thinned and Tom sat at the bar beside two Australian soldiers. When Jim spoke to him he looked round sharply, saw Susie, and slipped off the stool with the agility of a monkey. He grasped Susie's hand in both of his.

"Hello, young lady! You're looking prettier than ever!" He placed an arm around her shoulder and grasped Jim by the elbow. "Come on," he said, "let's sit over here." He called back to his companions at the bar: "Excuse me, chaps," and he led Susie and Jim to one of the tables.

They sat down, and Jim looked closely at Tom. "I expected to find you half-sozzled by now, Tom."

Tom was calling the waiter over, but he heard and looked round with a smile. "I would have been, but I met Mohammed."

"You did!"

"Yes, on Mohammed Ali Square. The young fellow is quite a capitalist now. He's running a taxi and is working his way into a bookselling business. The way he's going on he'll be wearing boots and a collar and tie soon."

"Yes, and before you get the thick stripe on your sleeve he'll own half of Egypt, or be the Prime Minister or something," retorted Jim with a rare touch of humour.

Tom looked quickly at his shipmate, pleasantly surprised. "You could almost be right at that, Jim. At least he'll get ahead better than we do."

They had one drink at the table. Sadness crept in as Tom remarked that Mohammed had shed tears on being told of Tim's death. However, Tom was in fairly good spirits during their meal in the restaurant. Afterwards, Susie and Jim walked back to the hospital. They left Tom in good company, for Mary Thompson and Torps had arrived at the bar, having just left a cinema show.

Jim caught the midnight boat. It was two minutes before the hour when he stepped over the gunwhale and joined Torps and Tom, who were standing in the stern.

CHAPTER 23

Mr. Mayson soon regained his strength. On the third morning after arrival in the harbour he was sitting up in bed writing a letter when Jim Kirklane called.

"How's it going, Harry?" asked Jim, taking a seat.

"Oh, not too badly, young fellow. The surgeon commander just left, and he seemed surprised that I've picked up so quickly. Actually, it's only been a cold—and I suppose I was a bit run down as well. He said I should stay in today and could get up tomorrow."

"Well, you take it easy. There's nothing you need to be up for."

"Isn't there? How's the work going?"

"Very nicely. We expect to go out of dock the day after tomorrow. The dockyard people have dished up several of the oil tanks and blanked off part of the oil fuel suction system. Lathom is in his element now. He was very excited yesterday after crawling around the oil tanks and watertight compartments. He said that everything you worked out on paper was right. He knows now why you had water at the burners so long before you got oil the morning after we left Malta, and he made a sketch to show how it happened."

"Dear little Lathom!" said the commissioned engineer. "I hope he gets something out of this. And I hope Heathcote does, too."

"Well, the senior is working on the recommends now.

And by the way, we have to assess the abilities of all the ratings for the past year. The service certificates are in the office, but there's no hurry. I suppose you'd sooner see to your own men."

"Oh, yes, of course. Tell the senior to leave mine till I'm up and about again. And now, how about you, Jim? Did you see Susie again yesterday?"

The younger man smiled happily. "I did, and this afternoon I'm going ashore to buy an engagement ring."

Mr. Mayson sat upright in bed. "You are! Come over here," and he reached out both his hands.

Laughingly Jim stood up and reached over.

"When is the happy day going to be?" asked Mr. Mayson, releasing the other's hand.

"Well, we have to talk a bit more about that yet. Susie doesn't want to hurry things. She feels she should carry on nursing for some time yet. And, again, I don't know what's going to happen to us chaps aboard here now. What do you think, Harry? Are we likely to go home, or what?"

"That's very likely, I should think. There aren't any dockyards away from the British Isles capable of repairing the ship—unless we go to America under the lend-lease scheme. In any case, I think you will go home."

"Me! Why?"

"Well, has it never occurred to you that you are the only warrant engineer aboard here young enough to be recommended for advancement to lieutenant (E)? Tom Langley is overage now; he's just turned thirty-seven."

"Well, what about that?"

"What about it! This ship has made a name for herself, my lad, and you had a good deal to do with it. If your recommend goes in—and I'm sure it will—you're a dead cert for two stripes."

"But what about you, Harry—and Tom? Why, both of you

can walk rings round me on the job below."

The older man smiled a little grimly. "Don't belittle yourself. You'll make a better lieutenant (E) than a good many I've met. I want to see you wearing two stripes. They're only promoting a few from our rank, but later on chaps like you are going to prove to the powers that be that they can make better use of men from the lower deck. Once they see that, perhaps they'll open the lock gates a bit wider; and who knows, maybe we'll live to see the flood tide, see this lousy warrant rank abolished and men from the lower deck rising on their merits in open competition with all comers. That flood tide will go a long way towards sweeping out the incompetence we find often enough in high places."

Mr. Mayson paused. The younger man sat leaning forward, elbows on knees, waiting to hear more, but the older man decided that he'd said enough.

"Let's forget that now, Jim. How about you and Susie?"

The warrant engineer stood up and leaned against the bulkhead. "You know, Harry, when I think of you and Tom, it seems I have all the luck."

"Never mind about that. You deserve it. There's one thing I'm sure about: You'd never have won Susie if you didn't deserve her; she's too levelheaded for that. I know Tom will wish you happiness, and he'll be glad if you are promoted, too."

"But Harry, isn't there any chance of the regulations being relaxed in favour of both of you after what this ship has been through? and especially in your own particular case since—in my opinion, anyway—you saved the ship?"

Mr. Mayson laughed a little. He was covering his embarrassment over the words of praise. "They'll relax nothing. If they did it would establish a precedent; and there are a good many chaps smarter than me wearing this one stripe, chaps who have seen a lot of action and done their stuff and still rank below sublieutenant. No. Admiralty will have to open the way for all—or none. But let's get away from this business; it's you and Susie I'm interested in. We shall be leaving here soon, you know."

"Yes, I know. Susie and I talked it over last night. She thinks the same as I do, that we should be married in England. And she doesn't want to leave the hospital yet. You see, she has been out here only a few months and feels it would be sort of letting our side down if she left the job now. She thought that if there's any chance of the war ending within a year or so it might be as well to wait, seeing I'll be moving about a lot."

Mr. Mayson wriggled down and leaned back on his elbows. "Well, as I see it, this is going to be a hell of a long war. I fancy some of us will be trampling on our beards before it's over."

Jim laughed. "I'll tell Susie that tonight—and now I'd better get below again."

"Right-o, Jim."

The commissioned engineer was taking up his writing materials when Tom Langley walked in.

"Hello there, Harry. You seem to be perking up nicely."

"Yes, Tom. I'll be up tomorrow. You're looking pretty perky yourself this morning. What's new?"

"Well, good news—and bad news, too, but I feel as if a load had been lifted off me. Look at this!" It was a telegram. Harry Mayson opened it. It read: "ETHEL SICK IN HOSPITAL RECOVERING WELL STOP HOME DESTROYED STOP CHILDREN SAFE WITH ME STOP LETTER FOLLOWS STOP NANA."

"Nana is Ethel's mother," said Tom. "I can only assume that Ethel was in the hospital and the children with their Nana during the blitz."

CHAPTER 24

Two weeks went by while the great vessel was being made ready for a long voyage. She had occupied the dock for several days and was now back at her old berth near the coaling wharf, while the dockyard men added extra stiffening to the stern. There was work in progress on the flight deck, too: Part of the landing-on equipment was being repaired, and the after lift opening was being covered, for she was to carry planes on her next trip. The date of departure was not yet known, but it was drawing near.

The ship's company had enjoyed the stay in Alexandria. The weather was fine throughout, and the men saw much of interest that had escaped them before, because their earlier leave had been limited. They found their way into gardens and into the museum, and they became friendly with men in some of the army messes, joining in at their dances and entertainments. Wherever they went they carried with them the splendid influence of their captain and their commander. Not all of them drank, but those who did consumed much Egyptian beer, though without once bringing discredit to the uniform they wore.

Stoker MacLeod (Speedy) and Dusty Miller were now close friends. Only once did they go to the canteen to play tombola, and then they stayed for only two "houses": It was no place for them now.

The assessment of abilities of the engine room ratings for

the past year had been completed. Another task had been undertaken by the senior engineer with the assistance of the other engineer officers: the making and forwarding of a report to the captain on the splendid conduct of certain men in action. It had not been an easy job, for only a few—the most outstanding men—could be included in the list. The captain's job would be harder still. He had to select the men he would recommend for honours and awards.

One of the things Mr. Mayson suggested to the senior was that he recommend Mr. Kirklane for advancement to lieutenant (E). He was surprised and pleased when the senior replied, "You're too late. Lieutenant Stanning suggested it a couple days ago, and the recommend is going in."

On his first trip ashore Mr. Mayson spent a pleasant evening. He had spoken to Eileen Hall over the telephone and had arranged to escort her to a cinema show. When he met her in the library the little sister seemed unusually serious. The first thing she did was pull down one of his eyelids; that set him laughing. Nothing daunted, she made him put out his tongue. After that she brightened up and, as they walked along the roadway, entertained him with a good deal of light-hearted chatter. Later, at the cinema, she took the raincoat he had carried and packed it around his back and shoulders, saying, "There's someone home there waiting for you, my lad, and you are not going to catch any harm while you are with me." Then, thinking of something else, she took his wrist and felt his pulse for a minute before sitting back in contentment.

Nothing was seen of Josie Weir outside the hospital until the day on which the repairs to the ship were completed, but each of the officers who had visited the hospital had seen and spoken to her. She was quieter than usual and did not smile so readily. It was Torps who started the movement that lured her out of the hospital. On the day the ship was made ready for sea, he set about arranging a party. As he said, it might be the last chance. He felt his efforts had been rewarded when a party of ten sat down at the Carlton that evening. Joining Torps and Mary Thompson were Jim Kirklane and Susie, Harry Mayson and Eileen Hall, Sublieutenant Kelling and Agnes Andrewes—and Josie Weir, as Tom Langley's partner.

Tom was a happier man that evening. Nana's letter had reached him several days after her telegram. Ethel was recovering from pneumonia and would soon leave the hospital, and the children were well. Accommodation had been found for them in Redruth, Cornwall, and the family would soon be taken there. Nana's home was undamaged.

Tom was greatly relieved to know that there was a civilian organization so efficiently aiding victims of air raids in England.

It was a pleasant party at the Carlton, though each knew that it heralded the parting of the ways. They dined and danced and saw the floor show twice. After the band stopped playing and the musicians packed up their instruments they remained at the table chatting until the place closed at 2:00 A.M. By 3:00 A.M. the officers were all sailing back to the ship in a felucca.

Later that morning the senior contacted the engineer officers and let them know when the ship would leave Alexandria.

"We're pushing off tomorrow morning at five," he said. "The captain wants the officers to know, but the ratings are not to be told yet. If you go ashore today keep the news to yourself."

Mr. Mayson was alone with the senior in the engineers' office when he heard the news. The writer, Saunders, had gone to the captain's office over some detail on service certificates.

"Thanks for the information, sir. Do you know where we are going?"

"No. We won't know for some time after leaving. Even the captain will be in the dark about it. Of course we shall go through the Suez Canal and be given part of our course." Then the senior became confidential. "Everything should run smoothly now, Mr. Mayson. We're a bit shorthanded on engineer officers, but with a long, steady trip ahead of us we'll need only one officer of the watch below."

Saunders returned and sat at his desk. The senior reached up to a bookshelf and took down an atlas. He opened it at a map of the world and Mr. Mayson looked over his shoulder. Both were thinking along the same lines. If the ship was to be repaired in England the route was clear: They would go through the canal, down through the Red Sea and round Africa. They would probably call at Aden, Durban, and Capetown. If the ship was to be repaired in America there were two possible routes: one eastwards via Colombo and Singapore and across the Pacific; the other, round the Cape of Good Hope and across the Atlantic. Mr. Mayson reached over and pointed to Durban. He spoke softly to the senior. "If we call there I'll show you around the place."

It was then that Fate played her old trick again—the one that shatters pleasant dreams. From the doorway behind them came the voice of Lieutenant Stanning:

"The chief's back!"

There followed a stunned silence, broken when Saunders flung his pen on the desk in a gesture of silent disgust. Mr. Mayson gazed in nauseated dismay towards the doorway.

The senior rose from his chair and turned. "He's back? Is he on board?"

"Yes," replied the lieutenant. "I haven't seen him but I heard him when I passed Commander Sands's office just now. He was telling the commander that he had pulled all the strings he could to get back."

The senior looked silently at Mr. Mayson and back to the lieutenant, then the sound of a heavy tread drew their eyes quickly to the door. The chief had arrived.

He was in uniform. His cheeks seemed rosier than ever and they shook, like the breasts of a hurrying woman, in harmony with his tread. Ducklike, his toes turned outward, he strode the length of the office. He waved a sheet of paper en route and let his voice be heard.

"Senior! Where the hell are the messengers? Blast it all! I'm trying to get this signal away!"

For a loaded, silent fraction of a minute, the air was charged with something that science may one day be able to name.

The senior answered in subdued, almost strangled voice. "There were two messengers at the door, sir. You must have passed them as you came in."

"Passed them be damned! They've disappeared somewhere. Saunders! Get hold of one of the blighters and send him in here!"

Saunders moved unhurriedly to the door. The chief thrust the paper down on his blotting pad and flopped into his chair. He picked up a pen, examined it, flung it away, and turned to the senior. "Is there anything here I can write with?" he asked resignedly.

The senior took up the discarded pen, opened a drawer of his own desk, and pulled out a box of nibs. He fitted the pen with a new nib and wiped the grease off it with a duster before passing it back to the chief.

Mr. Mayson moved quietly to a position near the door and looked back at the huge bulk of the commander (E), trying to sum him up. To think that this was the same man who had sat crouching in that air-raid shelter in Malta! He was then of less value than a scared rat. It was clear that the engine room department could run better without him. But now he was on top again, and it seemed that no one could do anything about it. He had pulled strings to get back. Strings! Here was a man born with strings. How else could he have reached the rank of commander? Strings must have got an obstreperous youngster in and through Dartmouth College, and later through Keyham Engineering College, to graduate as acting sublieutenant (E); and strings must have dragged him on to where he was that day.

The thought of it was too much for Mr. Mayson. He left the office to find happier surroundings.

There was no doubt that the chief was on top—at least in his own mind. In the wardroom before lunch he was a boisterously happy man. He drank gin and forced his conversation on anyone who did not openly avoid him. He was aware of little except his own importance. He had come from Malta in a high-speed destroyer, bringing his magnetic personality and unexcelled powers of command to boost the morale of his brother officers. He exercised his great gifts and gave the senior engineer much to put up with that day. In the afternoon he bounced into the office again. Only the senior and Saunders were present.

"Senior," he said, "I've had a hand message telling me to discharge any engineer officers who are still under training. Better tell Kelling to get packed; he'll have to leave today."

The senior rose from his chair. "But couldn't you give him his watch-keeping certificate, sir? He should have had it a month ago. Once he gets it he is no longer under training and we can keep him."

"Keep him! Who the hell wants to keep the useless blighter? Tell him to get packed!"

The senior left the office on his distasteful mission, and when he returned the chief was going through the list of engine room ratings. Beside each name the senior had written the assessment of the man's ability for the past year. There were one or two assessments the chief disagreed with, but it was not until he saw the word "superior" beside Heathcote's name that he showed real annoyance. He told the senior to alter it. "The man isn't even worth a 'satisfactory'; change it to 'moderate.' " When the senior told him that the assessment had already been signed by the captain and entered on Heathcote's service certificates, the chief was more annoyed than ever. He banged the desk and said it was not too late to alter it; it only needed the captain's initials. But for once the senior had a trump card. He told the chief that the captain was unlikely to agree to the alteration, seeing that Heathcote was included in the list of men recommended for honors and awards.

The chief's reaction was surprising. Instead of flying into a rage he pushed the list aside with a gesture of apparent disgust and rose to leave. He had accepted the inevitable, but before he left the office he thought of something else. "Look here, Senior," he said, "tell that messenger of yours he is not to carry his torch like I do. It was my idea to have a white lanyard spliced on to my torch and I don't want a bloody stoker copying me."

The senior said nothing.

As the chief left the office the offending stoker, Speedy, stood to attention outside the door. There was an ordinary white lanyard around his neck, to the bottom of which was secured an electric torch. Soon the lanyard was to be replaced by a piece of brown spun yarn.

The senior was relieved when the chief left. A few minutes later Saunders handed him a slip of paper. It was a request to leave the job of engineers' writer. As this final irritation was being assimilated by the senior, Mr. Kirklane entered.

"Those boilers we cleaned are closed up, sir," he said.

The senior replied without turning round from his desk. "Thank you."

The warrant engineer could see that the senior was not happy. Mr. Kirklane had turned to leave the office when the two lieutenants, Leyton and Stanning, entered. They were talking about Sublieutenant Kelling.

"I was surprised," said Lieutenant Leyton. "He seems to be quite happy about leaving the ship."

"Yes, it surprised me too," replied Lieutenant Stanning. "I thought he might have been upset about not getting his certificate. Apart from that, he knows he'll be better off away from here, and, what's more, he won't need to go ashore and say good-bye to a certain someone tonight."

It was Jim Kirklane who went ashore to say good-bye. He ran down the ship's gangway to catch the seven-thirty boat just as it was leaving.

From the moment he met Susie he lived up to his intentions and made the best of the remaining hours of the day, hours that were far too few and far too short. The time flashed by until, a few minutes after midnight, he was being rushed back to the ship in the last boat off. Soon he was alongside, and after a brief, hazy period during which he climbed the gangway and descended two ladders, he was alone in his cabin, looking at the framed photograph of Susie—Susie, to whom he had just said good-bye. It was hard to believe that the evening, which he had looked forward to so much, was now only a memory.

But what a delightful evening it had been. Not at all as he had expected it to be. He started to live it over as he undressed. He had spent four hours in the company of the serene young lady who was to be his wife. Susie had transformed what might have been hours of sadness into hours of joy. They had dined and danced and lived, utterly ignoring the parting that was soon to come. Their faith in each other was so great that the parting was a trivial matter. It would come, of course, and it would mean that a small span of their lives must go by before they experienced the greater joy of really belonging to each other. They had walked back along the seafront in the moonlight, lingering while the precious moments flew.

Jim slipped between the sheets and turned the photograph on his desk so that he could see it easily. Beside it a small clock ticked the seconds away. He left the reading light on and lay back on his pillow.

How lovely she had been when they had parted. What a wonderful thrill of mingled happiness and sadness had he known during those last five minutes. It was all stamped indelibly on his mind, and again, it seemed, she stood before him on the small veranda near the hospital's main entrance, holding the lapels of his coat. He removed her hat so that the moonlight might show him the full glory of her hair and he held her lightly at the waist, occasionally stooping to kiss her left eyebrow. They had made their arrangements for the future as they stood thus. It had been quite simple. Susie said, "Let me know when you are going to be based ashore for a time you consider long enough—and I'll come to you." She had looked up to him then, and he could still see that wonderful lovelight in her eyes.

He'd gathered her in. "Yes, I will, my love."

They'd clung to each other in that last kiss, but time would not wait, and Susie made no attempt to restrain him. He walked down the steps. At the bottom he looked back, and she smiled and lifted her hand in a tiny wave.

"Till then, Jim. Godspeed."

"Yes, Susie—till then. And God bless you."

He'd hurried away and now here he was—in bed.

He looked again at the photograph of Susie. After some time he glanced at the clock: 1:30 A.M. He had to be out at three-forty-five to keep the morning watch, but he didn't care whether he slept or not; and perhaps it was because he didn't care that Jim went to sleep almost at once, forgetting to switch off his reading light.

CHAPTER 25

Before dawn the ship was well clear of Alexandria harbour, and before sunset, after an uneventful trip, she arrived at Port Said. She carried two Swordfish planes on her flight deck, available for reconnaissance work and, if necessary, for offensive action against enemy vessels. At Port Said she anchored for the night, unable to start her passage through the Suez Canal until morning, for the enemy had mined the narrow waterway.

The mining had been a clever piece of work. Enemy aircraft had dropped magnetic mines first, and then they'd followed up with acoustic mines, which exploded at the sound of a ship's machinery. After that, to complicate matters, they dropped an improved type, which did not explode at the sound of the first ship, but made its presence felt when the second, third, fourth, fifth, sixth, or seventh ship went over. It only needed one large ship to be caught by one of the delayed action mines and the canal might be blocked for weeks. Already several wrecks—of small ships—had been dragged to one side of the waterway. The mine disposal parties were striving to cope with a situation that might become desperate. To add to the confusion the cunning enemy went a step further: He dropped paper bags full of sand. When the bags hit the water the watchers could not be sure that a mine had not been dropped there. And after the raid was over searchers would seek in vain for something that must be found. However, with praiseworthy determination and skill the authorities slowly but surely mastered the situation.

They had been working for many days and nights when the aircraft carrier arrived at Port Said, by which time they knew the answer to all the enemy's tricks. The carrier was delayed overnight because they were seeking the last mine—or what they thought was a mine. Certain instruments they had devised indicated that one was there, in the vicinity of one of the wrecks, but they didn't find it. They probed about the bottom of the canal all night to no avail. So with the knowledge that it might take days to remove this last menace it was decided to open the canal for traffic. Ships would have to be silent while passing over the spot. No attempt was made to set the mine off; the explosion might cause serious damage to the bottom and sides of the waterway.

At eleven o'clock in the forenoon the carrier entered the canal and became one of a long line of ships passing through. All the others were merchant vessels carrying important cargos. Later in the day it was a grand sight from the flight deck: There were ships ahead and ships astern as far as the eye could see along the straight, narrow waterway. The day was fine and visibility good.

Perhaps it was because of this particularly good view that the commander (E) had found his way up to the signal deck. This was the highest spot he could find in which to sit comfortably and at the same time enjoy the fresh air and the view. It was situated high up in the bridge structure, a place the commander (E) had probably never seen before. The signalmen were amazed when the commander (E) flopped his huge bulk into the chair and threw half a dozen magazines at his feet. As time went by they began to wonder what sort of navy they were serving. A steward brought the chief's tea up on a tray. The chief ignored the signalmen completely. He got on with his tea and grinned occasionally as he saw something humorous in one of the magazines. Once he fell asleep for nearly an hour. When he woke up he asked where the nearest lavatory was, and on being directed to one in the bridge structure he seemed pleasantly surprised and hurried away.

At 5:00 P.M. the ship had almost reached the spot where she must drift silently over what was thought to be a mine. All the engineers other than the chief were below, standing by to stop every piece of machinery that was working as soon as the order came from the bridge.

It was not necessary for all the engineers to be below; half of them could supervise the work, but the chief had ordered them all to get down there. It was bad policy, for if a mine exploded beneath the ship, somewhere between the engine rooms and the boiler rooms, it might put an end to all the ship's engineer officers—excepting the chief. But perhaps the chief had reasoned it out that a mine explosion at that point would so affect the ship that engineer officers would be superfluous. And in any case he would still be there to take charge. No mine yet devised could hurt him up there on the signal deck.

There was no explosion, and the ship passed through the canal in safety to enter the Red Sea. And on the stokers' mess deck the commander (E) had earned a new title: "The Marine Mountaineer."

On she steamed to Aden where she stayed long enough to take in oil fuel and stores. She remained unescorted until, on entering the Indian Ocean, she was joined by a cruiser. Both ships steamed on a southerly course, destination unknown.

And so the great vessel slips away from the scene of battle. She is physically crippled—and otherwise handicapped, for though a gentle breeze blows from the starboard quarter, with an unworthy senior officer on board she steams with her stem to the winds of Adversity.

But do not lose sight of her yet. Watch her as she steams away towards the smooth horizon, with the rays of the setting sun gleaming on the new paintwork at the starboard side of her upper decks. The bridge structure is casting a shadow directly across the broad flight deck. As she slips farther away you see that her sides narrow from her wide flight deck down towards a point at the waterline. She is emulating the great Prime Minister of her country of origin and, in this dark period of the history of the Empire, showing the "V" for victory.